Morning sunbeams lanced between the rock spires to illuminate William Covington's weary face. He raised his head from his rolled-up coat and sat up on the dusty, hard-packed ground. His throat was dry, and he took a swig from his canteen. A nicker caught his attention. Last night he had unsaddled his horse and slapped her on the rump to encourage her to run off, but there she stood this morning twenty feet away, nibbling at a bush.

"You better go, girl," he called out to her. "You won't be coming where I'm headed." The horse looked up at him and flicked her ears. When no other insight seemed forthcoming, she returned to nibbling at the sparse leaves.

Will sighed. He pulled some bread and cheese from his bag and ate half of his remaining rations. He would need the energy for the climb down this morning and could eat the second half for an added boost later. After that, there wouldn't be another later to worry about.

Breakfast finished, he crawled to the edge of the cliff face and peered into the valley below. He stayed low to avoid highlighting himself against the sun behind him, but he doubted his pursuers would pick him out from this distance anyway. Shadows of the hills and mesas blanketed the valley, but he could see that the posse had already broken camp and started up the winding path toward the pass. They were a bit ahead of the schedule Will had set in his mind, but he still had time for his final preparations. He scrambled back from the edge on his belly before standing and returning to his meager camp.

Last night he had separated out his gear. He strapped his gun belt with the dual rosewood-handled six-shooters heavy on his hips. He wrapped the one full and one half-full bandolier of bullets across his shoulders. In a small rucksack, he stowed the last of his food and one full canteen. He had filled two at a stream the afternoon before, and he now finished off the first canteen and dropped it on the coat next to his blanket and saddlebags. The last thing he did was hold a lock of black hair to his nose and inhale his lungs to bursting before tucking it in the breast pocket of his shirt. If somehow he managed to survive the day, his gear would still be here. If not, well, someone else would find it one day and put it to use, and if that preacher was right, by then he would be riding God's wide open plains. If not, then it was all down to darkness anyway.

It took him the better part of two hours to make his way down the cliff face and rock piles to his destination, a widened plateau halfway up the mountainside from the valley floor below. The road coming up the plateau was wide enough for the small wagon abandoned here to pass, but at this point the road became a rutted trail snaking a zigzag through a canyon pass whose sides narrowed in places so no more than two riders could ride abreast. The plateau was the last spot a wagon could travel.

Will's eyes shied away from the wagon and the red-brown stains in the back, baking away in the harsh sun. He did pick up the backboard of the wagon, discarded to the side, and carried it with him a few feet away to the natural depression in the earth he had enlarged two days ago. The depression lay across from the entrance to the canyon trail, but not so far from the wagon that the backboard could not have landed there or been tossed in haste. He took time to brush away his fresh boot prints. Settled, he ate the last of his bread and cheese and sipped his water. He checked his guns and laid them down atop the empty rucksack in the bottom of his hole. After taking one last breath of clean, fresh air, he hunkered down in the hole and lifted the backboard up and set it above his head, sealing himself off from the world.

Light filtered through the cracks in the boards above his head, but the air became stuffy and hot. A single bead of sweat ran down his cheek within five minutes, but he did not stir. His inner clock did not fail him. Within fifteen minutes of concealing himself, the voices of men echoed in the air and soon the sound of hooves pounded the ground and sent tiny dirt avalanches trickling down the walls of his hollow. Will dried his palms on his legs and took up a gun in each hand.

When the posse arrived, he could hear the consternation in their voices. They had not expected the narrow path and were none too eager to enter in search of their quarry. At least one voice rose in anger and a voice too quiet for Will to make out answered it. Some debate went on among the men until the voice of the leader told them all to dismount and take a break while a group rode on to explore the defile.

Pausing here had never been part of the plan, theirs or Will's. He waited there, crouched down in his hole. It was designed to conceal him from a group of riders passing through, not an afternoon picnic.

Boots crunched on the dirt, and a cowboy walked past Will's hole. He heard the man spit and then urinate over the side of the plateau not three feet from him. Will tensed, waiting to leap out as soon as he was discovered, but the cowboy finished his business and walked away.

The voices and sounds were garbled as they echoed down into his hiding spot, but Will heard none raised in alarm. These men were relaxed here on the plateau. In the defile, they would be nervous, expecting an attack from above or an ambush at every corner, but not here, not yet.

The abrupt sound of creaking wagon wheels to his left sent lightning bolts through Will's brain. They were using Janie's wagon. They were sitting on her wagon, where he had held her, where she had said she loved him, where she had...

The burning rage turned his vision black. They would die first. He would come up, guns barking, and kill them for desecrating her wagon. He should have burned it that day, protected it from unclean hands, but he had not, and now he would have to cleanse it with blood.

He closed his eyes and let his ears draw the scene out there on the plateau.

He had two guns, twelve shots before reloading. Coming up shooting to his left would expose his flank and back to the rest of the posse, but surprise was on his side. He could take down the two by the wagon easily. Turn right then, still firing. The original posse was two dozen men strong. Four, maybe five had already gone into the pass. He could hit with all twelve shots, but he was not as good as McPhail, and they would not all be kill shots. At best, that would leave seven armed healthy men when he had to reload, and he would never have a chance to reload in the hole. That would mean leaving his skimpy cover before he emptied his guns. If a man went down close enough, he could grab his gun and move toward the wagon. It would be little enough cover from seven or more guns, but there was no other cover on the plateau. Perhaps he could move toward the horses, but with all the gunfire, the big bodies were apt to panic and run. He could be trampled, but the horses might take out some of his foes.

In the end, none of it mattered. He would die here in these

hills far from his family and friends, away from McPhail, from Finn, and from Janie. His only regret was that his body would never lie next to hers again. Maybe they would bury him with the lock of her hair still in his pocket.

Will went to stand—his thighs tensed, his knees started to extend, and his hands came up holding his guns—but a voice, her voice, whispered in his ear. "Wait. Not yet. It's not time." He relaxed; knees refolded, arms lowered, and tension drained from his body. How long he crouched there he could not tell. Sweat still tickled his brow, but he did not move. He barely breathed.

Finally, voices came from the narrow pass. The scouts had returned. The men grumbled but gathered their things and re- mounted. The boss shouted out. They would enter in twos and threes, wait until the group in front rounded the first bend before following, spread out, and watch above for rock falls and ambush. Don't bunch up and make an easy target. As their guide had assured them, the pass was no more than three- quarters of a mile before they found open ground again.

The posse began to move out. In his hole, Will's senses buzzed alive and taut, hearing the sounds of men and horses, feeling the gentle rumble of hooves on the hard earth. He could imagine them, maybe twenty-one men pairing up and setting out, staying apart, not making an easy target to take out at once with a rock fall, watching for the attack from above. Their numbers dwindled on the plateau. Now Will could make out the individual voices, the different pitches of the jangling spurs and gear. They would not fall at once to an attack from the cliff tops, but now they lay in a long fuse, and Will would burn right up that fuse to the explosion at the end.

He could see it in his mind's eye. Five men on horseback waiting: two getting ready to enter the chute, three more spread out in wings to either side behind them. He waited for the lead man to say, "All right, let's get on with it."

Then, he rose from his hole, and the guns started to blaze.

PART

Two

ONE YEAR AGO

⟣ TRANQUILITY ⟢

For as long as he could remember, the valley of Tranquility had been William Covington's home. Finn and Kalirose Hennessy, his cousins from his mother's side of the family, were his brother and sister, and Margaret and George Hennessy were his adopted parents. Will's father had died while he was an infant, and his mother had moved to Tranquility just before Will's birth to be closer to her sister. Frontier life was hard though, and the grief and anger over the loss of her husband weighed heavy on Samantha Covington, something that baby Will could never placate, and she died when he was just two years old, too young to remember anything but vague impressions of his departed parents. Margaret and George filled those roles though, and Will grew up a happy child, or as happy as any orphaned frontier farming child could.

By the time Samantha and Will arrived in Tranquility, Margaret and George had already lost an older boy, Buck, to the pox as an infant. Finn was their second, a few months older than Will, a fact that he never let his "younger brother" forget as they grew. Kalirose came early, frail and tiny for her first year of life and gave her parents a fright; but after that, she grew hale and healthy, perhaps from having to keep up with the boys and survive their terrorizing ways. The Lord blessed the Hennessy family with pretty, bright Abigail two years later, but she too succumbed to illness before her first birthday, and the Lord sent no more after her.

The years passed. The crops cycled. The children grew. They worked the fields and tended the livestock. When chores allowed, the boys would go camping in the mountains above the valley. George took them when they were young, but as they grew, they camped without supervision, sometimes with Kali in tow. They learned to hunt and track and shoot. Finn perfected slowing his breathing and heart rate to take the long shot with the rifle, but at close range and with a quick draw, Will had the advantage. George would smile and shake his head when he saw Will with the pistol—"That's your daddy in you"—but generally would say no more.

The snow was still heavy in the high mountains when Will and Finn came riding home after a celebratory camping trip. Finn had completed his eighteenth year two months before, and Will would tie that benchmark in less than a week. For one more brief week, Finn reveled in being the older brother, now a man, and had spent the last couple of days calling Will "boy" and ordering him about like a child, though with few positive results.

Finn was the larger of the two in frame as well as age, much like his father: broad in the shoulder and arms with thick legs to hold him up and a mop of curly dark brown hair lying across his brow. Will was lean, and although not as big as Finn, had muscles well toned from the daily work of life on a farm. His hair was a wavy brown in contrast to Finn's darker locks, but with highlights that shone red in the late afternoon sun, a gift from his mother.

As the pair crested the last ridge, they could see a thin trail of smoke from the chimney and an extra horse grazing in the field with their plow horse.

"Looks like we've got company, boy." Finn urged his horse forward, and Will galloped after him.

Soon afterward, they trotted their horses into the yard and headed toward the barn. Kali sat on the stoop waiting for the boys and followed them into the stable. "Pa's still out in the back fields. Ma sent me to tell him Mr. McPhail was here, but he just said he'd be back by supper, and Mr. McPhail could just wait." Kali was excited, dancing from one foot to the other eager to tell her tale. "I don't really think he's here to see Pa anyway." She stared at Will with wide eyes and her voice dropped to a whisper. "I think he's here for you."

Will pulled a face. "Why'd some stranger want anything with me?"

"He was talking to Ma, asking after both of you, but 'specially you, Will. He knew your pa, and I think he has something in his duffle for you. Said something about you being a man grown soon."

The three looked at each other in silence. "He's a might scary if you ask me. Got cold eyes, he does. I bet he's killed people." Kali was speaking in a confidential whisper now.

The crunch of boots on the gravel outside made them all jump and stare at the door, only to find George Hennessy stopping in the doorway. He mopped his brow from the warmth of the day and the long walk back to the house. "Take care of your horses. They'll need a good rub down and water and feed. Hop to it now." He strode off toward the house.

Kali looked back and forth between her brother and cousin. "Well, get to it. I'm goin' in to help Ma and hear what they have to say." She hiked up her skirts and scurried after her father in an effort not to miss anything.

Mr. McPhail was standing on the porch when George greeted him. "David, you old dog, you're more'n a day early.

The boys just got back from camping, and I had to get the back fence put together again."

"S'all right," McPhail answered. "Molly and your lovely daughter have been keeping me company. It's good to see you." The two men embraced in a long hug and pounded each other on the back.

"Damn. Just as bony as ever, ain'tcha." George stood back and looked his friend up and down.

McPhail snorted. "Looks like Molly keeps you well fed. Always knew you'd go soft, George."

"Soft?" George looked offended. "I work this farm from dawn to dusk. I'm stronger than I ever was."

McPhail shook his head. "None of us are as strong as we were back at Vigilant; and you may be fit, but you're soft where it counts."

George returned McPhail's up and down appraisal. "Maybe so. You're as sharp and hard as ever, David, and a bad omen by half, as usual, I'll wager. Let me wash off and say hallo to my wife, and we'll talk." He walked around the side of the porch to splash water from the rain barrel onto his face and arms. Without another word, he walked past McPhail and into the house.

For his part, McPhail just leaned against one of the porch posts and stared out across the farm. His eyes alighted on Kali, who became flustered under his grey eyes. She bobbed a curtsy and ran past him into the house after her pa. The tall cowboy let her go. He pulled out a pouch of paper and tobacco, rolled himself a small tight smoke, and was soon puffing away while the sun crawled toward the mountains in the west.

An hour later, with the sun inching below those mountains, the five family members and their guest gathered around the dinner table. Molly and Kali had prepared fresh biscuits and gravy, and a bean and vegetable stew with bits of venison from one of Finn and Will's previous hunting trips. As usual, despite being decent hunters, the boys had not eaten a hearty meal for days, and they dug in with abandon. McPhail complimented the cooking and had seconds himself, despite George joking about the lean cowboy going soft.

George dabbed his lips with a handkerchief and leaned back in his chair. "So, where have you been all these years, David?"

McPhail shrugged. "Here and there. I went east first, but no one in the Federation cares much what happens out here on the frontier. As long as Hogg keeps the noise down, no one cares much what happened to the Rangers. 'Decommissioned' I think his cronies back east called it. After that, I tried up north for a while. Herded some cattle. Even went all the way up with some trappers past the border into French Canada, but I missed the dirt and rocks and heat down here. It's in my bones. Finally, I went west. Did a little prospecting up North Cali way and then a little south to see how Santa Ana is taking care of South Cali. Again, I missed my home, and I can't stand the thought of that man ruling over my land. He won't drive me out. Sometimes you got to make a stand, George, and so here I am."

Now it was George's turn to snort. "We made our stand, and we lost, David. Hogg won, and honestly, life's been quieter in these here parts ever since."

"Quieter because everyone's too afraid to say anything," Molly interjected. "And quieter until the Agents show up."

"Now, Molly—" George started.

"Don't you 'now, Molly' me. You know it's true, George. What do you think will happen the next time the Revenue Men show up here? They'll bring Agents with them next time, you can bet. You saw what happened to the Haskels last spring."

The three junior members of the table exchanged nervous glances. The Hennessy farm was successful enough. They kept themselves fed and clothed but not much more, and the original land grants in Tranquility Valley carried lasting taxes whose bills were coming due. Until now, they had managed to eke out the payments to the government in San Alonso, but this year had been tighter than most. Last spring, the Haskel family had fallen far enough behind that the Revenue Men and a group of Agents reclaimed the land, took the remaining livestock and crops as payment, and evicted the family. No one had seen the Haskels since, and though the story was they headed back east, the rumors persisted that the Agents had never let them leave the valley.

"Trouble in paradise, George?" McPhail asked.

George scowled at his wife. "Nothing I can't handle." He turned back to Molly. "We'll have the money in time."

Finn broke the silence that ensued. "Pa, maybe I should take Mr. Franklin up on his offer to ride on the cattle drive. It'll bring in good money and be good experience for me."

"I can go too," Will interjected. "That'll bring in twice the money."

George sighed. "I don't much like the idea, but the extra money would help. It'll leave your mother, Kali, and me to mind the farm, but I believe we could manage. You'd be gone more than a month though, and it can be tough out there on the trail."

"Not all the boys who go out on those cattle drives come back, either." The worry was plain in Molly's voice. "There're bandits and rustlers and Indian tribes out there to deal with."

"Governor Hogg has been dealing with the Indian tribes, putting them in their place. That's one good thing he's done," Kali added, not sure if she wanted that to help the boys go or make them stay.

McPhail's laugh was mirthless. "Didn't your father teach you anything? When the Rangers were the law, we were on friendly terms with all the tribes here about. After Governor

Hogg disbanded the Rangers, he started pushing the tribes off their land so he could sell it off to ranchers and farmers. If it weren't for him, we wouldn't have ever had any problems with the tribes."

Kali slumped down in her seat in crestfallen silence.

McPhail turned toward Molly. "As for rustlers and bandits and the like, there's not nearly as many of those as you'd fear, Molly. The main danger on a cattle drive is your own carelessness. Cattle are big animals, and when you got a whole herd of them moving, accidents can happen." McPhail wiped his mouth off with his napkin. "I'll go with them. I've done my share of cattle drives and can keep them out of most trouble. I'm sure your Mr. Franklin would be glad of another skilled hand."

Instead of calming her, this statement flared Molly's emotions. "Oh, yes, that's just what you'd like, David McPhail, to stir up trouble with my boys and get them to follow you off on some fool quest to restore your precious Rangers."

McPhail had the good grace to bow his head in assent, but that cold steel never left his eyes. "I cry your pardon, Molly. I'm not here to stir up trouble with your boy. I'm only here to keep a promise to Will's father."

"Boys, David. I've raised Will as well as I've raised Finn. They're both mine."

McPhail bowed his head again, but said no more. Will looked back and forth between his adopted mother and this strange figure at their dinner table. When he realized that neither was going to speak, he had to break the silence. "What promise did you make to my father?"

Despite the growing tension between them, George and Molly shared a worried look.

"It's about time you spoke up, Will." McPhail regarded Will with those cold grey eyes. "Your father was a Territory Ranger just like me and your adopted father here."

"David McPhail, I will not have you stirring up trouble with my boys." Molly stood and threw her napkin on the table.

"I'm following a dying man's wish, Molly. I made an oath, and I mean to fulfill that oath. After that, come what may." His words were even, but they brokered no argument.

"Well, I do not have to stay and listen to this folly. Finn, Kali, come with me," she ordered.

Finn's mouth fell open. "But, Ma."

George sighed again. "Finn's a man grown. He can stay if he likes, and Will permits it."

"Fine, George Hennessy. I will remember this. Kalirose, come with me." Molly grabbed her daughter's arm and despite her protests, dragged the girl off to the back bedroom and slammed the door shut.

The three men and one almost-man stared at the closed door. "After that, I may be sleeping in the stables with you tonight, David." George shook his head. "I'm not sure you're worth the trouble."

McPhail leaned back in his chair. Without asking permission, his nimble fingers rolled himself another cigarette and lit it on the candle closest to him. He took a few drags before continuing. "As I said, your real father and your adopted pa here and I were all Territory Rangers together out of Fort Vigilant. Joseph Covington was a good man and a good friend of mine. The three of us, we were pretty much inseparable from the day we enlisted. I'd never seen him so happy as the day he married your mother, nor as proud as the day we got word you were born."

McPhail puffed the cigarette a few more times and knocked the ashes onto the side of his plate. "By then, your adopted father here had up and retired from the Rangers and came back to Tranquility with your Aunt Molly."

George huffed. "We all knew what would happen when the

Federation appointed Hogg governor. Lots of us left then, David."

"Fine, you at least had the good sense to leave when you did, because that's when everything went bad for the Rangers." He took another pull and puffed a ring of blue smoke to the ceiling. "I was out on long patrol with Dick Warren and a green kid, Tommy Hopkins. Tommy got himself snake bit and was in a bad way. Made us three days late back to Fort Vigilant. By then, Governor Hogg's men had come and gone, and there were no more Rangers left."

McPhail stared off into the rafters. His voice remained flat. "I found your father among the survivors, belly shot and close to the end. Don't know how he managed to hang on as long as he did, except that he must have been waiting for me. He told me to keep an eye on you and your mom, and that when you reached manhood, he wanted you to have these."

The lean cowboy retrieved a bag from beneath his chair. It made a heavy sound when he set it on the table and slid it toward Will.

The young man found his hands trembling as he reached for the bag. From the rough cloth, he drew a package wrapped in linen and tied with string. Once he undid the knots, he found a leather gun belt and two heavy silver revolvers with rosewood handles. He could tell they were used, but well maintained, oiled and shining in the light of the lamps and candles in the room. Will heard a sharp intake of breath when he opened the package and realized it was his own.

"Those are your father's guns, Will." George was looking at Will with a mixture of emotions on his face and seemed older than he had three days ago before the boys left on their camping trip. "They match David's here and the ones I keep in a drawer back there." He nodded his head toward the closed bedroom door.

"Joseph wanted you to know about the Rangers and the work he did. Don't know for sure if he'd have wanted you to follow in his footsteps or find your own path, but he wanted you to have his guns, and remember him." McPhail stamped out his cigarette on the plate. "They're heavy guns, heavier than the ones you've been apt to use until now, but they'll shoot truer than any as long as you care for them right."

Will drew one of the guns. It was indeed heavier than the pistols he had taken camping, but the weight felt comfortable, the grip warm in his hand. He opened the cylinders, and they spun smoothly, unloaded. He hefted the pistol and sighted across the room. He thought he could feel his father's presence looking over his shoulder, sighting down the barrel with him.

"Looks like you know how to handle a gun," McPhail commented.

"I taught both of them myself," George said. "I dare say you'll have your own opinion about it, though."

McPhail nodded his agreement. "We'll see how well you use them come the morning."

Will pulled his eyes away from the guns. "Tell me about the Rangers. Tell me about my father."

George sighed, a smile creasing his face. "Guess it's time you both hear the story."

When Jefferson had just been a territory, not yet a state, the Rangers had been the law of the land. Like everyone save the original tribes who lived and hunted the lands, the men of the Rangers had come from somewhere else to the frontier hoping to build a new and better life, and they did come from everywhere: from the full-fledged states back east both free and slave, from Mexico, and even from the native tribes.

Not everyone who traveled to the frontier came for the peace and the work and the love of the land. Some came fleeing their own demons, and sometimes they were demons themselves. The world needed good men to stand up to those elements, and so the Rangers coalesced from the good men who banded together to root out the bad.

That was the legend, in any case—a legend McPhail whole-heartedly believed and one that George perhaps hoped to believe. It was the legend that they shared with the boys that night. From a motley crew of volunteers, the Rangers had become a true force. They patrolled the territory and checked in on all the homesteads and ranches and towns. They parleyed with the tribes. They served as arbitrators in disputes. They were all expert marksmen, and when called upon, dealt in lead with those who knew no other language.

Their main base of operations was Fort Vigilant, set atop Jericho Hill toward the western edge of the territory, where they could best monitor the borders to the west and south. From there, they trained and fanned out on their patrols across the lands.

Almost twenty years ago, the territory became a state with a governor appointed from the Federation of States back east, a man named Alistair Hogg. At first, Governor Hogg merely moved into his newly built residence in the fresh minted capital of San Alonso and made to get to know the territories and make friends. The Rangers and many of his governed may not have cared for the idea of an appointed governor from the Federals back east, but they came to pay their respects and offer their services as lawmen of the territories. For a time, all seemed well, but Governor Hogg had his own plans and own vision, and he brought with him his own lawmen, his own Agents, some recruited from back east, some wooed from the ranks of the Rangers, and some from the more unsavory elements of Jefferson State.

Less than two years after his arrival, Governor Hogg flexed his power and brought an end to the Rangers. George Hennessy had seen the writing on the wall and left six months before the end arrived, as had more than a few others. McPhail and Covington had remained committed to the Rangers until the end. McPhail was on patrol when the end came, while Covington had been on the receiving end of the hammer's blow that brought an end to the Rangers. Governor Hogg's Agents, with the support of regular army reserves sent in from back east, arrived at Fort Vigilant late in the day. They ordered the Rangers to stand down and submit to the state rule. A tense night ensued. At dawn, the order to stand down rejected, the Rangers made their stand. Three days later, McPhail returned to the burned-out wreckage of his home and family and friends.

Since then, Governor Hogg had been duly elected to four consecutive five-year terms. His Agents were the law of the land and the Rangers and their days of glory were a distant memory, a very painful memory for David McPhail, less so for George Hennessy, who had made peace with his past.

Outside, night fell over the Hennessy homestead just as darkness had descended on the Rangers.

In the end, the boys cleaned the table and began scrubbing the dishes, and George did not have to sleep in the stable despite Molly's frosty reception when she emerged from the bedroom. Kali goggled as Will showed off his new guns, unaware of the future those guns would hold for them both.

"Pa's got a set of his own," Will told her.

"You do, Pa? Where are they?"

"Put away safe, Kali-Kat. They're not for you to worry about."

"What about me, Pa?" Finn asked. "You gonna hand them down to me someday?"

Over by the sink, Molly groaned a little and flashed her husband a warning glance. George read his wife's mood without the look. "I'm not dead yet, son. You've got a perfectly good rifle and pistol of your own."

"Not like Will's got," Finn complained, but his complaints went unanswered.

"Finish up your chores, boys," Molly ordered. "And then get yourselves ready for bed. Kali, you can get your things and sleep in the boys' room tonight. Mr. McPhail will use your room."

Kali's eyes lit up at the idea, and she hurried off to collect her nightgown and blankets. Once her parents were in bed, she was sure she could convince her brother and cousin to spill Mr. McPhail's story.

"Now, Molly, I don't mean to be any more trouble. Just give me a pile of hay, and I'll be fine in the stables or under the stars," the cowboy said.

Molly glared hard at him. "What kind of host do you take me for, David? You are sleeping in a bed under a roof for a change." McPhail had the good sense not to object again.

The next morning, Molly kept her three children as busy as possible with chores, but determined as they were to get done, by late morning, the three marched off across the fields to find a place to try out Will's new guns. After the first few salvos of shots began echoing across the fields, the two men ambled after them, George to try and keep an eye on them and McPhail to evaluate.

The boys had found their favorite shooting spot, an old oak that had fallen over in a rocky glen less than a mile from the farm. The old tree trunk, lying at an angle against the rocks, made an excellent base on which to stack rocks and other debris. They took turns trying to hit their targets as they got the feel of the new guns. Finn even coached his sister on aiming and firing the big guns. They bucked in her hands like a rodeo bull, but being a frontier girl, Kali's aim became true before emptying the first pistol.

McPhail watched Will for a time, taking aim and knocking down the rocks again and again. "Not bad," he complimented, "but an enemy ain't likely to stand still and wait while you aim. How good are you at drawing?"

"Show him, Will," Finn whispered before he hurried over to set up more targets.

Will reloaded. "Passable, I imagine," he replied to the cowboy. "Finn and I do practice from time to time." Finn set up a new stack of rocks and ran back over. Will dropped the pistol into his right gun belt. He rolled his shoulders and flexed his fingers, and then quick as he could he dug the gun from his belt, drew it to shoulder level, and fired. His first shot went just wide, but his second hit the pile dead center, and rock chips flew everywhere, leaving a single stone atop the tree trunk. As he turned back toward McPhail, he smiled and dropped the pistol into its holster.

"Not bad," McPhail nodded. In a blink, he drew his own gun, shot from the hip, and dropped the pistol back into his holster. When Will whipped his head around to look, the last lone rock was gone. "You'll need to be a mite faster and truer, but I can train you on that." McPhail chuckled as Kali and the two boys stood frozen and staring open-mouthed. "George, let's show them what we used to do in the Rangers."

George sighed. "Molly will have my head for this." He acquiesced though and bent to pick up a handful of stones. "How many do you want?"

"Five should do," McPhail replied.

George walked to the center of the clearing and McPhail turned his back. "Throwing," George called and tossed all five stones up high in the air above his head.

McPhail spun about, drawing his gun as he turned, eyes already looking to track the stones on their upward flight. His gun snapped up and barked five times. All five stones shattered and littered small pebbles about the clearing. "That's what a properly trained Ranger can do." He re-holstered his gun. "You've got the metal, I think. Give me the time, and I can forge you into a Ranger like your father."

"Me too. Teach me to shoot like that," Finn said. He wore an anxious look more accustomed on his sister's face, as if afraid he was going to be left behind.

McPhail looked Finn in the eye. "Aye, you too, just like your father."

"She'll have all our heads," George moaned in resignation.

Kali sidled over to her father. "Can you do that, Pa?"

"Once upon a time, mayhap, but never as good as David."

They spent the rest of the morning and early afternoon practicing shooting and the quick draw. All three of the younger ones improved their aim under McPhail's tutelage, and Will was able to outpace Finn on drawing, though his accuracy from the hip still had a way to go. By the end, George could see the small smile in his friend's eyes that meant he was pleased with the material he had to work with.

At home, they supped on a quick meal under Molly's glower, and then McPhail, Will, and Finn headed down the valley into town to find the drover captain and enlist in the cattle drive. Indeed, Mr. Franklin was pleased to enlist an experienced cowhand and traveler like McPhail, and had space for both Finn and Will. The drive would leave in just over two weeks, driving the cattle north about four hundred miles to the rail yards for shipping east to the slaughterhouses of the large cities of the Federation of States, now too crowded to raise their own herds of cattle.

Those two weeks flew by for Molly as her boys tried to tidy up the last of their chores, help prepare the homestead for their absence, arrange what they would need for the cattle drive, and spend any other free time at target practice with McPhail. For the boys, those same days leading up to their departure crawled by with endless tedious tasks and sleepless nights fantasizing of adventures that seemed would never come.

Two days before they were to leave, the Revenue Men returned. Will, Finn, and McPhail had been out deep in the woods practicing and learning the lore of the Rangers. When they returned around supper, Kali was waiting outside for them in a tizzy of anxiety. "They was here again, three of them this time. Pa talked to the head one out on the porch. I stayed out in the garden with Ma helping with the weedin', but couldn't hear what they said. I did not like the way one of them kept looking at me. The other one was wanderin' round like he was addin' up everything we owned. I'm worried, Finn." All of this came out in a rush before the boys had even dismounted.

"It'll be okay, Kali." Finn hugged his sister when he alighted. "I'm sure Pa straightened out for now, and Will and I will be back in no time with some extra money."

"I hope so, Finn. They was scary lookin'." She hugged her big brother back and looked at Will over his shoulder. "Promise you'll come back soon, Will."

Will just nodded, distracted by the dark look he saw on McPhail's face. He followed the cowboy toward their cabin.

"She's got good reason to be worried," McPhail said when Will caught up with him. "One Revenue Man is a reminder. Three of them are a show of force. Next time they'll have Agents with them. It's time your pa and I had a talk."

That talk lacked the friends' previous collegiality. It happened after dinner. Molly ordered Kali and the boys to their room when the two men started to talk in low tones. Those tones started to rise, and they stepped outside into the cool evening air. The three young ones strained their ears by the open window to hear but only caught disconnected words. "Not leaving my home." "Hogg's Agents." "Damn fool." "Got a vendetta." "Never should have let you stay." "No sense." "Always were trouble." "Clear as day." "Sarah and Joseph." "Can't hide forever." "Death of us."

In the morning, McPhail was gone, his bed still made, his tall lanky frame a memory. Kali was the only one brave enough to ask what had happened to their guest. "He left," her father said. Neither he nor his wife would speak more on the matter, and Kali dropped the subject.

Finn and Will kept urging each other with their eyes to speak up. Finn gave in first. "Are Will and I still doing the cattle drive?"

Molly surprised them by answering before their father. "Yes, we'll need that money sooner rather than later. I don't see another way to come up with it in time."

"I asked them to give us another month and a half to make the payment," George said. "That'll give you enough time to go and come back."

Finn swallowed hard. "Yes, sir. Will and I'll do that."

George gave a wan smile. "Thank you, boys."

Their final day at home dragged by. A new tension hung in the air, and the excitement of adventure to come gave way to melancholy. The wind died down so not even a breeze ruffled the trees. Despite the cool of the late winter, the air felt oppressive, an omen of the day to come. Kali's bubbly smile faded and her laughs echoed hollow. The boys helped tidy up the last of the chores around the house and packed their final bags in preparation for their sunrise departure for the cattle drive, but morning would not arrive for everyone in the Hennessy household.

Will tossed about in bed that night. With McPhail's departure, Kali was sleeping in her room. In typical Finn fashion, his cousin was snoring softly within minutes of his head hitting the pillow. That skill would serve him well on the trail. Will on the other hand was always the more high-strung of the two, more sensitive to his emotions, and tonight his emotions were afire. He would leave on the morrow for a long journey of demanding day and night work lasting three to four weeks with dangers large and small, real and imagined, at every turn of the trail. Every step would take him farther away from his home and family, and that home was in looming danger. Beyond that lurked the enigmatic figure of McPhail, a mysterious Ranger and his only link to a father he had never known. In all his years growing up with the Hennessys, they had spoken often of his mother but only of his father in dribs and drabs. Yet all this time, his adopted father had known Will's father, been his comrade-in-arms, been a lawman and peacemaker with him, and that legacy had been left to the side.

Exasperated, Will sat up in bed. He cast an envious glance at his cousin and then looked out the window. Clouds covered most of the moon and starlight and a gentle breeze had kicked up to rustle the leaves. One of the horses nickered, and another whinnied in reply, but the horse chatter was not coming from the corral. Boots tromped down into the dirt as men started to dismount their horses. His window looked out onto the side yard, not the front of the house, but Will was able to spy the edge of a silhouette of a dark-clad figure.

Will rolled out of bed and started to pull on his pants while whispering at his cousin. "Finn. Finn. Wake up. There's someone outside. Maybe it's McPhail. Wake up."

Finn grunted and smacked his lips. "What's up?"

"There's someone outside, maybe a couple of someones. Get up and get dressed." Will strapped on his gun belt and stepped into his boots. He started when their bedroom door swung open.

George stuck his head in the room. "You're up. Someone's here. Stay in your room and let me handle this."

"What's the trouble, pa?" The sleep and muzziness dropped from Finn's voice.

"No trouble, just a misunderstanding." George swung the door shut, but the shotgun in his hand belied the ease of his voice.

Finn needed no more urging and swung out of bed. "Why's McPhail creeping 'bout at night? Is it time to leave?"

"I don't think it's him."

Finn pulled on his clothes and was stepping across the room to reach for his gun belt when a voice thundered from outside. "All right Hennessy, it's the governor's Agents. We've heard about your plans. There'll be no skipping out on your debts. Come out quietly now, or we're coming in loudly."

No sooner had the last word left the speaker's lips than boots slammed against the front door.

"What's going on?" That was George's voice, but the sound of men entering the house muffled his words.

What had been terrifying dissolved into chaos.

"Gun," one of the invaders yelled. Three different sets of pistol shots echoed in the front room. George's cry of pain, and the thump of a body onto the wood floor were followed by the roar of a shotgun blast and the sound of shattering crockery.

From the other side, Kali screamed and another door burst open. "George," came Molly's anguished cry.

"Get the women, and kill the boys if you need to," the voice in charge ordered.

Will and Finn had drawn back from their bedroom door when the men first invaded their home. In the moonlight through the window, Finn's face was a pale death mask, but something cold had awakened in Will, and it paused still, lying in wait, poised like a rattlesnake with its yellow slit eyes staring down a bobcat. Maybe it was the legacy of his father flowing in his veins or the habits McPhail had endeavored to ingrain over the past short weeks. The rosewood revolvers appeared in Will's hands without the memory of drawing them.

When their door burst open and the dark figure stormed in, firing his gun into Finn's empty bed, Will's guns rose to meet him. The man must have caught Will's shadow as the door swung farther open because the invader's gun hand started to track toward Will, but the man was too late. That cold creature took over, and Will fired both pistols, their thunder deafening in the enclosed space. The man slammed into the side wall and collapsed, leaving a dark stain on the wall.

Shouts went up from the other rooms and more screams. "Phillips is down," someone yelled, and two shots came through the doorway, missing both boys as they dropped to the floor. From outside the door came sounds of a scuffle, Molly screaming for George and her boys, a shot, more screams, another shot, and the screams became a gurgle.

Will aimed out the door toward the gunman but did not fire for fear of hitting his family. Beside him, Finn's body trembled with rage or fear or sadness, Will could not tell; but his cousin now held his pistol in a sweaty palm.

"Get 'em out," the original voice shouted. More dark figures went past the doorway, at least one of them holding a struggling form. Then, a new gunman spun into the doorway to fire. His shot went wide, but neither Finn's nor Will's did, and a second man went down.

By now, all the interlopers had retreated to the front of the house. The two boys went through the doorway, Finn high and Will low. Their shots scattered off the front door frame and into the night but found no flesh and blood targets. There were no more intruders.

"Ma. Pa. Kali," Finn yelled. He went back down the hall

toward the other rooms, while Will crouched in the doorway, watching the front door. Off to the side, a familiar booted foot stretched into his field of view, and it did not so much as twitch at the commotion all around it.

"Ma." Finn's cries had turned to anguish now. Will glanced back at the door one more time and turned toward his parents' room.

Outside the men shouted, and their horses' hooves began pounding on the dirt. Scarcely had he turned than Will skidded to a halt. Finn sat in the hallway cradling their mother in his lap, but by the lolling of her head and the crimson stain on her chest, Will could tell she was gone. In her hand dangled a gun belt with a duplicate of the guns Will held in his own hands.

Will had time to take in the scene, and then bullets began flying again, this time from outside. The riders outside were shooting into the house. Most lodged themselves in the log walls, but some shattered the windows. He dropped to the ground as a bullet whipped overhead. A voice outside yelled, "Light 'em up." The sound of breaking glass outside cut off the gunfire, and then the glow of fire began to dance up the walls.

"They must have thrown oil lanterns on the walls, Finn. They're gonna burn us out." Will crawled over to his cousin, but Finn did not respond.

"How you like that, you brats?" the voice Will identified as the leader yelled. "Come on out and play or roast in there with your pappy and mammy. Makes no never mind to me." His laugh was deep and grating. "We'll show you what happens when you traitors mess with governor's Agents. If you come out nice though, maybe we won't have to take it out on little sister." Now Kali's scream of pain pierced the night, and that shook Finn from his stupor.

"Get Pa's guns," Will ordered while he reloaded his two pistols. "We gotta find a way out." The home had only the front door, and while they might be able to scramble out a window, they would make easy targets doing so. They crouched at the entryway to the main room. The invaders had left the front door open, and the boys could see flames licking around the porch. Beyond the flames, men on horseback pranced about the yard, brandishing their pistols. Tendrils of smoke ran up through cracks in the logs and from between the roof beams as the shingles began to catch fire.

"Do we throw out our guns and surrender, or do we go out shooting?" Finn paused midway through the sentence to cough. His head cocked toward Will, but Will suspected that was to avert his eyes from the body lying to the left of their kitchen table.

Will's eyes were red and watering. Later he would swear that had been the smoke, nothing more. "Shooting." He had hoped to sound confident but his voice broke on that single word.

Finn swallowed hard and blinked back his tears. "Blaze of glory. You go left, and I'll go right."

Not trusting his voice, Will nodded. The two boys began to cross the front floor in a crouch, hoping the smoke and flames outside would obscure their movements. They did not. Will could see the Agent closest to the door raise his pistol toward them. He raised his own in return, disappointed that they were not even going to make it to the door before the shooting started.

A crack of gunfire echoed, and the Agent pitched forward to the ground, a dark rent in his back. The horse bolted. More bullets followed the first, all coming from off to their right, and cries of pain and the thump of bodies came from the left.

"Murdock's down," someone hollered.

"Let's get out of here," another voice yelled, and the hoof beats began to recede.

A tall lanky figure strode into sight through the doorway. His guns were still pointed to the left after the retreating horses. McPhail began calling. "George, Molly, Finn, Will, anybody still in there?"

Neither boy hesitated. They burst from the doorway, one after the other, and danced across the flaming porch. McPhail glanced at them but retrained his eyes after the fleeing Agents. "Keep your eyes out. They'll regroup and be back any minute. Get your horses. We need to get out of here now."

"But Ma and Pa are still in there," Finn objected. "And they took Kali."

McPhail's eyes were cold. "No time for the dead now, else you plan on joining them. I told your father it was time to leave, and he didn't listen. Now it's your turn to choose." He strode back toward the stable from behind which his horse peeked.

Finn looked back at his burning home in despair but allowed Will to guide him to the stable. Their horses kicked and snorted in their stalls, disturbed by the gunfire and smoke and flames in the air. Calming and saddling the animals took extra minutes Will feared they did not have, but soon the boys joined McPhail outside in the smoky air.

The homestead was a roaring bonfire shooting licks of flame twenty or thirty feet in the air with embers raining down about the yard. One pile of hay had caught fire and the oak tree between the stable and house was starting to catch.

McPhail wheeled his horse around and started heading into the hills.

"Wait," Will yelled. "They went the other way."

"Which is why we're going this way," McPhail snapped.

"What about Kali? What about making them pay?" Will's voice broke with fury.

"Those are trained Agents. I took them by surprise and killed their leader. They'll regroup though, and be back for revenge themselves soon enough. If we're still here when they get back, you won't be the ones making them pay. You're not ready yet." McPhail spurred his horse and galloped off into the night, and Will and Finn had to follow or be left.

They were deep in the hills before McPhail slowed their pace and started turning to the east and the distant town. "We'll have to get you boys out of here for a while until things cool down. We'll take the long way, and I'll meet up with Franklin in the morning. The Agents may know you boys were going on the drive. We'll send you two boys ahead one or two days' ride and wait for us to catch up. Unless I miss my guess, Franklin's not a fan of Hogg or his Agents. Once word gets out about what happened at your farm tonight, I'm sure he won't mind helping you hide out for a while. If not, we can strike out on our own for a time."

"Just like that?" Finn glared at McPhail. "They just killed our parents and burned our house and took our sister, and we're just gonna run off with our tails between our legs?"

"Being dead with them won't help." McPhail shrugged. "Your choice. Stay, fight and die; or come with me, learn some things, and then we'll take it to the man pulling all the strings. Either way, I'm taking some cattle north."

After that, they rode through the night in silence.

ᕦ *TEMPERANCE* ᕤ

Two weeks later, Will and Finn were riding tail with two other young men behind a herd of almost one thousand cattle. Their job in riding tail was to prod the stragglers along and eat their dust. At some point in the past week, their sense of smell had deadened enough that they no longer noticed the odor except when they ate when everything had the faint taste of cow manure. They wore their bandanas across their noses and mouths but even then, by the end of the day, were spitting out thick brown and black mucus.

Given his experience, most days McPhail rode point up at the front of the herd near Mr. Franklin, the trail boss, and the chuck wagon. Sometimes, though, he would take up swing or flank position farther back along the sides of the herd. He also had the first choice at the horses, while being the tail riders, Finn and Will tended to get the nags of the lot when their own horses needed to rest.

The days were long, plodding, and boring while at the same time tense in an instant. The cows were stupid, fearful, and at turns cantankerous. The slightest noise out of turn could stop them dead in their tracks, requiring much cajoling to get them moving, or flip them off into a dangerous stampede that could take hours to control and get the herd back on track.

The terrain was rough with rocks, narrow gullies, steep hills, and wide open plains dotted with hidden prairie dog holes seemingly designed to catch the unwary hoof and break a steer or horse's leg and perhaps a rider's neck.

Then there were the rivers. Even a narrow creek could hide a submerged rock or sinkhole, and after the cattle drank, what remained for the drovers was thick enough to chew. Trying to wash off some of the trail dirt in those was apt to leave the bather worse off than when he started.

The wide rivers were the worst. On the positive side, there might be clean water to drink afterward, but crossing with one thousand head was trying. From the shore, the river might look calm enough, but get far enough across and the current could kick up and sweep away the unwary steer. At one broad but calm-appearing river, they lost several young steers and almost lost one of their cowboys to the current. Mr. Franklin, back from scouting the trail, was able to lasso the young man from out of the center of the river.

During the day, the sun beat down relentlessly. In fact, the only saving grace of riding tail was that the dust plumes of the herd sometimes blocked enough of the sun to make the heat bearable. At night, when the sun dropped below the horizon, the wind would kick up and knife through blankets and clothes alike. They all huddled as close to the campfire as possible on those nights.

The nights, though, did not mean rest. The ground was generally as hard and rocky as the air was cold. When Will was not tossing and turning and waking to the sounds of the night, he was pulling watch duty, making lazy circles around the dozing cattle and keeping an eye out for rustlers or bandits, but also for the all too common wolves and coyotes that were liable to sneak in under the cover of darkness. Nights were the worst for the risk of stampede. The cattle, jittery during the day, were downright panic-stricken if awakened from sleep by a strange noise, distant thunder, the unexpected clang of a cooking pan, or even the snap of a branch in the middle of the night.

Given the continual drudging work, neither Finn nor Will had much chance to dwell on Tranquility, their last terrible night at home, their parents left unburied, or their sister gone without a trace. When they did see him, McPhail refused to speak of those subjects, saying, "What's done is done," or "Reckoning will come when it will and no sooner," if pressed. Worse, the trail curtailed their training with the guns. They had no time or energy to practice, and even if they did, shooting off six-shooters anywhere near the cattle was likely to cause disaster. In fact, at McPhail's urging, they kept their guns wrapped up and hidden among their gear. Most of the men on the drive did not carry firearms on their person, though at night, Mr. Franklin would pass out rifles for the men on night watch in case of wolves.

For all of the hardships and the heaviness hiding below the surface, the cattle drive was cathartic for both young men. Their fellow drovers were pleasant fellows with colorful lives and tall tales to tell around the campfire. They welcomed Will and Finn into their midst without question and would spell them or their fellow tail riders from time to time.

Eddy Krummhorn was the horse wrangler in charge of the remuda, the riding horses driven along with the cattle. He was an old hand at cattle drives, and he and Alejandro Diaz, the cook, had been riding with Mr. Franklin for the last eight years on these drives. Eddy was always willing to share riding tips and the best ways to earn a horse's trust and when to know to trust the horse. Alejandro laughed at everyone's jokes, even

McPhail's poor dry ones. Much like their mother had, he prodded the young men to eat second helpings to keep their strength up, and his cooking made those second helpings worthwhile though, by noon and dinner, all the cowboys were hungry enough that taste was a secondary criterion.

At night, interspersed among the stories, they sang trail songs about the long days and nights, the cold and the rain, the heat and the dust, the mercurial nature of the steer they shepherded, and more than a few ribald ballads about the women they had left behind and the women at the end of the trail. They played poker for matchsticks and twigs because, on a cattle drive, all cowboys were paupers until the end of the trail.

Two weeks on the trail broke Will and Finn down. Farm life had not been easy, and they were strong, but life on the trail was harder and made them shed all the softness McPhail had seen in their father. Complacency fled. Senses tightened. Reflexes heightened. An hour of tedium shooing stray cattle back into line could turn to life versus death reactions when a big steer took umbrage to the prodding or a group of the big animals took it into their mind to turn and bolt at the wrong sound or the wrong smell. The next two weeks served to build them back up stronger than before. When the cattle drive rolled into the stockyards at the railhead in Temperance, they were seasoned cowboys and weathered men, or so they felt.

Growing up in Tranquility on a farm, Will and Finn were unprepared for Temperance. The largest gatherings they had ever seen were the local barn dances which consisted of maybe fifty men, women, and children from the surrounding homesteads, and even then the animals at the dance outnumbered the people. Now with one thousand or so cattle rolling into Temperance, the animals still outnumbered the people, but the town was several hundred strong.

Temperance marked the westward end of this branch of the transcontinental railroad. Workers were still extending west, but for now, the town was booming with banks, rail men, farmers, and ranchers shipping out their stock, dry goods men shipping in new wares, shops, hotels, a physician and a barber-surgeon, blacksmiths, real primary and secondary schools, a post office, houses, a sheriff's office, jail, magistrate, and of course, saloons and brothels and gambling houses located just south of the rail tracks not far from the rail yard.

Mr. Franklin's drovers stuck together to drive the cattle into their pens for counting and waited for him to settle up with the railroad officials. Then they all met by Alejandro's chuck wagon to settle out their wages.

The trail boss counted out the bills into two piles in front of Will and Finn. "Sixty-two dollars each," Mr. Franklin declared. "Not bad for four weeks of work for young men of your age." He covered the piles with his hands before Will and Finn could reach for them. "A word of advice before you take them." He eyed both boys. "Some of your companions on this ride would have you come out with them and spend these wages on dice, cards, booze, and women. If you do that, you're liable to come off with empty pockets, a headache, and a bad case of something in your nethers." Now his voice dropped lower. "Someone else on this drive might have other plans for you. I knew your pa, not well, but I knew him. My advice is get yourselves a nice hot bath, a good meal, and a room for the night. In the morning, buy yourselves a ticket and head east or north or west, I don't care, but don't head back south. Only misery lies that way."

Finn looked unsure, but Will's eyes blazed. "Thank you

much for your advice, Mr. Franklin, and all your teaching during this drive. We'll take your words to heart." His eyes told a different story, and Mr. Franklin read it there.

"Aye, I hope you do, Will. I hope you do."

Finn swallowed and shifted his weight from side to side. "Really, Mr. Franklin, thank you. We'll think hard on your words. You've been good to us and always steered us right."

Will pushed past his cousin and put his hand on his stack of money. "But in the end, Finn and I will be making our own decisions."

Mr. Franklin resisted for a heartbeat and took his hand away. "Godspeed to you, Will. You'll need it."

Both boys scooped up their money and walked back toward McPhail, who as usual stood on his own. "Let's go, boys." Will joined him, walking by his side while Finn trailed two paces behind, his head down and sending self-conscious glances back toward Mr. Franklin and the rest of the drovers.

The trio's first order of business was to stable their horses for the night and find bunks for themselves. They deposited their gear in a cheap hotel near the stables before heading into the town proper. Piano music mixed with the sounds of shouts, and laughter filtered out of the saloons lining the roads. The smells were of beer and whiskey, burnt breads and meats, and the pungent tang of cigarettes and cigars. Some of the famous painted ladies of Temperance displayed rounded calves from doorways or called and waved to them from the windows above.

"There you are. Will, Finn, McPhail, been looking all over for you three." Vega, one of the other cowboys from the drive, waved to them from one of the saloon doors. Boyd, his comrade-in-arms, was swaying in the door with him. "Come on in. We need to celebrate."

McPhail looked to his wards.

"One drink can't hurt." Finn shrugged, and so the other

two assented.

"Yeehaw," yelled Vega. He dropped an arm each around Finn and Will's shoulders. "Gonna make men of you boys tonight."

Inside they found a crowded saloon with lines of blackjack, poker, and craps tables in the back, a bar crowded two to three bodies deep redolent with the smells of alcohol and sweat, and of course more of the famous painted ladies who from time to time would lead a cowboy up some stairs to a private room. At a little table off to the side crowded Eddy the wrangler, Royce, another cowboy from the drive, two other men who seemed to be old friends of Eddy's, and three ladies. A few used food plates littered the table, but mostly it was covered in beer and whiskey bottles and shot glasses.

Eddy whooped at the sight of the three and invited them in with open arms.

McPhail was polite, shared two shots of whiskey, bought a round for the table, gently declined one of the lady's advances, and faded from the scene before Will realized what had happened.

By then Will's head was abuzz. Like most frontier boys, he had drunk his share of beer or spirits around their old homestead, but never in such quantities and with so little food in his stomach. He still had enough sense to be grateful McPhail had insisted they lock up most of their wages before coming into the town. Mr. Franklin had been right about how easy it was for money to slip through a cowboy's fingers. He did not have enough sense though to know when enough was enough.

Boyd pulled him over to a craps table and did his best to explain a surefire strategy to win every time. In both of their alcohol-addled minds, every bet seemed perfectly clear, but despite that, Will's meager coffers shrank with every roll of the dice. Next, he tried a couple of hands of blackjack before stumbling back to the table empty-handed.

"Here you go. Wash away the pain." Royce offered him a shot of whiskey, and Will threw it back just like his mates had shown him. It burned terrible going down and even worse as it sat there in his stomach. "Rotgut," someone, maybe Boyd, had called it, and Will had to agree with that assessment. His eyes watered and blurred for a minute before he could see straight again.

Meanwhile, Finn sat there with the biggest grin his cousin ever had seen stretching across his bright red face. The grin was directed at the lady who had plopped into his lap at Vega's behest. She was laughing and pouring more whiskey into Finn's glass and whispering into his ear. Finn nodded to her with more of that vacant grin. Soon, she led the dazed boy up the stairs in the back. In all of that, since returning to the table, Will never heard Finn say a word.

"Be gentle with him, Mavis," Vega called after them. "It's his first time."

Mavis gave a theatrical wink and disappeared upstairs with her charge.

Vega clapped Will on the back. "Don't worry, hijo. Once Mavis has broken in Finn there, she'll give you a spin if you like." Will smiled and then puked on the floor. "Well, maybe some other night, then," the cowboy conceded.

Not much more than fifteen minutes later, Finn came back down the stairs with an even wider grin on his face. He whooped in greeting to his trail mates when he bellied up to the table. He grabbed Will and shook him. "That was amazing, Will. We have to find you a lady friend." He leaned in close. "I think I'm gonna get some more money and go again." In close, he got a better whiff of Will and then leaned back. "Or we could just take you back to the bunkhouse."

Vega and Royce poured one more round into the boys and then laughed themselves red in the face as the cousins stumbled out of the saloon and into the streets. "Think they'll find their way home?" Vega was holding his side in laughter.

"Not likely. Probably find them passed out in some alley come the morning." Royce elbowed his friend. "Course if Finn does find his way to the bunkhouse, I think he'll be stumbling on back for more of Mavis or one of her friends."

The two cowboys clinked their glasses. "Told 'em I'd make men of them," Vega declared.

Outside, the sun had set long since and the heat of the day had disappeared into the bright, wide-open field of stars that hung like a canopy over Temperance. Neither Will nor Finn noticed the stars, though. Finn looked through muslin-covered eyes up and down the street to get his bearings, while Will just concentrated on getting one boot in front of the next without vomiting again.

Despite some laughs from neighboring saloons and gambling houses, the two young cowboys wove unmolested through the streets of Temperance toward the stockyards and McPhail's chosen bunkhouse. Their downcast eyes and gait made it clear to anyone they passed that these two cowboys had exhausted their funds.

In an uncommon display of courtesy, McPhail did let the boys sleep off some of their hangovers the next morning. When he did wake them, he brought along a pot of mud-colored coffee that was better than anything on the trail. Less courteous was his plate of hot eggs and bacon. The greasy smell permeated the room and made both boys groan.

"I do believe Mr. Franklin warned you about the headaches, among other things." McPhail was leaning back in a chair, shoveling eggs and bacon into his mouth and chomping away with his teeth like train wheels beating along the tracks, and smacking his lips. "Get on up and have a cup of coffee. It'll help."

Will groaned and covered his ears. "Do you have to chew so loud?"

"Loud enough to get you boys moving, anyway. Once you're up, we got to load up on supplies for the journey back. We'll be needing more ammunition if you two are going to get any better at shooting."

The thought of improving his shooting did break through the drums pounding in Will's head, and he was willing to sit up. He promptly leaned back over and put his head between his legs. "I think I'm gonna be sick again."

"Chamber pot's under the bed," McPhail told him. "If you miss, you're cleaning up the mess."

It took a few minutes, but the green faded from Will's face, and he managed to find his way to the offered cup of coffee. Warmth spread out from his stomach. He plopped back down on his bed and continued to sip.

Finn was sitting up in bed too. "You think Mavis will be at that same saloon again tonight? I'd like to make her company again."

"No," McPhail said. "She may be there, but we'll be on the trail by then. Can't have you two boys wasting another night of debauchery here in Temperance."

Finn looked over at Will. "What if Will and I aren't ready to head back to Tranquility? Maybe we could find some work here or maybe head east or somewhere?"

To Will, his cousin looked forlorn, lost, and not like the older brother he claimed to be, but Will had no sympathy in that moment. "They killed our parents, and they took Kali. You can do what you will. Go run off like Mr. Franklin says if you want, but I'm heading south with Mr. McPhail."

"I ain't saying we should run away." Finn looked hurt. He wished he had Will alone to talk with him. On the trail, when McPhail had been up at the front and they had been at the tail, Will had been himself. Whenever McPhail was around, though, Will had a hardness in him that scared Finn more than a little. "They wuz my parents, more'n yours. I'm just saying maybe we need more time. Anyway, I ain't sure Pa'd want us trying to go after a bunch of Agents. He and Ma'd want us to stay safe."

Will was looking at the floor, unable to look his cousin in the eye. He was afraid Finn would be able to read the contempt in his face. "What about Kali? You think she's safe? You think Pa would want us to just forget about her? We have to find her and protect her."

"Aw, they wouldn't hurt Kali. She's just a kid." Even as he said it, Finn knew he did not believe that statement one bit. Kali was more of a woman now, even if she would always be his little sister, and certainly, the Agents had shown little concern for anyone's safety when they came calling that night. "Okay. We'll go back. For Kali."

McPhail did not say a word. He finished his bacon and eggs and waited for the boys to get themselves ready for the day.

By midafternoon, they had saddlebags laden with fresh blankets, rations, full canteens, coats, a change of clothes, and ammunition aplenty. McPhail even purchased a small pack mule to lessen the burden on their horses. Precious little of their scrip remained, but the trail back across Jefferson toward Tranquility, the Agents, and Kali would not cross any towns where they could spend that money in any case. They bade their farewells to Temperance, set the sun to their right, and rode out across the plains.

The cattle drive had taken just over four weeks to travel the distance from Tranquility to Temperance. Unencumbered by a thousand head of cattle, the journey home could have taken a quarter of that time. After an initial grueling push to make plenty of distance from the distractions of Temperance,

McPhail made sure they traveled slow and began their indoctrination in the ways of the Rangers.

They were sitting around a campfire the second night, their hangovers burned out by a day and a half of hard riding. Finn was still making frequent breaks to pass water and swear from the burn. McPhail had picked up a bag of medical supplies at the apothecary in Temperance, and he passed a vial of tincture of quinine to the stricken young man. "Two swallows morning and night'll put you right as rain."

"The morphine'd help more," Finn complained but took a swallow of the quinine and grimaced.

"Deadens the pain but also the mind. You need to stay sharp now. Quinine'll burn out the infection."

McPhail sat back and puffed on his cigar. He stared into the fire, deep in his own thoughts. "You have to understand there were never more'n a hundred of us Territory Rangers, but of course, there weren't that many people around to look after back then. Some of the larger towns might have a local man serve as sheriff when needed, but he'd be spending most of his days farming or ranching or shoeing horses or whatnot. Most disputes people just settled themselves and usually civilized-like. Just like in Tranquility, you depend on your neighbors, and if you don't do them a good turn, then they're liable not to do you a good turn when the time comes."

McPhail puffed some more and then spat. "But some feuds get too big and there's always some men'll take from the weaker. That's where the Rangers came in. We patrolled the land back then, visiting the towns and cities and farms. We arbitrated the disputes as fairly and wisely as we could, and the people listened to us and respected us. When called upon, we dealt with the bullies and ruffians and rooted out the bandits and thieves and murderers."

"I won't say we were perfect. We were men, and men make errors, but we were honest, and if we made a mistake, we tried to make amends. Much more'n not we did right. The people respected us and young boys wanted to grow up to be Rangers." The cowboy's eyes glistened in the firelight, lost in reminiscence.

Then a shadow blew over his face. "Now Governor Hogg's Agents may pretend to walk in our boots, but you saw what happened in Tranquility yourselves. They are not peacemakers. They are not men of justice. They are the iron fists of Governor Hogg ruling over our state." He puffed some more. "The good news is that not all the Agents are what you'd call quality fighters. Most of them are just bullies grown too big for their britches, swaggering about and putting on airs. Hogg has a core posse of about a dozen hard men loyal to him, and most of them would've had the skills to be true Rangers back in the day. Hell, a few of them used to be Rangers. They'll be hard men to kill." Now McPhail gave a rueful smile. "Of course now there's one less. That was Claude Murdock at your farm unless I miss my guess, and he won't be troubling anyone no more."

"How can there only be a dozen? We've seen and heard of Agents and Revenue Men all over." Will was leaning forward, intent on the story.

McPhail puffed his cigar some more. "Each of Hogg's personal Agents recruits his own posse. Every man's different, but most have five or ten men of their own, some even twenty, I'd guess. Most of them's a mixed bag. You got some good shots, some quick draws in there, and any man can have his lucky day with you. That's where you get the bullies, though, just men too full of themselves, thinking they look good in Hogg's black, thinking they can lord it over the rest of us. Some'll stand and fight, but once you take out the real leader, most of them'll scatter like gnats."

"So are we going to war against Governor Hogg?" Finn looked worried. "I mean, there's only three of us against an army, it sounds like."

McPhail stared at Finn with those cold hard eyes. "I'm a

Ranger. I set things right. It don't matter the odds. I've got a job to do, and I've left it alone for too long. If you're willing, I'm gonna make Rangers of you and Will here. Your fathers were Rangers. George Hennessy and Joseph Covington were my friends, and in our day, we were some of the best of the Rangers. A Ranger is worth ten of any regular man. There's three of us now, but there'll be more in time. We're gonna make sure Hogg knows his tyranny is at an end."

"We're with you," Will said. "Finn and I are with you. I want to be a Ranger like my father. We're gonna find Kali and then we're gonna make Governor Hogg and his men pay for what they did to our family and all the families in this state." He looked at Finn with wild eyes. "We're gonna be heroes, Finn. They'll be singing our songs and telling our story forever."

To that, Finn had nothing else to say. When he glanced to McPhail, he saw the same fierce light that flickered in Will's, the same obsessed expression.

In the morning, the next stage of their training began. "It's all well and good to aim and shoot a target or even to draw and shoot." McPhail was puffing his morning cigar at the top of a shallow arroyo. "In a firefight though, you're on the move, and targets can be everywhere. Now I may not be able to get your targets moving, but I can get you moving." He pointed with the cigar. "Down there, I've arranged some prickly pears along the route. You follow the creek bed, and I'll call out which side. Your job is to find 'em and shoot 'em quick as I say." He eyed the two young men. "Who's first?"

Of course, it was Will. He traversed the course upstream and got seven of the ten targets on the first shot, two with his second shots, and ran out of bullets by the time he got to the tenth.

"Nine out of ten, whoopee," Finn whooped for his cousin.

"And the tenth one killed him." McPhail spat. "Your turn,

Finn. Thatta way." He pointed downstream.

Finn sighed and jumped down into the arroyo. He got eight of the targets before running out of bullets and time.

"We keep this up until you can get them all," McPhail declared.

They practiced all morning, taking turns setting up the routes the other would take. Prickly pears gave way to sticks and stones and whatever other debris they could find. By noontime, both boys had successfully negotiated their routes at least once hitting all ten targets. They ate a small meal in the scant shade provided by a tall yucca plant. Then McPhail ordered them to saddle up, and they continued south until nightfall.

They made camp near the base of a mesa with a little copse of trees struggling in the dry earth. The trees produced ample firewood for a warm meal and a little light to lengthen the day.

Finn was poking at the campfire logs with a stick. "So when we get back, how do we find Kali?"

Will shrugged. "If they let her go, she'd go home. Of course, there's no home left to go to." He sighed a melancholy breath into the night.

"There'd be no reason to keep her, right?" Finn kept poking at the fire, sending sparks dancing up into the night air. "She's just a kid. So she'd go home, looking for Ma and Pa and us. Once she found the house burned down, she'd probably go to the neighbors, maybe the Smiths. She and Theresa are friends."

Will nodded. "Okay, so we head back to the house, make sure she's not camping in the barn or something, and then check with the Smiths and everyone else in the valley. Someone's bound to know where she is."

McPhail said nothing, just lay down on a rolled-up coat and pulled his blanket up over his shoulders.

"You don't think she's there, do you?" Finn asked the

prone form.

McPhail turned his head to look at Finn. "The Agents do not generally leave witnesses to their crimes. They also don't take kindly to losing some of their own. You killed two of their men, and I killed their leader and wounded at least two others." He let that hang in the air. "If she's able, I agree, she'll go home. We look there first." He turned on his side, his back to the cousins, and was soon asleep.

The two young men stared at each other across the fire. "She's okay, Finn. Kali's okay. We'll find her and set things right." Will spoke with conviction, but inside another worming, whining voice disagreed. He looked at McPhail. The cowboy knew something, but he was keeping that knowledge to himself. Will doubted it was the first time, or that it would be the last.

The next day followed a similar pattern to the previous. McPhail arranged a course of targets for the boys to follow. Will leapt to point position first and drew his left gun. He was good with both hands, but his slow left hand needed more work, and in a firefight, he wanted to have both hands available.

"All right, Will, go get 'em," Finn said.

Will moved forward, gun up.

"Left."

Will swung left, spied a red fruit wedged in the fork of one of the trees, and watched it explode when he shot it.

"Up."

Higher in the branches, he spied the next target and the next target disappeared in a shower of pulp. He moved forward.

"Right."

Will swung right and the gunshot startled him as dirt and rock kicked up not a foot from his boots. "What the...?" He spun around to stare at McPhail whose own pistol was still smoking in his hand. Finn stood agog not two feet away from their mentor.

"Your targets will move, and they're likely to shoot back. Continue."

"Right," Will muttered to himself, and turned back to the task.

It surprised both boys how quickly they could grow accustomed to bullets interrupting their course. McPhail's random gunshots kicked up dirt and stone or bit into wood and sent small shards of shrapnel into their boots, pants, and cheeks if the shot hit a higher tree branch. Will would grit his teeth against the anger growing inside him and take out his targets. Finn took a bit longer to stop flinching, but he took to the target practice with a kind of glee, whooping and hollering and cajoling his targets. "That all you got?" "Missed me." "Eat lead."

Again, around noon, they called it a day, had a bite to eat, and hit the trail. In the evening, they camped atop a hill with only a few dry bushes and small twigs with which to make a fire. As the sun set and the fire burned down, McPhail had them practice loading their guns over and over until their fingers grew numb. They did not talk about Kali or their plans that night.

It took the trio ten more days to finish the journey back to Tranquility. By the end, both Will and Finn had honed their skills to near perfection. The courses involved drawing and shooting now and only seconds to reload when needed. The targets became smaller and better hidden. They started hunting, mostly rabbits, both to eat on the journey but also to improve their tracking and shooting skills. Hitting a running hare from a distance became the norm. They worked on their speed, trying to bare hand grab the ubiquitous lizards that patrolled the deserts. McPhail kept them busy, too busy to contemplate what awaited them in Tranquility.

The farm was gone. The house and stable had become ash, and the broad oak between them sported charred and yellowed branches. Out of the ashes at its base, a single green shoot pushed up through the ground. The fences lay broken open. The animals had disappeared. Whether that initial night or later on, the barn had also burned, leaving only skeletal fingers of wood to support a roof half collapsed to the ground.

It looked as though no one had been there since the night of the fire. They poked about among the ashes of the house and found intact only a few metal pans and the potbellied stove. They found no bones in the remains of their homestead. Either someone had come and buried them, or the fire had burned hot enough to consume them. None of the three looked hard: Will and Finn because the memories of the night were still too painful and encountering their parents' bones would be too horrible, and McPhail because the dead were beyond the cares of this world, and only the living could be helped.

Of Kali, they found no sign.

The Smith's homestead occupied a plot of land three miles southwest. As they rode around the bend toward the house, they spied Mrs. Smith outside hanging laundry while the littlest child played at her feet. Mr. Smith chopped wood while his two older boys stacked it in rows under the eaves. Theresa sat on the porch sewing the hem of a dress.

At the sight of the three riders, Mr. Smith ordered the family back inside. Then he took position in the center of the path, arms crossed, axe leaning at his side, and waited.

"Afternoon, Finn, Will." He nodded to the boys when they reined in their horses but did not acknowledge McPhail. "I didn't expect to see you two back. We don't want no trouble 'round here."

Finn and Will exchanged a surprised look. Will nodded his head a fraction to his cousin, and Finn took the lead. "We're not here for trouble, Mr. Smith. Our families have always been friends. We're looking for Kali. We thought maybe she would have come here since she and Theresa are close."

Mr. Smith frowned. "Haven't seen your sister since before that night. She was a sweet girl, but like I said, we don't want no trouble. She's not welcome 'round here no more, and neither are you boys if you don't mind me saying, and even more so if you do." His frown had now become an outright glare. "Now do me the favor of getting off my property and don't come back."

Finn sat agape on his horse.

"But, Mr. Smith," Will began. "We've been neighbors—"

"We ain't neighbors no more." His eyes narrowed to slits. Behind him, the front door of the house opened and the two older boys stepped onto the porch with rifles in hand. "You're riding with trouble, and I'll have none of it on my land. Now git." His right hand reached down to grab the handle of the axe.

Will's eyes flicked from the father to the two boys, people he'd known all of his life, now rejecting him. Anger flared in him and his right hand started to move toward the pistol on his hip.

McPhail's quiet voice overrode him. "Will, Finn, time for us to be on our way and leave Mr. Smith to the rest of his day."

Will returned Mr. Smith's glare for a few more heartbeats but put his hand back on the reins. "Aye." He wheeled his horse around and headed off down the road.

For his part, Finn sat there bewildered, a pained look spreading across his face.

"Come on, Finn," McPhail ordered, but there was an uncharacteristic softness to his voice when he spoke.

Still dazed, the young man turned his horse to follow Will.

McPhail nodded his head to the farmer and rode after his charges.

When they rounded the corner, Finn's confusion spilled out. "What's going on? Why won't he even talk to us? What did we do to him? We were the ones attacked and driven out of our home. We didn't do nothing wrong."

"Says you and Will," McPhail replied. "You think that's the story the Agents and Revenue Men have spread?" He urged his horse forward to a faster trot, and the others sped up to follow him. "Maybe the Agents have been saying you two boys had a fight with your parents and killed them and burned the house down. Maybe they said someone, your pa or one of you, had gambling debts and that someone came to collect, and you ran away. Maybe they said you were fomenting a revolt against Governor Hogg. Doesn't really matter. Even if none of the families in the valley believe it, not one of them is going to stand up to the governor's Agents for you. They all have too much to lose."

"So what are we going to do about it? We have to clear Pa's name." Finn looked more distraught than Will had seen him since the nights after the fire before they had joined up with Mr. Franklin and the cattle drive.

McPhail turned his horse off the road and began taking a narrow trail up into the eastern foothills. "What do you think, Will?"

Will's eyes were livid, but the anger stayed contained for now. "We get out of here. If Hogg poisoned our home against us, someone here, maybe one of the Smith boys, will go tell the Agents that we're back. Even if the people here don't be-lieve we did anything wrong, we probably have a reward on our heads for killing those Agents. We aren't safe here."

The boys could not see his face, but McPhail smiled, satis-fied that his lessons had taken root.

"What about Kali though?" Finn's voice was still breaking

with emotion. "If she comes back, they'll turn her in too. How are we going to find her?"

"She's not coming back, Finn." Will's voice was laced with bitterness. "They never let her go. Probably killed her."

"Mayhap," McPhail agreed. "But dead, she's worth nothing. Alive, she might still be useful. Depends on which of Murdock's lieutenants took over and how many brains he had in his head."

"Where do you think she is?" Will asked.

"Could be anywhere really, but the closest place to put a young girl to work is Chastity. If we cut through the mountains here, we can be there in three days."

⌒ *CHASTITY* ⌒

The journey through the mountains cleared Finn's head and washed out the morose mood that had settled over him after being rejected by his childhood home. The mountain air and trails reminded him of happier times camping with Will and living off the land. Even at the best of times, Finn was mercurial by nature, but a night in the high mountain air to wash out the smell of ash in his heart and a destination to navigate toward, and Finn reverted to his ebullient self.

For all outward appearances, Will seemed at peace too. In some sense, he had always been an interloper or beloved guest in the Hennessy household, part of the family but not really. No one ever told him that, and Molly and George had never treated him that way, but Will felt it just the same. He was never a Hennessy, always a Covington. He took the anger he had felt down in the valley and wrapped it up tight and stored it away for later use. He could tell that McPhail carried his anger deep within him, and if it worked for the Ranger, it would work for Will.

When they crested the pass and saw the plains and Chastity laid out before them, Finn whooped. "Whooee. Look at that down there. We're becoming city slickers, ain't we, Will." Will laughed with his cousin.

"Look at everything going on down there and all the people. Maybe we need to settle down in a place like this. The farm was all right, but I think the city is for me." Finn urged his horse ahead.

McPhail grunted. "If you want to see a city, Finn, you got to travel back east to the coast or maybe out to San Francisco. Even San Alonso isn't much of a city compared to those places, and Chastity is just an ugly pimple in the desert."

Finn's horse trotted well ahead of the others. "Don't really matter for now. I guess I'll just have to work my way up," he called over his shoulder. "Now let's go have some fun."

"And find Kali," Will added to his cousin's back.

The town of Chastity lay on the opposite side of the mountains from the Tranquility Valley. It was not as big as Temperance by any means but was still a bustling town compared to any other town Will and Finn had ever visited. Located on the banks of a river rolling off the mountains, it was a waypoint for travelers heading east to the distant capital of San Alonso or southwest around the mountains toward South Cali and Mexico. Traders and trappers followed the route, as did highwaymen and bandits and mercenaries and Hogg's conscripted men. Telling the difference amongst the latter groups could be an exercise in futility.

Being on the main line of the railroad, more legitimate business interests dominated Temperance, while Chastity specialized in the bawdier end of the spectrum. There was a single general store and plenty of flophouses and bunk rooms as opposed to the nicer hotels of Temperance. A surfeit of saloons and gambling dens, and more than any town's fair share of houses of ill-repute, and many of those establishments all wrapped into one, made up the remainder of the buildings. A lone church stood on the outskirts of the town, its bell tolling against the heedless sin and vice before it. All of those businesses provided a plethora of employment options for a young woman, be it washing, cleaning, cooking, serving meals and drinks, or selling her feminine charms. Many times, a job involved all of the above.

"Chastity is a bit wilder than Temperance," McPhail told his protégés. "Keep your guns with you, but generally there'll be no trouble 'less you win too much gambling and get accused of cheating." He looked at Will. "Course if you lose all your hands, they'll be more'n happy to have you at their table."

They hitched their horses outside one of the bunkhouses not far from Chastity's lone church. The journey back from Temperance had divested the team of most of their supplies, and the mule carried little more than their bed rolls, which they redistributed to the horses.

"You boys can start asking around about your sister. I'm going to see what we can get for the mule," McPhail said, and led the mule over to the nearby corral.

Finn led his cousin into the office of the bunkhouse. The proprietor, a thin balding man with a scraggly beard, squinted at them when they entered. "Need beds for the night?"

"Not right now. We're looking for someone," Finn replied.

"Lots of someones around here, but I'm not the lost and found office."

"She's a young girl, name of Kalirose Hennessy." The proprietor just stared at Finn. "Sixteen. Blond. About this tall." Finn held up his hand at shoulder height.

The man stared back without expression. "If that's what you're looking for, they got all shapes and sizes and colors 'round here, but this ain't that sort of place. Try down the block."

Finn's eyes narrowed. "She's not like that. She's my sister."

The proprietor just stared back with those squinting eyes. Will laid a hand on his cousin's shoulder. "Sorry, sir. We just think she might have been brought here looking for a job, maybe cleaning rooms, washing up, that sort of thing."

"Lots of young women 'round here. Hard to tell them apart."

Will pulled a coin out of his pocket and slid it across the counter. "Maybe if you just thought a little harder, you might remember her."

The coin disappeared under the counter. "Still haven't heard of her. Now, if you're not looking for a room, I'll ask you to be going." When the hand that had absconded with the coin came back up, it rested a weathered-looking pistol on the counter.

Will grimaced. "Thank you kindly." He turned and dragged his cousin out with him.

Outside, they waited for McPhail to finish his transaction with the stable owner. Will sighed. "Okay, so I'm about as good at bribing as I am gambling, and the people here are not the helpful upstanding citizens we grew up with."

"Oh, yeah, the Smiths were real upstanding," Finn said. "Let's try across the street."

Will and Finn asked in two other boarding houses, a dry goods store, and one of the hotels, with similar success.

After the long ride into Chastity, Finn's antsy, inattentive nature began to assert itself. Frustrated from the lack of results, his mind moved on to other distractions. He stopped the group outside of the Broken Mare, a large building whose music and signs made it clear that it served all the many and varied tastes a man could desire in Chastity: food, drink, cards, dice, and female companionship. "I'm hungry and thirsty. Let's eat."

"What about finding Kali?" Will asked as they headed to the doors.

Finn shrugged. "Maybe she's serving drinks in here. Anyhow, we need to eat."

Tables and a bar occupied the front half of the room, while gambling tables dominated the back half. Above them, a flight of stairs led to a landing on the second floor that stretched in an *L* along two sides of the building. The corner of the second floor seemed to be offices of the managers, but multiple doorways through which men came and went dominated the rest of both wings. Some time later, a delicate hand might reach out to flip a sign by the door, or the woman herself might step out and wave to a gatekeeper at the foot of the stairs. Soon another man would head up the stairs to the designated room.

Will and Finn found a table near the bar and ate and drank. They scanned the waitresses but did not find Kali among them. Not long after their food arrived, McPhail caught up with the cousins. He had not located Kali in any of the establishments he had visited, either.

Finn was on his third beer and second shot of whiskey. Will had joined Finn for a single shot and nursed a beer with his food. Unpleasant memories of Temperance danced in his head, but on the other hand, the weight of the last few weeks and the fruitless search for Kali demanded some numbing solace of its own.

"I know what we need to cheer you up, cuz. Come on." Finn grabbed Will's arm and pulled him to his feet. "We're gonna find you a lady friend and make you a man like me."

McPhail let out a tiny puff of air and his head shook a fraction, but he kept eating in silence.

"I don't know, Finn." Will pulled back and did not follow.

Finn came back, this time with a firmer grip to drag him along. "You'll thank me for this later. You'll love it."

Will shot a glance over to McPhail, but the Ranger did not meet his eyes and continued to chomp mechanically at his food. Will would have to make his own choices. "Just like you loved cursing in the bushes every time you pissed and all the quinine you had to drink?"

Finn wagged a finger in Will's face. "Shut up." He continued to pull his cousin along and then turned back with a smile once more. "And it was worth it."

A small knot of men clustered in a rough line near the foot of the stairs. As each man's turn came, he handed over money to the gatekeeper and headed up. Waiting, Finn shifted foot to foot, rolled his shoulders, and gabbled on to Will's quiet, downcast countenance. Soon after, Finn bounded up the stairs to a brunette who greeted him at her door with a laugh.

When the next room opened up, Will demurred and let man after man pass in front of him until Finn came back down from his rendezvous.

"What are you still doing here?" He shook his cousin's shoulders and then leaned in close. "We're out there shooting and training and planning on taking on the world. Hell, you've even killed a man, two of 'em, and you're scared of a woman?" Finn pushed him back to the man at the base of the stairs. "He's going next," Finn declared and slapped the money down on the stand.

The man gave him a gap-toothed leer. " 'Bout time, boy. Don't worry though. First time's always the scariest. Oh, looks like room nine is ready." He pointed along the landing branch over the bar about midway down. A pale hand had just flipped the sign and darted back in. "Might need a firm hand to get her started, but then she'll be fine."

Will swallowed hard and lifted one leaden leg after the other to scale the mountainous stairway. Inside he was as aquiver as Finn, if for different reasons. Back a few months ago, he had been just a normal boy, not yet a man of age, curious about the opposite sex and being a farm boy aware of the basic anatomic material, but still considering girls and women a bit mysterious. He had fancied Kali's friend Theresa and hoped to ask her to step out with him at the next barn dance. Now he was heading upstairs to lay with a woman he had not even seen. Half of him wanted to run up the stairs, and the other half wanted to throw up.

Will kept his eyes glued to his boots marching across the polished wooden floor. Then there he was standing at the door to room nine. Not knowing what else to do, he rapped on the door and stepped inside.

Down below, Finn rejoined McPhail at the table. He could just spy the top of Will's head before he entered the room. "Whooee, go get her, Will." He grinned at McPhail and took a swig of beer. "You're looking mighty sour there. Maybe you should have a go yourself. Really brightens your day."

McPhail regarded Finn with his cold steel eyes. "I don't like my women bought and paid for."

Finn had to laugh at that. "Well, Mavis and Miss Bea upstairs sure don't seem to mind. Had plenty of fun, they did."

"Because their livelihood depends on you thinking they enjoy the experience as much as you."

"It's not like that."

"Isn't it?" McPhail asked in his flat voice.

Finn shook his head and took another swallow of beer. "Always takin' the fun out of everything, ain't 'cha."

"You have a great deal to learn about the world, Finn. Live a few more years and maybe you will."

"Spreading happiness wherever you go," Finn muttered

under his breath.

Upstairs, Will had let the door close behind him. The room was small, with hardly enough space for the narrow bed and a dresser with a mirror and a rickety chair where a lady might do her hair or makeup. There were no windows, and under the perfume was the smell of sweat and something sour. The woman, more of a girl really, was sitting near the head of the bed in white petticoats with bare cream-colored shoulders peering out at him. Her face was turned away, curtained off by her blond hair adorned with frayed pale blue ribbons.

Will cleared his throat. "Ma'am?"

Her shoulders gave a little shudder and then a sigh before she turned to him with sad blue eyes and a false smile on her lips. "You can put your things there," she started to say while pointing to the table and chair, but then her voice caught and her eye grew wide. She grabbed the covers and pulled them up over her chest. "Will?"

Will's jaw dropped. "Kali?" Beneath the smeared makeup, curled hair, and red eyes, he recognized his younger cousin.

"Is it really you, Will?" She was starting to cry now and held out her arms to him and let the sheets fall away.

He ran to her and encircled her in protective arms. "What are you doing here?"

She was sobbing now, a rush of tears, more than he had seen her shed in her entire life back in Tranquility. "It's been horrible, Will. After they took me, they told me Ma and Pa were dead all because of you and that you and Finn burned up in the house too. They beat me, and they... they did things to me. Then they brought me here and said since I'm all that's left I had to work off all of Pa's debts. They make me work here all afternoon and all night... taking care of the men." She buried her face in his shoulder, muffling her cries as her tears soaked through his shirt over his heart.

Will held her to him and rocked her. "It's okay. It's okay," he kept repeating, hoping somehow that would make it true. "Finn and I are here with McPhail. We've been looking for you, but I never thought..." Tears streamed down his cheeks too, but underneath anger was growing, not doused by the tears but inflamed by them. "We're going to get you out of here. Now."

He pushed away from her and wiped her eyes with the cuff of his shirt leaving dark streaks on her face, but at least removing some of the hideous powder and makeup. "Get on whatever clothes you have." He stood up and started to go the door but stopped. He unholstered one of his guns and dropped it on the bed by her lap. "You may need that." He ran a hand through his hair and paced the small room.

"How many ways out of here other than the main staircase?"

Kali had not moved or touched the gun. A confluence of emotions ran over her face: joy, fear, shame, hope, despair. "There's a back stairs through the offices in the corner to our rooms, but they're more like cells really. That's where they take us when our shift is over, but there's doors out to the back where deliveries come in for the kitchens and things."

"Okay, so down the main stairs where everyone sees us, or out through the offices."

"There's always men in there, Will. That's where the boss is if he isn't on the floor."

"We need Finn and McPhail. I can go get them, but I'm not leaving you here a moment longer." Will went to the door and opened it a crack. From his vantage, he could not see the table near the bar they had been sitting at. How to signal them then? He could step out to call to them, but that would look strange to the guards and give away the plan. Maybe if he and Kali just went out together, McPhail and Finn would see them. They could rush them, but there was a long distance from here to either set of stairs or exit. If he left the room, how much time before they would send another client up to Kali? He would not let that happen. He could not even think how often that must have happened in the past month and a half. These men had to pay. Hogg's Agents and Hogg himself would answer for this. Will would see to that himself.

Behind him, Kali's eyes drifted down to the gun on the bed. She picked it up, feeling the alien weight of it. A distant part of her remembered standing in the forest with Will and Finn and Pa and Mr. McPhail and learning to fire that gun, hitting those targets, maybe not as quick as her brothers, but hitting them. Her thoughts tumbled on to her ma and pa and the fire and everything that had happened since then: the beatings, the men, the medicine they had made her take three weeks ago when her monthly failed to come on time and terrible cramps and thick blood that had come after that, and the lines of men, always another man at her door, in her bed, on top of her. She cried herself to sleep every night. Even the laudanum they gave her did little to dull the pain inside or the shame of what those men made her do. She dreamed of Will and Finn coming to rescue her. She had never believed they were dead, and now here was Will going to take her away. Only when he had come into the room, Will was not there to rescue her. If there had been some other girl in here, Will would have climbed right on her and done his business and left, just like that line of men did to Kali every night. But Will was here showing her the way out. Kali never hesitated. She put the barrel of the gun into her mouth and pulled the trigger.

In the enclosed space, the unexpected thunder of the gun shook the room and started Will's ears ringing. He spun about, confused that somehow Kali could have accidentally set off the gun and now whatever plan he could devise would be ruined, and then he was horrified. "Kali," he screamed. "Kali! Kali!" He ran to her, pulled the gun from her lifeless fingers, and tried to lift her limp bloodied body. He screamed her name until he was hoarse and the crimson curtain of anger descended over his eyes.

Downstairs, even above the noise of music and glasses and groans of despair and cheers of joy from the gambling tables, the sound of the gunshot was loud and distinctive. All sounds stopped in the room except for the wail of a despondent voice from upstairs. "Kali!"

McPhail and Finn jumped to their feet, and the noise came back into the room. McPhail grabbed Finn's shoulder. "Go get the horses."

Finn looked bewildered. Whatever alcohol-induced sedation he might have been feeling fled. "But that's Will."

"I know. Go get the horses. We need to go, now."

When the gunshot went off, the guards who lingered on the upper floor started moving along the balcony to locate its source. The cries made that easy, and two of them converged on room nine.

Around the bar, most patrons scrambled for the door or ducked below tables. Some laughed and pointed and cheered the drama unfolding upstairs. Others only shook their heads and told the dealer to deal. McPhail grabbed Finn's shoulder one more time to get him to focus. "Meet us out back. Hurry." Finn ran.

The despondent wail had now turned deadly. One of the guards kicked the door to room nine open only to be greeted by Will, guns drawn, coming the other way. The first guard collapsed with a bullet in his chest. Blocked by his partner, the second guard could not get off a clear shot before Will's gun found him. He fell back to the railing, keeled over the side, and smashed to the floor just feet from where Finn had been standing moments earlier.

A red haze of anger and hatred flooded Will's mind. He turned to his left toward the office at the end of the hall and the three guards who were coming toward him. He roared and charged.

Will did not see the one guard at the end of the landing behind him, but McPhail did. He shot the man before the guard could take aim at Will, and then the Ranger ran across the room to the stairway to the second floor.

Upstairs Will and the guards started to exchange gunfire, but with all of his training, Will's aim did not fail, and all three went down. Before he got to the office door, it flew open and two more men came out, one brandishing two pistols and the other a shotgun leveled at Will's face.

Instinct took over. Will dropped into a slide on his back. The shotgun roared and buckshot whipped by overhead, some of the balls in the expanding cloud grazing through his chestnut hair.

Even sliding on his back along the slick wooden floor, Will's shots flew true. His right gun thundered twice and the shotgun wielder went down. His left gun, the one covered in gore, fired once and then clicked on an empty chamber. The pistol-wielding guard stumbled back clutching a shoulder but tried to bring that hand back to bear. Will's right pistol spoke once more, and the man went down.

Will pulled himself to a crouch on the wall outside the office, dropped the left pistol into his holster, and began reloading the right.

Boots pounded on the stairway. Will snapped the gun closed as another guard crested the stairway. No sooner had the guard made the turn than more shots rang out. His body twitched and collapsed, and McPhail rounded the stairway behind him. The two nodded to each other. While the Ranger closed the distance, Will reloaded and locked his second pistol by the time McPhail arrived at the end of the hall.

They stood on opposite sides of the doorway. "They had Kali," Will said. "They're going to pay."

McPhail nodded, but there might have been paternal pride blooming behind those cold steely eyes. "You go left. I'll go right."

Guns ready, the two men charged into the room beyond.

It was a small salon with a stairway down to the left and an office door hanging open to the right. A quick look confirmed the boss had deserted his office. The sound of receding footsteps and yells and screams from the first floor echoed up to them.

Will and McPhail followed.

At the bottom of the stairs, they found another branch point: to the left a set of double doors leading back to a kitchen area, to the right a corridor of rooms out of which various ladies peered, and straight ahead a set of heavy doors that were swinging open. At the sight of Will, McPhail, and the drawn guns, the women shrieked and withdrew. Through the swinging doors in front came three more armed men. They didn't last long, and then Will and McPhail burst through into the room beyond.

It was a counting room. Most of the workers dove beneath their tables and cowered, but in the back of the room, three more guards had turned over a table in a corner sending coins and bills spilling across the floor. In the center of them hunched a heavyset man in a tan suit, the owner of the Broken Mare.

Will and McPhail had no sooner passed the doorway than the three guards started firing, which sent Will and McPhail diving for cover of their own.

Will felt a bullet whizz past his ear. His shoulder impacted the floor a moment later jarring his gun hand. He fired twice with the other hand, his shots going wide, but close enough to make the shooters flinch back. McPhail's guns roared, and two of the men jerked back and fell. Will scrambled up to his haunches at the edge of one of the other tables. The third guard fired at him and missed, but Will did not.

"Stop. Stop," screamed the man in tan. He cowered back behind the table, trying to hide beneath the bodies of his guards. "Take it. Take all the money and go. Just let me be."

Will took a few cautious steps toward the overturned table, pistols still leveled at the man. Behind him, he could hear McPhail sweeping the room, shooing the money counters into another corner. The sniveling in front of him rolled up and down like a musical scale. The man was shielding his face with his arm, only one bulging brown eye peering out from under the crook of his arm and a large runnel of snot hanging from a bulbous nose.

"I'm not here for your money," Will said. "Kali was my cousin. I was here for her." He emptied both pistols into the tan suit, staining it crimson, and continued to pull the triggers on empty chambers. Finally, he dropped his arms to his sides and turned around to McPhail.

The lanky cowboy had tossed knotted pairs of money bags over each shoulder. "Will, reload. We gotta get out of here before the local law arrives."

Will ignored him and just tromped toward the doors.

McPhail hit him, not an open-handed slap but a hard fist to the side of the face. "Wake up, Ranger." McPhail's cold eyes were alight with anger now. "You're going to get yourself and the rest of us killed. Now reload, and let's move."

Will stumbled back and rubbed the side of his face. He could already feel the swelling rising on his cheekbone, but the pain cleared away the shock of the last few minutes and brought him back alert. This time he listened and reloaded in a trice.

When they arrived back at the foot of the stairs, the

women ducked back down their corridor, all except for one.

"Quickest way out, ma'am?" McPhail asked her.

She jerked her head down the ladies' corridor. At the end, they found a locked door, but the lock could not hold up to two bullets from McPhail, and then they found themselves in the back alley. Shouts went up all around them, but Finn was waiting astride his horse and leading the other two alongside.

They rode out into the main streets to more yells behind them. "That's them over there." A moment later, a shot rang out and then a second.

Will ducked down along his horse's neck and spurred her on. The shots, haphazard at first, began to grow more accurate, but distance and speed were the trio's friends. McPhail was in the lead and turned his horse at the corner of the next set of buildings to take them out of the direct line of fire before turning down the next street to head back out of town.

Will glanced back, and about two blocks away saw a cluster of horsemen, guns drawn, galloping after them. "They're after us," he yelled just before more bullets started flying. Still trying to keep his horse galloping after McPhail, Will pointed his pistol back and fired off two ineffectual rounds.

"Don't waste your bullets," McPhail called back. "Ride."

They rode, weaving in and out of buildings closer and closer to the edge of town, but their pursuers were gaining. Even on open ground, Will was not convinced they could outdistance their hunters.

McPhail knew they could not. They were galloping toward the edge of a large barn, when McPhail said to them through gritted teeth, "Get ready to stop." He turned his horse sharply at the edge of the barn, yanked her to a stop, jumped off, and slapped her rump to send her running again.

Will and Finn followed McPhail's lead with less alacrity than he had but still managed to get their horses moving and back themselves up near the wall of the barn before the posse rounded the corner.

The posse's eyes naturally followed the fleeing horses for half a second or more before realizing that the horses had no riders. It was that first second that turned the tide. The Ranger and his protégés opened fire with a precision born of their training and the instinct to survive. Only the last two men rounding the corner managed to get off any shots before they too were cut down. One of those shots grazed Finn's bicep enough to draw blood but not enough to bite into the meat of his arm.

"There'll be more coming. Let's move." McPhail did a quick sweep of the bodies and collected two more sets of pistols and a shotgun with shells while Will and Finn ran down their horses. "We'll head into the mountains north for a pace," he said when they returned. "Hopefully, they'll expect us to head south, and we can throw off any pursuit across the river. Then we have to make plans."

The sun had been setting when the firefight started and long shadows now cradled Chastity and the surrounding foothills, making their progress slow, but McPhail's band pushed on ahead of the next wave of pursuers. They forded the river west of the town and pushed on deep into the night. Most of the pursuit did seem to head south, but they could still hear the sounds of men and horses echoing in the nighttime hills. The winds off the mountains kicked up, biting into them despite long coats pulled tight, and a slow drizzle dampened their bodies and spirits even more. They spoke little lest their voices reveal their presence.

Will spent the night in his own personal fog, replaying the last few minutes of Kali's life and the terrible vision of her when he had turned around. Sweet, beautiful Kali brought low by Governor Hogg's men and now dead. She would never smile at him again, laugh with him again, tease him about the looks he gave Theresa, or annoy him with her endless prattle about nothing. And there he had been with her in those final moments, never knowing what she was thinking. He had been there to rescue her, and instead, she had chosen a gun for solace. She had lost faith in him. He supposed after more than a month of torture, he might have lost faith in him too. He and Finn had failed Kali. They ran away when she could not. Their efforts to find her had been halfhearted at best. He deserved to have that final image of Kali burned into his heart forever.

When Will shot the Agents in Tranquility, he had acted on instinct to protect himself and his family. He had not thought of himself as a killer after that night. Tonight, he was a killer. How many men had died by his guns tonight? The red fog of rage had taken over and the details of the fight were lost except at the end, the man in tan. By then, Will had taken control over his rage, had held in check that great beast snarling and seething like a rabid wolf. He had looked at that man, sniveling and defenseless but still the nearest cause of all of Kali's suffering. Calculated and cold, Will had released the bonds of the beast inside and let it consume its prey. Everything before may have made him a killer but that had been rage out of control. The man in tan made him a murderer. By Will's calculations, though, there were more men out there in need of killing.

By morning, the horses needed rest, and the sounds of pursuit had since died away. McPhail chose a small cluster of trees to offer some concealment and with nearby grass for the horses. The trio unsaddled and made camp but lit no fire.

Will stared at his boots with tears streaming down his face and told Finn and McPhail about Kali in as few words as possible.

"I don't understand," Finn said. "Kali would never do that

kind of work. She's just a kid and not that kind of girl anyway. Why was she there?"

Will's anger flared again. "She didn't decide to do it, Finn. The Agents sold her. They beat her and raped her and sold her as a whore." He looked back down at his feet. "And I gave her the gun she used to kill herself. I'm as guilty as them."

"Those bastards," Finn muttered. He hadn't heard or chose to ignore his cousin's last words. "We'll make them pay."

"We should have gone after her that night." Will looked up to glare at McPhail. "I wanted to go after her, and you wouldn't let us. We could have stopped them from hurting her."

McPhail maintained the same dispassionate face he always wore in the face of their anger. "If you'd gone after them that night, you'd be dead, and she'd still be sold. At least now, she's free, and you're alive to get justice for her."

"Free? She's not free. She's dead." Finn was now listening again.

"Death is freedom, Finn, a freedom she chose. No one can hurt her again," McPhail said.

Will broke the ensuing seconds of silence. "You knew she'd be up there. You knew I'd find her."

Now McPhail's eyes flared in indignation. "Did I believe the Agents would take her to a whorehouse? Yes. That's why we came to Chastity. A young girl, and attractive to boot, was going to make them more money on her back than she would scrubbing floors or waiting tables. You're the ones who refused to even imagine that. Did I know you'd take it into your head, Will, to go whoring yourself in the very house they'd sold her, and that out of all the women and girls there, you'd pick her? No, I did not." His eyes flashed back and forth between the cousins. "You still haven't grown up yet. Despite everything, you still live in that sheltered little valley."

He shook his head. "Finn, do you think any of those painted ladies in Temperance or the ones in Chastity chose that life? I very much doubt it. Maybe they weren't all forced the way your sister was, but they were forced into it by life and circumstances. I don't know any girl or woman who'd choose to sell her body if she had another option. Life is hard that way. Think on that next time you go into one of those pleasure houses."

He stood up and stamped his boots. "There's evil out there, a rot in the world. It's always been there, and always will be. Right now, in our little corner of the world, the source of that rot is Governor Hogg, his Agents, and their corruption. Half the places in Chastity like the Broken Mare belong to Hogg or his cronies, and the other half pay him and keep him in power. A good man's job in life is to stand up to evil in the world. We Rangers weren't perfect, and we couldn't cure all the evils in the world, but we stood up to them. That's our job: to stand up to evil, to stand up for people like your sister."

He surveyed the two young men. "We need rest. I'll take first watch; Will, you second; and Finn, you third. We'll head out again at noon." The cowboy stalked out of the copse to take up his station.

Will and Finn said nothing more to each other but laid down to a restless sleep.

⟶ MERCY ⟵

Without new supplies, McPhail, Will, and Finn skirted the foothills north for another two days over the rough terrain, in and out of gullies. They hunted and lived off the land. At that point, believing that they had lost any pursuit from the south, McPhail turned them east across the rolling hills that lead out into the plains of central Jefferson. The Ranger was vague on their destination, only that they needed to find a town to re-supply using some of the money appropriated from the Broken Mare.

The sun was shy of its zenith when the trio rode into the town of Mercy. It was a familiar version of most of the towns that served the surrounding homesteads and ranches: a general store, bank, sheriff's office, saloon, blacksmith, barber-surgeon, and church. They planned to pick up some supplies and check to see if word of the firefight in Chastity had followed them this far.

For such a flotsam of buildings, the town center was packed today with a crowd hailing from the entire region. When the three turned onto the main street, they could see why. A gallows stood in the center of the town square, its fresh wood still redolent of pine with runnels of fresh orange sap drying in the sun. The guest of honor had not yet arrived, but from the size of the crowd, the arrival seemed imminent.

McPhail rode up next to the hitching post outside the general store where a thin balding man in an apron stood on the porch in the shade of the awning. The porch was high enough that the proprietor stood level with McPhail on his horse. "Mornin'." McPhail nodded.

"Mornin'," the man replied. "New to Mercy, I see."

"Just passing through with my boys. Finished a cattle drive up north and now on our way to Diligence hoping for a bit of work." McPhail rubbed his chin. "We've used up a fair spot of our supplies on the way here and were looking to pick up a few things. We've got a little scrip and some coin still."

The merchant nodded. "Well, I mainly deal in barter, things being what they are 'round here, but I'm always willing to take the Gov'nor's coin."

"I'm mighty glad to hear that." McPhail looked out at the square and nodded at the gallows. "Looks like you been having some trouble 'round here with bandits. We need to be careful 'round these here parts?"

The merchant shook his head. "Aw, I wish it was only that. Bad business that there. Bad business." He spit over his right shoulder. "Keep the devil at bay." McPhail waited until the silence induced the man to speak again. "You ain't likely to run into bandits 'round here any more than you will anywhere else in these territories. We may be a ways from San Alonso, but we got order 'round here."

"Good to hear."

The two stood in silence a while longer staring at the noose dangling above the trap door six feet above the ground.

"Well, you'll be seeing the show soon enough. No sense tryin' ta keep a secret." The merchant mopped his brow. "That there is for Janie De Casas. Sweet girl really, barely nineteen. She put her pappy in the ground though, and that's a sin in the eyes of the Lord as well as the Gov'nor. Don't know what the Lord will say when she's standing afore him, but the Gov'nor, he demands the rope."

McPhail frowned. "Awful hard to see how a sweet girl would go and put her pappy in the ground just so she could dance the hemp jig."

The merchant clicked his tongue. "That's 'cause you ain't never met Arthur De Casas. Always was a mean drunk, that man. Married Maria Montello when she were right young, he did. Course he was handsome back in the day. Anyway, they had little Janie a year or so later, but no other children after that. You ask me, that was a 'cause by then Maria knew what kind a man Arthur was and made sure no more little De Casas would come runnin' round."

He heaved a sigh. "Anyway, all is as well as it can be for ten years or so 'til Maria caught her death one winter. Ill for three or four weeks racked with the ague and coughin' up blood until her body couldn't take no more. Arthur and little Janie buried her under a pinyon tree up by their homestead. Arthur tried for a while to keep himself straight and sober for his little girl. Only girls don't stay little forever, and a man like Arthur, well, he's got his needs. All the women in town knew what a temper he had, and they stayed away, but little Janie didn't have much say in that, I reckon." He spat again.

"I guess Janie decided five or six years of her father's attentions was more'n enough. He come home drunk one night from town callin' for her, and she put a bullet through each eye from twenty yards in the dark, they say. Then she walked on over and put a few more a mite down lower if you catch my meaning."

McPhail pursed his lips. "So this young lady, this Janie De Casas, after she had enough of her father's ministrations, which no one else cared to put a stop to, she decides to end it herself. And after that, the sheriff here decides she's got to hang for getting some justice for herself?"

"Well, you ain't from 'round here, and so I can see how you'd say that and thars many here including me mayhap that take that side too. But Arthur, well, he was a Gov'nor's man. Used to be on Hogg's posse hisself. Poor bastard prob'ly taught Janie how to shoot so good hisself. Sheriff Daniels didn't have much choice. He and Deputy Dave and Deputy Samuel went on up there to have a talk with Janie and see what could be done quiet like. Well, Janie, she ain't a quiet one, at least not no more. She warned 'em off, but they kept coming. Told 'em if they kept coming, where she'd put the next bullet, and then she did it. Took off one of Samuel's ears all calm like. Then put a bullet through Dave's knee, ended up losing the leg, he did. They went on home after that, but Gov'nor Hogg went and sent som'a his Agents on down. By then Janie was done warnin' and killed four o' them afore she ran outta bullets. So now, the Gov'nor says she hangs, and that she will."

McPhail and the merchant remained in companionable silence. "Aye, bad business that is," McPhail agreed after a time. "Shame to see a young lass treated so, 'specially one such a fine shot if what you say is true."

The merchant snorted. "Oh, I seen the evidence with me own eyes. Shame it is though."

Murmurs started to run through the crowd when the door to the sheriff's office swung open. Two hard-looking men in Governor Hogg's black, one with a paunch and one lean, came out first to flank the door. Behind them followed a slim woman, her long black hair tangled, a purple bruise swelling her left eye shut and a deep scratch running down that left cheek. Her hands were tied in front of her torn and dirty dress. She squinted her good eye in the bright sunlight and scanned the crowd until her eye alit on the gallows. Her throat bobbed in a swallow, but then her face turned blank as stone. Two men followed her out. Given the silver star on his brown vest, the older man was most likely Sheriff Daniels, while the other man with the bandage about his head and ear must have been Deputy Samuel.

The group started their march past the crowd to the steps leading up to the gallows.

McPhail nodded to the merchant. "Guessin' we'll need to do our business a mite later."

"Aye." The merchant nodded, and McPhail rode back over to Finn and Will.

"What's going on?" Finn whispered

McPhail nodded toward the woman ascending the stairs. "She's coming with us," he whispered back. "Wait for my signal. I don't think the sheriff and deputy will be a problem, but we'll likely have to kill the Agents. Finn, you'll cover me from over there." He nodded toward the saloon on the other side of the street. "Will, be ready to go get her."

The two young men looked at each other wide-eyed but nodded and drifted off to the side of the crowd, still astride their horses. McPhail took up position in the middle of the street, staying ahorse in order to view the proceedings above the heads of the crowd.

The sheriff and deputy made to climb up the stairs, but the heavier of the governor's Agents at the top held up a hand and shook his head. The other Agent led Janie to the center of the platform and placed the noose over her neck. She looked pale, but her visible eye burned a defiance McPhail could read despite the distance. Her nostrils flared as the black hood came down over her head, but she made no sound.

Assured his charge was secure, the lean Agent stepped over to the handle that would open the trapdoor while his partner stepped to the front of the gallows to address the crowd. While that was happening, Finn edged his horse over to the saloon side of the street and slid his rifle out of his pack but let it dangle down his leg, concealed by the body of his horse. Meanwhile, Will urged his horse around the edge of the crowd and closer to the gallows.

The heavier, senior Agent looked out across the crowd. "Good people of Mercy, we are here today to carry out justice on Miss Janie De Casas." Murmurs swirled among the crowd. "With premeditation, she took the life of her father, Arthur De Casas, former Agent of the governor." The murmurs were louder, but no one spoke back to the Agent. He glared at the crowd until the whispering quieted. "When Sheriff Daniels and his deputies came to arrest her, she again with premeditation grievously wounded two sworn deputies of the law." At this point heads turned behind the gallows to the entrance to the sheriff's office where a thin, pale man stood on a pair of crutches with the stump of one leg wrapped in white bandages. "Again, the law came to her, and in cold blood, she killed four of Governor Hogg's sworn men: Agent Drisco, Agent McFadden, Agent Scott, and Agent Walker. For those crimes, she has been sentenced to hang by her neck until dead." The crowd remained silent under the Agent's harsh gaze. "Does anyone here have anything to say in the matter?"

For several seconds, the only sounds in the square were the wind blowing in the hills above, the rustle of dust along the planks of the buildings, and the nicker of a horse. The Agent opened his mouth to continue, but McPhail beat him to it.

"It seems to me, Agent Garland, that the young lady deserves a medal. She killed an incestuous drunkard. I do feel grievous bad about the two deputies, but four dead Agents is a good start in my book."

Agent Garland shielded his face from the sun to make out the figure on horseback, and his eyes went wide.

"There'll be no hanging today. You can untie the young

lady and let her go right now, or you'll deal with me, Garland." McPhail's words rang cold, calm, and deadly over the hush of the crowd, but his hands still rested lightly on the pommel of his saddle.

Tense as the yoke on a straining ox, Finn raised his rifle but kept the barrel below his horse's neck and out of sight.

Will rounded the crowd and rested his right hand on his pistol.

"David McPhail," Garland sneered. "Sheriff, arrest that man. He's wanted by Governor Hogg himself for crimes against the state. As for hangings, McPhail, this may just be the first of the afternoon." Garland gestured to his fellow Agent, and the man pulled the lever.

The action happened so fast that even Finn, who had the best view from his position to the side and behind his mentor, had trouble seeing it at all. The lever snapped forward and the trapdoor began to move. Before it could, McPhail drew and leveled his revolver at the platform. The gun barked once. The noose around Janie De Casas's neck started to go taut as she fell, but McPhail's bullet severed the rope eight inches above her falling head. The sound of the bullet echoed in the square. Garland flinched and grabbed at his chest, sure that the bullet had been meant for him. Janie landed with a thud and a cry of pain on the hard ground beneath the gallows. A woman in the crowd screamed, and everyone scattered.

As soon as he saw her fall, Will spurred his horse through the crowd and leapt off at the gallows. He drew his knife from his belt as he ran toward her sprawled form.

The panicked crowd jolted Finn out of his daze, and he raised his rifle and pointed it toward the sheriff and deputy who were fighting their way through the crowd.

McPhail kept his gun leveled at the platform. Garland had not moved, but the second Agent reached for his sidearm. McPhail shot him dead and pointed the gun back at Garland.

"Sheriff Daniels," McPhail yelled above the crowd. "I am Territory Ranger David McPhail, formerly of Fort Vigilant. I have no quarrel with you, but I need you and your deputy to stand down now before we do have one. My business is with Agent Garland."

Under the gallows, Will scrambled over to Janie. She gagged and kicked in the dirt, unable to free herself from her bonds. The noose had not broken her neck, but it endeavored to complete her strangulation on the ground. "Hold on," he hissed into her ear. She kicked and writhed away from him. "I'm trying to help you."

She heard him and quieted enough to let him loosen the noose and pull the bag off her head. Her look was a mixture of menace and gratitude, and Will was unclear which would win out. "Let me cut your ropes," he said.

She stared at him but then held out her hands to allow him to remove her bonds. "We need to get out of here. Can you walk?"

She looked down at her right ankle, which had started to swell, but nodded and let him pull her to her feet. Together they scrambled out from under the gallows. Will climbed on his horse first and pulled her up behind him.

Finn and McPhail saw the two mounting the horse. The sheriff and his deputy saw it too, but stood with their hands up and only watched. "All right, then, Sheriff Daniels, my boys and I will be going. I hope we don't see each other again anytime soon."

Will and Janie galloped past, heading back out of town the way the trio had arrived. McPhail nodded, and Finn turned and followed them. The Ranger clicked his tongue, and his horse started to back up down the middle of the street.

Garland stood seething atop the gallows until he could take no more. He roared and reached for his gun. It cleared his holster just before McPhail's bullet smashed into the metal to send it flying and set Garland screeching and clutching his wounded hand.

"Give my best to Governor Hogg, Garland." With that, McPhail turned and galloped out of town in pursuit of Will and Finn and their damsel in distress. None of them would think of Janie De Casas in that way for long.

Will rode hard for the hills in the distance with Janie's arms wrapped around his waist. Unencumbered with a passenger, Finn caught up with them not far out of town and whooped. "Did you see that?" His face was flushed with excitement, and he looked back to McPhail who was just exiting Mercy. "He shot out the rope! That was amazing. I wish I could shoot like that."

Will shook his head. "I just wish we didn't have to keep running out of every town we visit." He glanced back over his shoulder toward Janie, but her face was buried against his back. "No offense meant, ma'am." She did not answer, and they kept riding.

McPhail caught up with them where a trail started to wind up the hills. No pursuit appeared evident from Mercy, and they slowed their horses to a trot for the ascent.

"So who's Agent Garland?" Will asked.

"Someone you don't want to trifle with," McPhail answered.

Finn and Will exchanged a look. "And that wasn't trifling with him?"

McPhail's gunmetal grey eyes bore into Finn. "I'm better than him. You aren't, not yet anyway." The Ranger turned back to lead them up the trail.

Will shrugged at Finn and spurred his horse closer to McPhail's. "But who is he? How do you know him?"

"I have had encounters over the years with most of Hogg's Agents. Seward Garland is part of Hogg's personal posse. He killed Rangers."

"Why didn't you kill him too?"

McPhail's face remained stony. They rode for a space in the mounting tension. "I didn't kill him because it wasn't necessary, and I wanted him to go back to Hogg with his tail between his legs and admit I got the best of him again."

Will and Finn exchanged another look but remained silent this time. Now that they had slowed their pace, Janie leaned back away from Will, but if she had any thoughts on McPhail or the boys or her rescue, she kept them to herself.

When they reached the crest of the first hill, McPhail called a halt to rest the horses. No sooner had Will reined in his horse than Janie's hands snaked down and drew both his guns. She pressed one to the small of his back and cocked the hammer and pointed the other one at McPhail. "I don't know what your boys' plans are, but they don't involve me anymore."

Finn's hand dropped to his gun belt, but Janie cut him off. "Do it, and I put a bullet through your brother's kidney." Finn's hand hung there just above his waist, but Janie's good eye stayed locked on McPhail, and her gun never wavered.

Will lifted his arms, palms spread wide. He swallowed. "Cousin, actually. Finn's my cousin." He turned his head a fraction toward Finn. "Listen to the lady, please."

McPhail nodded, and Finn put his hand back on the pommel of his saddle. McPhail and Janie regarded each other for a time. "Well, miss, we certainly had no intention of inconveniencing you, but I would have thought a word of thanks would be in order given how your township was treating you."

"Well, for that, thank you, but I won't be passed around between the three of you either. I think it's time we parted company." Her gun hand remained as unwavering as her voice.

"I understand." McPhail nodded. "For what it's worth, I was a Ranger once, sworn to protect the citizens of these parts, and we were not in the habit of raping women. As for the boys here, Finn's sister was sold by Governor Hogg's men to a whorehouse in Chastity to pay off her father's debts. Will here got to see her put a bullet in her brain for the trouble. After that, I don't think either of them has much of an interest in rape neither."

Janie just glared at him.

"No cause for you to trust my word, I know, but for now I think our offer is better'n you'll get from your friends in Mercy." McPhail inclined his head back down the trail. "For the moment, I'd say we are traveling in the same direction and would benefit from the safety of numbers."

Janie did turn back toward the township laid out below them and could see the dust plumes of riders heading their way.

"It looks like Agent Garland finally roused enough men to form a posse." McPhail drew a cigar from his shirt pocket, bit off the end, and spat it into the dirt. "Now, if you'd like, I can ask Will there to climb off, and he can ride with Finn. That way you'll have your own horse."

Janie's eyes darted from McPhail to Finn and then off to the side where the riders were coming across the plain. "No," she said. "He'll stay here with my gun in his back in case you decide to cross me."

"As you wish." McPhail looked at Will. "Will, be so good as to pass back your gun belt so she has a place to put them." He looked at Janie. "We're gonna have to ride hard. You'll need to hang on."

"Don't worry about me, old man." She slung Will's offered gun belt over her shoulder and holstered the guns. She wrapped her left arm around Will's waist but kept her other hand near the butt of one of the revolvers. "Let's ride, Will."

"Yes, ma'am," Will grunted, and the quartet galloped off,

deeper into the hills.

They pushed on through the afternoon, winding in and out of the hills around Mercy. Janie's knowledge of the area shied them away from a box canyon and soon had them outdistancing their pursuers. By the time the sun set, McPhail declared the pursuit over. Garland would only be able to drive the sheriff and men of Mercy so far in tracking down an escaped girl the townsfolk felt some sympathy for and a group of outlaws who had nothing to do with the town.

At some point during the flight, Janie moved the gun belt to her hips and stopped hovering her free hand near the guns. While not exactly friends, at least the initial animosity seemed to be behind them.

They made camp in a small hollow before full dark. Janie winced when she climbed off the horse and limped about as she helped make camp.

"Do you want me to take a look at your ankle?" Will asked her.

Janie gave him a withering look. "Are you some kind of doctor?"

"No, but I've had to bandage up Finn enough times." Will gestured to his cousin who was unsaddling his horse. "He can be pretty clumsy."

"I'll be fine." She grimaced though when she lowered herself down to the ground on her bedroll.

McPhail was busy breaking out their rations and portioning out the food for the night. "Better to have someone look at your hurts now. We're still on the run, and we need you in as good a shape as possible in case that posse does catch up with us in the night."

Janie narrowed her eyes but relented. "Fine, go ahead." She stuck out her ankle toward Will.

He knelt next to her and poked and prodded. "I don't think anything's broken," Will concluded. "Just twisted is all." He retrieved some cloth from McPhail's medical supplies and bound her ankle. "That'll keep down the swelling and give you some support. We'll need to get you decent boots though in the next town. Now let me look at your neck."

Janie rolled her eyes at him but tipped her head back in assent.

"Some nasty rope burns, but they'll be all right." He reached into the pack and pulled out a salve. When he reached to tip her head back again, he caught the look in her eye and handed over the jar. "Here, rub this into your neck. It'll help it heal."

Janie snatched the jar out of his hand, but then shook her head and sighed. "Thank you, Will," she managed. "Much obliged." She looked over toward Finn and McPhail. "Thank you, all of you, for rescuing me. I owe you." She paused. "But I'm still holding onto the guns for now."

"You're welcome," Will answered with a small smile. "Thank you for not shooting me in the back."

Janie gave him her first smile of the day. "When I'm ready to shoot you, Will, I'll do it to your face." She rubbed the salve into her neck and a little into the scratch along her cheek. "This sure does reek. It better work."

Will cocked his chin at her face. "How'd that happen?"

Janie gave him another withering look. "Clumsy me must have tripped in my cell. That's what Agent Blandish would have claimed anyway. He would have done worse too, 'cept Sheriff Daniels walked in on him. After that, either he or Deputy Samuel camped out in the office to keep an eye on me and those Agents. Despite what I did, they were decent like that. Didn't want to see me molested anymore, even if they were gonna string me up." She laughed a little, but without humor.

"Well, no one's gonna lay a hand on you here," Will said.

"No, they will not." Janie patted the guns by her side.

Will looked wistfully at those rosewood grips, but he knew he would not be getting them back that night.

McPhail handed out the food: dry bread, cheese, and smoked jerky. They spoke little except to split up the night watches, in which Janie insisted on participating. Will took the first shift and had to settle for strapping on a pair of McPhail's extra pistols.

Janie would take the second watch. "Make sure you wake me in time, Will. I can handle anything you boys here can." Without waiting for a reply, she lay down and pulled up her blanket to go to sleep.

Being the least recognizable of the quartet, a day and a half later at the town of Charity Will and Finn went in alone. They bought more food, an extra bedroll, and some better riding clothes, boots, and a cowboy hat for Janie. There was only one horse for sale, an older mare, serviceable for distance travel if not speed. Despite their best efforts, Will and Finn knew they needed the horse, and so did the seller. Negotiations ended with them parting with much more than they had hoped. Will consoled himself with the thought that it was somehow Governor Hogg's money paying the price. That thought just made him think about what Kali had been through to earn that money and plunged him back into a dark mood for the return ride to McPhail and Janie.

At the rendezvous, Janie regarded the clothes and mare with a jaundiced eye. "Next time I do my own shopping," she said before going behind some trees to change. Her limp was better today and the swelling around her eye had subsided a fair degree, but red welts peered out above her shirt collar. She tucked her long black hair under her hat. She had consented to return Will's pistols and wore McPhail's extra set of guns strapped to her hips. The shirt and pants ballooned about her, and she had to cinch the latter with a length of rope. At least the boots seemed to fit well, and the clothes were an improvement for riding compared with the woolen dress she had been hanged in.

"We need a place to lie low for a space and plan our next steps," McPhail said when they had redistributed the gear amongst the horses. "There's a place northeast of here that should do. Mount de Dios, they call it." He looked at Finn and smiled. "Your father and I once tracked some bandits there. Gave us quite a fight, but in the end we walked away, and they didn't."

Mount de Dios was the largest and northernmost of the Mescala Mountain range bordering the eastern edge of Jefferson. It rose out of the plains in gentle waves at first, but deeper into its foothills and higher up its side rose steep walls and crumbling cliffs. A wide trail started near the bottom, undulating up and down at first and then weaving back and forth in wide switchbacks. About a third of the way up the wide trail ended at a narrow defile that zigzagged through the rock walls above them for almost a mile before it opened out into rolling hills that descended the far side of the mountain into the desert badlands on one side and a steep climb toward the summit on the other.

McPhail took them up the steep branch of the path to another broad plateau three-quarters of the way up the mountain. A stream cut across the plateau with berry bushes on the far side. Past the berry bushes rose the stands of firs that lined the mountain at this elevation. In the mountainside, a cave mouth yawned. Whether natural or mined, time obscured its genesis. Inside the cave was musty, but it contained some crude cots with molding straw mattresses, some old canned goods, a strong box, and a few beat-up dishes including plates, pots and pans, and tin mugs. Someone had put together a makeshift door that could shut out the worst of the wind and cold but not the rodents and other wildlife that had used the cave in absence of humans over the years.

To the south and west off the plateau stretched the central plains of Jefferson State. Their stream cascaded down the side of Mount de Dios, where in time it joined other streams and brooks of the rest of the Mescala Mountain range stretching to the south. Together those streams formed the Grand River that flowed west toward San Alonso. There it made a hard left toward the Mexican lands in the deep south. Shielding their eyes from the sun, the quartet could make out the far distant smudge that represented San Alonso in the elbow of the thin shining ribbon of river.

"I've never been anywhere more beautiful," Janie said. "It's like standing up in Heaven and seeing the world all laid out before you."

"The mountains around Tranquility are pretty beautiful," Will said. "But the view isn't nearly as grand."

McPhail snorted. "It also has shelter and is far enough out of the way, no one's going to come wandering up on us; and if they do, we can see them long before they get here and be ready for them." He stalked back toward the cave home.

"He's a practical man," Finn said. "And not one to let happy thoughts get in the way of bad ones." He sighed and shrugged. "Oh well, at least we get a warm meal tonight. Hey, Will, want to see if we can hunt up some deer?"

They were unsuccessful hunting the first evening, but by noon the next day, Finn bagged a young buck. After lugging their prize back to camp, they spent much of the rest of the afternoon butchering the carcass and processing the meat.

Janie helped out with the deer but otherwise kept to herself the first day. McPhail busied himself putting their hideout in order, cleaning the dishes so they were fit to eat off, and scouting the surrounding area.

The next day, Will and Finn took some moldy old rags of clothes from the hideout and fashioned themselves target practice dummies by stuffing them with pine needles and sticks and hanging their crude scarecrows from the trees. Their experience in Chastity had driven home the fact that their targets were people, not rocks, flowers, or rotten fruit.

The two young men had been shooting for ten or fifteen minutes under McPhail's watchful eye when Janie wandered over. She squatted down on her haunches and watched for a time.

Finn and Will exchanged a look with each other. "Hey, Janie, you want to take a try?" Finn asked. He nodded toward their latest mannequin. "Let's see how good you are."

Janie stood up and walked over near the boulder where they had laid out the ammunition. Without preamble, she drew one of her pistols and fired. The first two shots hit the straw hands. Her second two shots went through the dummy's face where the eyes would have been. The last two shots went into the dummy's putative heart. She dropped the gun into her holster, picked up the shotgun from the boulder, and fired it into the dummy's groin. The blast echoed across the mountainside, and the lower half of the dummy collapsed to the ground. Janie put the shotgun back down and stomped off, back toward camp.

Finn and Will stood staring at the dummy. "Damn." Will whistled.

Finn shook his head. He yelled over his shoulder after Janie's retreating form. "That is low, Janie. That is not okay. I am not okay with that, Janie."

Will made a face at his cousin. "Let up, Finn."

Will caught up with Janie near the stream. She was sitting on a rock tossing pebbles into a small pool stirred by eddies off the stream.

Choosing a space a handful of paces away, Will plopped down cross-legged on a rock. They sat in silence for a space, long enough to hear Finn in the distance resume shooting. Will sighed. "Finn and I grew up together in the Tranquility Valley most of the way west across the state. Finn's parents raised me. My parents died when I was a baby." He scooped up some pebbles and started tossing them into the water.

"We had a little sister too, Kalirose. Well, Finn's sister, my cousin. Anyway, Pa got behind on his payments for the land, and Hogg's Agents came one night and killed our parents and kidnapped Kali. McPhail saved Finn and me; otherwise, we might have roasted."

Janie eyed him, but kept up her emotionless stare and threw more pebbles.

"Kali wasn't so lucky. They took her to a brothel in Chastity and put her to work. I found her there a little over a week ago now. She must have been broken inside. I gave her my gun." He pulled out one of the rosewood-handled pistols. "This is the one. She put it in her mouth and pulled the trigger." He put it back in its holster. "I wanted to save her, but I couldn't. I gave her the gun she used to kill herself. If I hadn't given it to her, she couldn't have done it. It's my fault she's dead." He tossed the last of his pebbles and sat staring at the stream.

"Do you think you know about me because of what happened to your cousin?" Now there was emotion on her face, anger.

"No." Will shook his head. "I don't know anything about you except some people wanted to hang you." He shrugged. "That and you're a damn good shot." He laughed a little at that. "You're angry though. Maybe you should be, maybe you shouldn't. I don't know. Maybe if Kali had been angry instead of sad, she wouldn't have done what she did. I'm angry too, but I think if you don't have somewhere to direct that anger, it'll eat you up inside just like sadness will." He shrugged again and gave her a half-smile, half-grimace. "That's what I think anyway."

"And where are you directing your anger, Will?"

"Governor Hogg. His Agents. I'm gonna make them pay for my parents and Kali."

Janie laughed. "That's a tall order for a boy like you. I bet that will get you killed just as well."

"Maybe so, but at least I'll take some of them with me and go out in a blaze of glory." He looked Janie in the eye. "I couldn't save Kali, but we managed to save you."

"I didn't ask you to save me."

Will shrugged. "I didn't ask McPhail to save me either."

They stared at each other until Janie gave in and sighed. "What is it you want?"

"A truce. To be your friend. I don't have a family anymore except Finn. It doesn't look like you have one either."

"I'm not your cousin."

"No, you're not. You're nothing like she was, but you still seem like someone who could use a friend." He stood up. "When you're ready." He walked back into the forest toward the sound of Finn practicing in the distance.

Janie watched him go and sat brooding for a while afterward.

Alistair Hogg lived up to the first half of his name but not the second. He dressed to the nines and spoke in a sharp, crisp accent like his English ancestors. In contrast to other hogs, he stood six and a half feet tall and lean with stilt legs and long wiry arms. His valet kept his custom suits crisp with sharp lines and nary a trace of dust or lint, even on the white linen number he wore today with its white vest and white shirt underneath. The only splash of color was the crimson bolo tie around his neck. His signature luxuriant waxed mustache hung a bit thinner than in his early years as governor and was now a speckled salt-and-pepper as was his thick head of hair. While he leaned back in his chair, his cinnamon eyes roved back and forth between his secretary, Horace Weatherwax, and Head Agent Dick Warren.

The two advisors sat across the desk from Governor Hogg in the upstairs office of his vacation home in the resort town of Humility. Dick shifted in his chair. "I know you and McDougal go back from before he was governor of North Cali, but I'm a little worried about sparing the men, sir. General Santa Ana seems preoccupied with North Cali and its gold, but he may turn his eyes to us any time."

"Oh, old Mexico'll turn our way, Dick, I can assure you of that." Hogg leaned forward again. "They're focused on North Cali now, though. They want to retake what they lost to the Federation, especially now with all the gold up there. They're not stupid, either. They recognize the utility of the sea for trade and war, the more ports the better. San Francisco is too tempting right now."

"But you do think they'll come for Jefferson?" Horace's voice quavered a bit. He had read rather colorful stories about how the Mexican soldiers treated their captives that kept him awake at night despite the questionable validity of those tales. Well, perhaps the stories of what the conquistadors had done to the Aztecs were not exaggerated, but that had been hundreds of years ago, or so Horace tried to convince himself.

Hogg's eyes shifted. "Well, of course, they will. This land was all part of Mexico until the Federation got Manifest Destiny on the brain. Conquistadors founded this town on the site of one of the old pueblos. They'll be back. We need time. Time for North Cali to soften them up, and time to pull in more troops from the Federation."

"How likely do you think that is, sir?" Dick's tone suggested he did not think reinforcements to be forthcoming after they sent their own men away.

The governor shrugged. "I send men to McDougal. McDougal sends me Californian gold. The gold greases palms back east and with the right pressure applied to the right individuals, I can siphon off more troops than we're sending to North Cali before the Federation goes to hell."

Dick shook his head. "The Federation won't fall apart."

"Yes, it will. This great experiment in democracy and the common man choosing his leaders will last less than a hundred years. Mark my words, in the next one or two election cycles the Federation will split, north and south, over the slave issue. It will be a long bloody war, friend against friend, brother against brother, and we out here on the frontier will be left to fend for ourselves against Santa Ana and his armies."

"Then won't we need our men here?" That was Horace again.

"As I said, if I play the game right, and I always do, we can get more men from the Federation than I send to help North Cali."

Horace wrinkled up his face. "How, sir?"

Hogg sighed. "Let's just say, that I am not the only one who sees the powder keg ready to be lit. If a civil war is inevitable, and you could ship off a few regiments of your future adversary's troops before the war started when everyone was still friends, wouldn't you?"

Dick smiled. "You've got friends in the north who can deploy some southern soldiers out here to keep an eye on Santa Ana."

"Dick, I have friends all over. If we move soon enough, we'll have all the soldiers we need, northern and southern."

Hogg looked back and forth between his lieutenants. "Satisfied?"

The Head Agent nodded, and Horace flourished a paper from the folder in his lap. "Here's the agreement with Governor McDougal for you to sign, sir."

The speed with which Hogg's pen scampered across the page belied the bold loops and whorls of his signature. He pushed the page back to Horace for blotting. "What about Chastity?"

"I have the condolence letters right here." Horace produced another sheaf of papers from a separate folder. "Pat Chapman will be taking over management of the Broken Mare. His contract is the last page, your standard agreement."

"Which one is Chapman?"

"The freeman, sir."

"Seemed like a solid man. Good choice, Horace."

The shadow of a subdued smile glossed over the secretary's lips, the closest to beaming the little man ever came.

"Who's in charge of the investigation, Dick?"

"Julio Palliser and his posse were closest."

While continuing to sign condolence letters, Hogg raised eyebrows at the Head Agent.

Warren snorted. "No, I still don't like him, sir. I would have preferred Pryor or Reynolds, but Conviviality was farther away, and I thought the sooner we had Agents on the scene, the better they'd be able to track down the robbers."

"And if he fails, you can subtly imply I never should have promoted him to my posse in the first place." One of Hogg's brown eyes flashed a wink. "You're shrewder than you look, you, Dick."

"No, sir. Just trying to do the best I can to serve the state and governor."

"Good response, Dick. Any other business?"

The governor's tone indicated that he hoped not, and Dick dropped his gaze and rubbed his nose when he cleared his throat. "One more thing, sir." He looked back up into the governor's eyes.

"Yes?"

"Agent Garland just came back from Mercy. He has something to report, and I think you need to hear it from him."

"Ah yes, the De Casas affair." Hogg sighed and gave a vague wave. "Send him in."

While Dick went to fetch Garland and Weatherwax fussed with his folders, Hogg neatened the last of the papers on his desk and leaned back in his chair. He remembered Arthur De Casas from back in the early days of his governorship. Arthur was a swarthy man, an excellent shot, charming when he was sober and with an appetite for the ladies, but a mean drunk who by the end was spending more time drunk than teetotaling and was more than once accused of going a long step too far with the ladies. The man had come crawling back two days after his dismissal, whining about having a wife and daughter back in Mercy to support, but Hogg had no sympathy. Arthur De Casas had become a liability. The man had been lucky to walk away, let alone walk away with the small pension Warren and Weatherwax had arranged on the side.

Agent Seward Garland entered and stood at attention before Hogg's desk. His middle paunch pushed at the golden buttons of his black jacket like it might send them shooting off as fireworks at any moment.

Hogg nodded for the man to commence but kept a wary eye on those buttons.

"Good afternoon, Governor Hogg, sir. I am here to report on the death of Agent Arthur De Casas."

"Former Agent."

Garland nodded. "Once an Agent, always an Agent, sir."

Hogg contained his eye roll. If Governor Hogg personally dismissed you, you were no longer an Agent, but he had more important agenda items for the rest of the day than prolonging this visit by making a point. "Fine. So what was it, a bar fight? Gambling? Jealous husband?"

"No, sir. Killed by his daughter. Shot him through both eyes and then more'n once a might lower if you catch my meaning." A wrinkle of distaste disfigured his pocked nose.

Now that did raise Hogg's eyebrows. Killed by his own flesh and blood. "And why would she do that?"

"Don't rightly know, sir." Garland's ears blossomed pink. "Don't really matter much either. Arthur De Casas was an Agent and a friend, and the penalty for killing an Agent is death."

"So, no questions asked? You just strung her up?"

"Well," Garland shifted foot to foot. "She also injured two deputies, and then when my men and I arrived to take her into custody, she managed to take four of my men unaware and killed them too." Garland swallowed hard and pushed on. "After that, we had no choice."

Governor Hogg blinked. Killing four men from Seward's posse was no small feat, and it did make clemency for killing a drunk bastard difficult. Given where in her father's anatomy the girl had apparently emptied the rest of her chambers, it did not take much imagination to guess the crux of her grievance with him. A pity, though, as she sounded to have possessed her father's marksmanship. Hogg could have used her. "So she hung, and Arthur De Casas and your men are avenged." Hogg sat forward. "Thank you for the information, Agent Garland."

"She didn't hang."

Hogg was already turning back to his papers and almost did not catch the last phrase. He arched an eyebrow at the Agent.

At the apex of his discomfort, Garland focused his eyes on a point above and to the left of the governor's head. "We had the noose around her neck, but David McPhail showed up and rescued her at the last minute."

"David McPhail?" Hogg placed both palms on his desk and narrowed his eyes. "That addled-brained former Ranger who caused all that trouble after I decommissioned them?"

"Yes, sir."

Hogg slumped back in his chair and pulled on his chin. "Last I heard, they refused to listen to him back east, and he huffed off into the prairies, but that was more than fifteen years ago. I'd assumed his irritating personality would have got him planted six feet down ages ago. Why is he back here?"

"Can't say, sir, but he seems to be causing more trouble."

Garland's eyes stayed glued to that spot on the wall.

Hogg felt the worry lines smooth on his face as his sigh ebbed the unease from his body. "Well, I never thought him a Sir Galahad rescuing damsels in distress, but maybe old age really has softened his brain." Hogg sat up. "He escaped, I take it."

Garland gave a curt nod. "With the De Casas woman and two young men."

Something about that tickled at Hogg's brain but gentle enough to ignore for the moment. "Wonderful, a cozy little gang. I wonder which one is his Sancho Panza." He shrugged. "Well, for their sake, given what she did to her father, I hope they don't try and molest the lass. As long as he's playing the white knight, perhaps he'll stay out of our business." He afforded Garland a sly smile. "To catch him, you may need to put guards on all the windmills."

Garland's face scrunched up in confusion, but a snort from Weatherwax showed Hogg had hit the mark with at least one person in the room. "Read a book, Garland," Hogg told him. "No, better yet, you're in charge of tracking down McPhail."

"And De Casas?" Garland's eyes darted to the governor's but could not tolerate the heat and skittered back to the wall.

Hogg's fingers drummed on his desk for a full five seconds.

"Yes, and the De Casas woman. You can take McPhail dead or alive, but I want Miss De Casas alive and brought back to me."

"I'll be glad to see her hanging on the capitol lawn for what she did to Arthur and my men."

Hogg's eye blink lasted an entire second. "Yes. Dismissed, Agent Garland."

The remaining three men watched the Agent spin on his heel and march from the room.

Warren cleared his throat in the silence. "Seward's a stickler for the law."

Hogg waved a hand. "The laws are for the little people, to give them direction and order in their lives, to keep their baser instincts in check."

"The laws don't apply to us, sir?" Warren asked.

"Laws are guidelines, but they do not bind us. We serve a higher purpose here, Dick." He looked over to Horace. "Give my best to Mildred. I look forward to seeing her this evening before we head back to San Alonso."

Horace bowed, and he and Dick Warren took that as their cue to leave.

⟡ HUMILITY ⟡

Toward dusk, a company of four rode into the town of Humility. Dust from their travels coated their clothing, which was to be expected. On the three men, those clothes hung ragged and threadbare, while the young lady accompanying them wore clothes two sizes too large and scandalously included pants rather than a dress or skirt. Perhaps that was because she chose to ride like a man, not sidesaddle like a proper lady.

Mildred Weatherwax sniffed at the sight, but out here in the frontier, you found all types, even in a town like Humility, second in grandeur in Jefferson only to San Alonso. Of course, even the grandest city in Jefferson would barely qualify as a real city back east in the Federation. Not for the first time, Mildred admitted that her mother had been correct that allowing Horace Weatherwax to move her out west so he could become an advisor to Alistair Hogg was a mistake, second only in magnitude to agreeing to marry Horace Weatherwax in the first place.

Now, twenty years of marriage, fifteen years in Jefferson, and five children later, Mildred despaired of ever achieving the life she deserved. She had managed to impress upon Horace the need to have their children properly educated on the coast. Elaine, her eldest, seemed to have done Mildred better and caught herself a handsome lawyer from Boston, no less. The two would marry in six months, thankfully in Boston and not out here in this dusty, culture-forsaken corner of the country. At least it would give Mildred the chance to take the train back east in a few months to help with the wedding and visit her other children and escape riffraff like the four ragamuffins that rode past her in the street. She sniffed again after they passed and hurried on her way home, parasol raised against the setting sun.

Although San Alonso was the cultural center of Jefferson, Mildred preferred the more relaxed pace of life in Humility, this resort area at the foot of the Mescala range, famed for the natural mineral springs that cascaded down and pooled above the town. A good soaking in the mineral springs did the constitution and digestion good and helped repair the damage the sun wrought on the complexion. At least three times a week, Mildred journeyed up to the highest pools, reserved for the wealthy and elite, to soak and replenish her spirit. Of course, the pools were strictly divided to keep the men and women separate and the pools lower down the cascade served the less well-off locals and tourists. On the other days of the week, she would lunch with friends at one of the three fine chateaus that catered to visitors in Humility. Ostensibly, she stayed to keep up their home here in Humility, but she and Horace both knew the real reason was that it kept them in their own separate life orbits which was precisely the way they both liked it. Oh, she would show her face for state functions when needed. There would be the dreadful summer ball coming up next month, but after twenty years of marriage, Mildred and Horace had seen quite enough of each other, thank you very much.

Horace had visited Humility two weeks before. Governor

Hogg had taken a break to visit his mansion in Humility, and of course, his personal secretary and advisor, Horace Weatherwax, had come along with a handful of other lieutenants. Mildred had attended one and hosted a second dinner party as well as an afternoon tea for the ladies. Mildred used that term loosely, given the habits of some of Governor Hogg's associates, and she and Horace had once again managed to navigate the shoals and submerged sandbars of their marriage. Now the whole cadre of them was back in San Alonso, and Mildred was glad to be rid of them. As usual, Horace had left his study a mess with sheaves of papers and calendars. Being her fastidious self, she knew she would find herself going in one of these days soon to straighten and file them away, but for now, she allowed herself to be irked by her husband's disarray.

Behind her, in the gathering dark, the four riders, who had taken no notice of the plump woman and her parasol, stopped their horses outside one of the smaller, less ostentatious hotels in the center of Humility. The older gentleman, a lanky cowboy, handed the reins of his horse over to one of the young men to secure to the hitching post, and he and the young woman went inside. The two young men followed a few minutes later. By then, Mildred had rounded the corner, well on her way home.

Cal Winthrop II, the proprietor of the Silken Crane, suppressed a sour grimace when McPhail and his companions came into the foyer. The Crane was not the most upscale of hotels in town but neither was it the lowliest. The busy season had not yet started though, and any customer with cash was likely better than no customer at all. So he hid the initial dip in his stomach at the sight of them and put on his professional, if pompous smile. "Good evening, good sir. How may I be of assistance?"

McPhail smiled back with his mouth but not his eyes. "Looking for two rooms for a couple of nights and stable and feed for four horses."

"I see." Cal shuffled some papers on his desk. "May I ask the purpose of your visit to Humility?"

"Mostly just passing through. My boys and I are on our way to Diligence, but it's been a long journey, and we're in need of a rest for a day or two before pushing on."

"You and your boys?" The man looked past McPhail at Janie.

McPhail laughed. "She's the daughter of a friend. We're from up by way of Denver. Her mom and dad were killed in an avalanche last winter just after the last big storm. Her father, Arthur, was a passing acquaintance of mine, so my boys and I agreed to escort her down to her aunt in Diligence. Hell of a journey, but can't let a young lady travel all this way alone."

The man behind the counter just nodded.

"So one room for the lady, and my boys and I can share a room I imagine."

"You know, sir, there are some less expensive rooms to be had on the west end of town."

Now McPhail gave a deeper laugh. "Well, don't you worry about that, sir." He reached into his duffle bag and pulled out a large mound of bills. "As I said, it has been a long journey that has taken its toll on our looks." He leaned in and spoke in an exaggerated whisper. "And truth be told, not a bad thing to look a little down on your luck when you're traveling through some dodgy territory." He stood back up with that same broad smile that refused to touch his eyes. "Now that the journey is almost done, we'll also be in need of sprucing ourselves up a bit come the morrow. Can't be bringing a young lady to her aunt and uncle looking like a rag doll, now can we?"

"Of course not, sir," the proprietor answered, but his eyes remained fixated on McPhail's stack of bills. "And I could suggest a fine establishment to help with all your needed accouterments." An establishment that would also pay Cal Winthrop II a nice finder's fee for sending the four his way.

"Thankee kindly," McPhail said.

It took a bit more time to settle the horses in the stables with grooms who promised to rub them down and water them for a tip. The companions left the saddles but carried the rest of their modest gear upstairs.

The rooms lay across from each other on the second floor. McPhail had already handed a key to Janie, and he and Finn were heading into the larger of the two rooms.

Will stopped before following them. "Will you be all right on your own?" he asked.

Janie raised her eyebrows at him with what Will thought of as her haughty look. "I'm a better shot than you or Finn, Will Covington." She patted one of the guns on her hips. "I'll be just fine."

"That's not what I meant."

Janie narrowed her eyes over a sly smile. "Are you worried I'll get cold and lonely?"

Will's face pinked. "No." He looked shocked. "I didn't mean that either."

"Good." Janie reverted back to the icy look she usually shared with the rest of the world. "Because I don't need that kind of attention from you."

Will could feel himself starting to mirror the same cold look back at her and fought the urge to just turn away. He won the staring contest.

"Ugh." Janie rolled her eyes and shook her head. "I'll be fine, Will. I'm not going to start weeping and shoot myself as soon as you turn your back, you know."

Will frowned at her.

"I've got debts to collect on too," she told him.

"Okay, Janie," he said. "Goodnight." He turned and headed into his room.

"Goodnight, Will," she said to his back. She rolled her eyes again and locked her door behind her.

In the morning, the first order of business was new clothing. Despite her protests, McPhail insisted Janie outfit herself in a dress to blend in with the rest of the ladies in town and refused to let her wear her guns over her skirts. As much to spite him as anything else, she chose the most expensive outfit she could find, a maroon affair with layers of ruffles and frills. Finn, Will, and McPhail all dressed themselves as dapper gentlemen in new pants, shirts, vests, coats, and hats. To Janie's consternation, all three proudly wore their rosewood-handled guns.

"Whooee," Finn whistled when he saw Janie. "You sure can clean up nice."

She glared at him. "You wouldn't be saying that if I still had my guns."

Finn laughed. "But you don't. Just gonna have to rely on us boys to keep you safe from now on."

McPhail cut off Janie's response and the rest of the bickering. "Enough, we have a job to do."

That job today was reconnaissance. Governor Hogg and several of his lieutenants kept vacation homes in Humility. McPhail planned on surveying the homes in preparation for a later raid when he hoped to gather more information on Hogg and his assets and later use that information to cause the governor as much damage as possible.

While McPhail detailed their plan of attack for the day, Will sidled up to Janie and offered her a rather large crocheted black bag. She gave him a questioning look. He shook the bag at his side, and she could hear metal clinking on metal. Realization dawned on her face, and she took the heavy bag from him, replete with her pistols tucked out of sight, but nearby for easy use.

"We'll split up and explore the town," McPhail said. "Don't be too obtrusive, but get the lay of the land, and find out if the homes are occupied." He looked at the three. "Finn, you'll come with me."

"Aw," he complained. "Why can't I go with Will?"

"Because a young couple is less likely to draw attention than Janie and I would, and I can't trust you and Janie not to get into a shouting match or worse if I leave you alone. We'll take the south side of town and Hogg's mansion, you two take the north and the Weatherwax house."

"Yes, sir," Will said. Then he turned to Janie and offered his arm. "My lady?"

"Don't push your luck, Will." She did put her hand on his elbow. "Just blending in."

Will glanced over his shoulder and saw that Finn and McPhail had turned their backs already. "Once they're out of sight, we'll stop off somewhere to get you some better riding clothes."

Janie raised her eyebrows at him. "Why suddenly so thoughtful?"

"There hasn't been a town we've been to yet we haven't had to make a quick get away from. You'll never get far on a horse dressed like that."

"Good point." She gave Will one of her few genuine smiles. "I like someone who plans ahead."

Later that day, Mildred hosted Daphne and Catherine for afternoon tea on the porch of her home. Under a broad awning, they reclined facing east, which afforded them a view of the mountains and the cascading pools in the distance.

"What a handsome young couple there," Catherine said while sipping her tea. "I don't believe I've seen either of them around here before."

Mildred and Daphne both glanced up at the two young people. The young lady was dressed in a deep maroon dress, perhaps a bit overdone for the day, but quite fetching with her long black hair stirring along her back in the breeze. Her beau wore a black coat and pants with fine grey ticking and a red vest almost the color of the young lady's dress.

Daphne sniffed. "I don't recognize them either, but I do believe I saw that dress in Manitu's shop the other day. Seems a bit ostentatious for the season in my opinion. Looks like it's not even tailored properly."

Mildred and Catherine both laughed at that. "Now, Daphne, I distinctly remember you admiring that dress yourself not one week ago," Mildred chided.

"Well, now in the sunlight, that is clearly not my color," Daphne said. "And if I were to wear it, I would not wear it for a stroll in the middle of the afternoon. I had considered it for the spring ball, but I can see that would have been a poor choice."

Catherine reached across to pat her friend's hand. "Oh, you know we're just teasing, Daphne. Yes, that color is rather garish." She turned to her hostess. "So where will the money from the ball go for this season?"

Mildred was in charge of arranging the Spring Ball in Humility and traditionally the proceeds from the ball went to a needy cause. "Oh, I believe the committee wants the money to go to some poor Indian children to build them a school or some such. It is our Christian duty to help educate those poor people."

Her friends pursed their lips and nodded in agreement, though the expression on all of their faces made it clear none had a personal interest in providing that education.

While the three women chatted, the young couple ambled past on the opposite side of the street and down the block. The young lady would titter at something the young man said or demurely turn her head away from his attentions. The sound of their voices did not carry far. "From what McPhail said, that should be the Weatherwax house with the three ladies on the porch," Will said.

"Looks big and the front is pretty open to the street. Easy to be seen." Janie glanced up and down the block. "At night though, there's likely no one around. Let's circle the block and see what's on the backside."

The rear of the estate consisted of a high, walled-off garden with a single locked gate that opened into an alleyway behind some of the businesses on the main street. The lock would stop a causal snoop but not impede a serious interloper, and the alleyway would offer some concealment as would the night. All in all, that entrance looked promising, but the wall was too high to identify what they might find between it and the house itself, and there were too many people about to risk scrambling up to peer over the wall in daylight. They had already gotten a disapproving glance from one of the shop proprietors when he spied them in the alley. Of course, that might have been from the impropriety of the two young people appearing to skulk off together out of sight.

"Looks like we're not going to find out too much more here," Janie said. "Better stop loitering about before someone gets suspicious."

By midafternoon they met Finn and McPhail at the hotel. Those two had located Governor Hogg's holiday mansion, and other than a lone caretaker, it seemed to be deserted. It was also isolated, sitting apart from the adjacent homes by a large plot of land and trees. They ought to be able to enter the mansion without being observed and look for the information McPhail wanted. Failing that, they could make an attempt at the Weatherwax home, though the danger would be greater with Mrs. Weatherwax and her household in residence.

"We'll turn in for some early rest this evening," McPhail said. "Pack all your gear. We'll bring the horses in case we need to leave in the night."

Will leaned a fraction toward Janie to whisper out of the side of his mouth. "Told you."

The moon had peered over the mountains before sunset and dipped to the horizon by the time the quartet rode onto the Hogg estate. A screen of bushes and trees obscured the house from the street, but no gates barred their passage. They tied their horses to some trees just inside and crept toward the dark two-story home.

The caretaker had bolted the front door and the kitchen entrance, but Finn found a parlor window ajar. McPhail had brought along a hooded lantern that he lit once they slipped inside. The parlor held only chairs, a divan, and an upright piano, but no paperwork. A quick reconnaissance of the downstairs revealed a kitchen, dining room, and game room with a billiard table. At the end of the hallway across from the kitchen, a closed room looked to belong to the caretaker, so they avoided it and headed upstairs.

The second story consisted of three empty bedrooms and a study replete with bookshelves, drawers, and desk. Janie remained in the hallway to watch for any late-night guests, while the other three closed the door, drew the curtains, and opened the lantern to search the room.

Will perused the bookshelves that consisted of history books, a few almanacs, atlases, tomes of works including Shakespeare, Homer, Ovid, and Cervantes, and books of poetry. Shifting the books failed to reveal any hidden locks or doors.

In the desk, Finn found a calendar empty of entries for the majority of days and nothing going past April where a looping hand had scrawled "Weatherwax, 6p" on the final filled line. The remainder of the drawers contained blank paper, pens, ink, and extra oil for the desk lamp. A humidor on the desk held a handful of cigars until McPhail appropriated them.

McPhail took more time to flip through a file cabinet and set of drawers, but in the end, their contents were sparse and what little remained appeared to be household bills and old invitations to parties and meetings in Humility. "Looks like Hogg clears everything out with him when he goes." McPhail surveyed the room looking for a concealed space for a safe or hidden drawer, but the room was as plain as it appeared.

Will shuffled along the walls tapping here and there. He moved the framed painting of a desert vista but found no safe. "Doesn't look like anything to me either."

McPhail frowned. "We'll need to check out the Weatherwax house."

"There's people living there," Will said. "It won't be easy. We could use a distraction."

The three stood in silence. Finn stared down at the open desk drawers. "How about a fire?" He looked up. "If there were a fire, people'd come from all over to try and help put it out. Things are dry enough, one wrong spark could set off the whole town." He held up the bottle of lamp oil. "We douse the room here, or maybe the parlor downstairs, light it up, make enough noise for the caretaker to wake, and head out. He'll raise the neighbors, and they'll raise the town. In all the yelling, we hit the Weatherwax house."

McPhail pursed his lips. "Not a bad idea."

"I didn't know you were so sneaky, Finn." Will gave a little laugh. "I'm gonna have to watch out for you."

They rejoined Janie on the second-floor landing and slipped back downstairs. With two bottles of lamp oil from the study, Finn and McPhail coated the parlor and game room to make sure the caretaker would not be able to put out the fire himself and would have to go for help. Meanwhile, Janie and Will brought the horses closer to the house.

Finn lit a match and dropped it into a puddle of oil near the parlor door. He had expected a satisfying whoomph of noise, but the orange flame leapt into the air without a sound and snaked across the floor onto the divan, across the chairs, and up the window curtains. As it began to eat into the fabric, it made a low crackle, and the room began to fill with grey smoke.

When he turned around, he could see that McPhail had set the billiard room ablaze and was loping for the front door. The Ranger nodded to Finn and fired two shots into the floorboards. "Fire. Fire," he yelled, and the two ran outside.

The horses shied away from the flickering lights in the windows and the growing smell of smoke. They were more than glad to gallop away from the acrid smell and the sound of the gunshots. As he turned the corner, Finn looked back to see a dark stick figure, silhouetted against the flames, run from the house, flailing its arms.

In her dream, Mildred listened to the pastor's sermon, only the pastor was Catherine Montague, not Father Samuel as it was most Sundays, and the sermon was not so much a sermon as it was a lecture about the history of the tribes who lived and hunted the lands near the Mescala Mountains which somehow intertwined with the latest fashions that were coming out of the Federation. The mention of fashions made Mildred realize how fetching the new hat she wore was, but every time she turned her head, the bells on it clanged away. The more she turned to get a good look at herself in the full-length mirror Catherine had so thoughtfully brought to church for her, the more they clanged. Now even the church bells had begun to chime, drowning out the sound of the bells on her hat, which irked her to no end. How dare the bell ringer try and upstage her on her wedding day. Mildred would have to go have a word with him, but when she turned to do that, Catherine and Father Samuel had begun to stomp out a jig up in front of the altar, pounding away with their boots.

Mildred sat up in bed when her bedroom door swung open. It was Marissa, the maid, holding up a lamp. "Mrs. Weatherwax, I'm so sorry to wake you, but there's a fire."

Outside, the church bells peeled a warning to the town.

"Where is it?" Mildred swung her legs out of bed and stood up. "Do we need to flee?"

Marissa shook her head. "No, ma'am. It's down on the south end of town, but Mr. Banyan and Mr. Fredericks are going to help out. They told me to wake you and let you know."

Mildred sighed in relief. At least the fire was not close yet, but that could change. She knew stories of whole towns burning to the ground over one errant ember. "We'd best get dressed, Marissa. Then you'll help me pack some bags just in case."

As she dressed, Mildred realized neither she nor Marissa would be able to wrestle her chests into the wagon or hitch the horses were the need to flee to become acute. Helping the neighbors was all well and good, but surely Mr. Banyan or Mr. Fredericks ought to have stayed to make sure she was safe and well taken care of. It was their job, after all. She made a note to have a serious talk with the two of them and maybe a sharp letter to Horace. If he was to expect her to keep living here, he really had to find reliable help.

It took Mildred just ten minutes to get dressed. After that, she busied herself and Marissa roaming the house and filling her three traveling chests with her essentials: one trunk full of her dresses and coats, another with jewelry and hats and scarves for various occasions, and the third for paintings of her children and baubles. That left far too many dresses and knick-knacks in harm's way, but with only three large chests, there was not much hope for more, and one would just have to make do under trying circumstances.

The first two trunks were loaded and sitting by the front door, and Mildred and Marissa were halfway through the third trunk when they heard the back door in the kitchen open. "Well, it is about time, Mr. Banyan and Mr. Fredericks," Mildred called out. "We might have all burned up waiting for you." She barged into the kitchen, ready to continue reprimanding her help, but the sight inside pulled her up short.

There were four figures in the kitchen: a tall older man; two younger men, one broad and one slim; and a young lady dressed as a man. All four wore guns on their hips save the tall one who had drawn a pistol. "Pardon our intrusion, Mrs. Weatherwax, but we're going to have to detain you for a space."

Mildred's mouth fell open, speechless for once.

"Are they back, Mrs. Weatherwax?" Marissa asked as she tailed her mistress into the kitchen. She let out a little screech and would have turned to run, but the slim young man jumped forward and grabbed her arm.

The older man regarded both women. "Now is there anyone else left at home, ladies?"

Marissa had turned as white as the china in the kitchen hutch, but she shook her head.

"Good," the man said. "Now, if you will be so kind as to point us the way to your husband's study, Mrs. Weatherwax, we can finish our search and be out of your hair quick as a jackrabbit."

Mildred had recovered her composure and drew herself up to her full five foot one. "I don't know who you think you are barging into my home like this, but I will have you know, my husband is Horace Weatherwax, secretary to Governor Hogg, and he will not stand having the likes of you storming into his home and molesting his family."

The cowboy sighed. "We know exactly who your husband is. That's the reason we're here. Let's tie 'em up, boys."

And so Mildred found herself tied to a chair, back to back with Marissa, with a bandana tied across her mouth while the four intruders ransacked her husband's already disorderly study.

"Look at this," the familiar-looking dark-haired young lady said to the others. She was thumbing through one of Horace's green ledgers. "It looks like it's a list of Hogg's business assets and income."

"And I've got a calendar over here with appointments," said the young man who had grabbed Marissa.

The tall cowboy spent a few minutes more thumbing through more papers, a few of which he stuffed into the duffle bag over his shoulder. "Looks like we have what we need. Time to go."

The other three slipped back out of the study toward the kitchen, but the tall cowboy stopped by the two ladies. "Sorry again for the inconvenience, ma'am. When you see your husband and Governor Hogg next, please tell them Territory Ranger David McPhail sends his regards." He gave a little bow and disappeared out the door.

Boots clomped across the floor and the back door swung shut with a bang.

Mildred and Marissa sat there by the light of the lamp on Horace's desk for almost an hour before Mr. Banyan and Mr. Fredericks returned from their gallivanting about town. Yes, they were dirty and covered with ash, but Mildred could tell when a man had been neglecting his duties. Horace would hear all about this little episode, and Mr. Banyan and Mr. Fredericks would be looking for new employment very soon.

BENEVOLENCE

Humility was two days behind them, and to Will's relief, they escaped unmolested and without any pursuit. As near as they could tell, only Governor Hogg's mansion had burned during the night, but the distraction had been all they needed. Knowing that they had burned Hogg's personal residence gave Will and Finn a sense of satisfaction, their first step in retribution for the wounds Hogg's men had inflicted on them.

Before they delved into their catch from the Weatherwax house, the quartet made their way back to their base camp on Mount de Dios. The spring sun shone on the little plateau, but a cool breeze ruffled the branches around them. Birds twittered in the trees and a butterfly flitted across their stream. Up here in the fresh mountain air, Will could forget some of the filth he had seen. From the way Janie carried herself, Will thought she felt the same. She scowled less, and in unguarded moments, he even saw her smile if she thought no one was looking.

They spread out near the stream to look through the papers. Janie had the ledger in her lap. "This looks like a copy.

The dates are all different, but there's these long blocks of entries all in the same color like they were written together and then another block later with a different ink."

Finn leaned over her shoulder to look at the entries, which made Will feel an annoying twinge of jealousy. He had been sitting on a log with ample room for company, but when Janie came over, she chose to sit down on a rock not far away from his cousin. He pushed the thought down and went back to the papers in front of him. They appeared to be a list of stage stops and cargo manifests between San Alonso and a San Francisco broker in North Cali.

"So those are all Hogg's holdings?" Finn asked Janie.

"It looks like it." She brushed her hair back behind her ear. "It's monthly ins and outs from a bunch of businesses."

Finn snorted. "The Broken Mare. We know that one. Looks like he's got plenty of other places in Chastity." He looked up at McPhail and Will. "Maybe we should go back there and burn a few of them down for good measure."

McPhail just shook his head. "Too dangerous there. We'd be recognized like as not by someone before we got far. That's not what's filling San Alonso's coffers anyway, even if they do help line Hogg's pockets. The real income comes from taxes and the Revenue Men."

Finn went back to the calendar. "Yep, and tax time is coming up. There's a big star there two weeks from now when the Revenue Men bring in their booty to San Alonso."

"Hmm." McPhail rubbed his chin and shuffled back through his papers until he found the page he wanted. "And according to this, an armored stage leaves from Benevolence two days before that with the profits from the southern counties."

Finn wrinkled his brow. "We could hit the stage along the way."

"There's more than one route through the mountains between Benevolence and San Alonso. If we guess right, it's doable, but if we guess wrong, we miss out." Having replenished his supply in Humility, McPhail sat back and chomped on a cigar.

Janie stopped flipping through the ledger. "What's the goal? Do we want the money ourselves or just make sure Hogg doesn't get it?" All three looked at her. "What if we hit them in Benevolence before they leave? At least the town and building won't be moving, and we could just burn it all down if we want since Finn here has caught the fire bug. Seems easier than trying to steal it."

"Well, if that's the case, maybe we could just drop the coach off the side of a mountain or something," Finn said. "Still easier than attacking the building."

Janie shook her head. "Depends on how many guards, and if you just knock it down the side of the mountain, all someone has to do is climb down and drag it back up. Burn it and it's gone."

In his funk, Will was not paying much attention to the conversation, or to the papers in his hands for that matter, but a word on one of the papers caught his eye and he stopped to reread the entire letter. "Why are we sending troops to North Cali?"

The other three turned to look at him. "What?" Finn asked.

"This letter from the governor in 'Frisco is thanking San Alonso and Hogg for agreeing to send more troops. He says when the troops arrive, they'll send back payment." Will held up the letter with an official-looking seal at the bottom and a flourish for a signature.

McPhail squinted at the letter for a brief second. "There's a battle line of sorts between the Mexicans in South Cali facing off against our sister state, North Cali. Santa Ana didn't appreciate being kicked out of half of California, especially after the gold rush. Mexico stills thinks North Cali ought to belong to them more than the Federation. The Federation and 'Frisco disagree, Manifest Destiny and all, but the Federation is sometimes a little slow with warm bodies to back them up. I wonder why Hogg agreed?"

Will pointed to the paper. "A whole lot of gold, it sounds like. If this is right, should be coming in another month or so once those troops arrive."

McPhail leaned back and took another few puffs from his cigar. "All right." He clapped his hands and rubbed them together. "We're hitting Benevolence the night before the coach heads out. We'll take what money we can and burn what we can't. There will be Revenue Men and Agents there for the transport, but we can handle them. After that, we keep heading west and see if we can't pick up a line on the gold shipment before it gets to Hogg."

Finn smiled and laughed. "Wouldn't Pa be proud of us, Will? He and Ma raised a couple of bandits."

Will grimaced and turned back to his stack of papers.

They descended the mountain a week later. Janie had been raised in the plains and hills of north-central Jefferson and had never traveled more than a half day's ride from her home until now. The mountain vista, the trees, the birds, the water cascading down from the snows above, and the feeling of being able to reach up and touch the clouds, to touch the sky, were experiences she had never even imagined. Trekking down the mountain was a fall from grace, a return to a life tethered to the ground, pulled into the drab, dirty drudgery of life. With each clomp of her horse's hooves, she could feel her mood settling back to earth.

She considered turning around and riding back up, maybe

even climbing all the way up to the mountain's top, into its sharp grey peaks covered in sparkling white snow.

Before her mother had died, Janie's life had consisted of work, but work wound up in people, neighbors, visiting, and other children. After her mother's death, Janie's world shrank to their little cabin and her father. At first, that had been a comfort, closed away with her mother's familiar things: dresses, cloth, weaving, dishes, spices, and her smell. Later, those things had faded too, replaced by clouded days, building grime, dank smells, and her father's yeasty burps and sweat. In those times, she had wanted nothing more than to be alone, away from the painful memories of her mother and the conflicted feelings for her father.

Now she had the choice to be alone, to be up above all the world and the dirt and the pain, to be closer to the sky where her mother's soul now must fly, and yet she chose to stay in the company of people and return to the earth.

McPhail was like the father she had known between the ages of ten and thirteen. He was stern and dark, beset by sorrows of his own, much as Arthur De Casas was beset by grief for his wife. McPhail had a purpose and goal in life that her father lacked. Just like her father, Janie could see the pride McPhail took in his younger charges as they learned from him.

The closest Janie and her father had ever been was when she took an interest in shooting and excelled under his tutelage. Back at eleven years old, shooting was something she could do to please him, to lift the both of them a bit from their grief, something that did not remind them of Maria De Casas or their struggle to eke out a living on the plains. Even later, when his dark side emerged, they continued to hunt and practice shooting together, as if trying to recapture that time when Arthur De Casas had been happy for Janie to just be his little girl before he took pleasure in her in other ways.

Finn was little more than a large boy, neither handsome

nor disagreeable. He and Janie tolerated each other, but there was little closeness, only a vague companionship that consisted of two people traveling in the same direction. Of the quartet, he seemed least affected by the demons that swirled about them. He could be sad and moody at turns if they dwelled on subjects too painful, but mostly his spirit bubbled up into smiles and jokes within minutes. Their entire existence seemed a lark to him. He would be just as happy to ride off north or east and explore the world as he was to head west or south to seek revenge. In fact, Janie thought it was not so much revenge as adventure that drew Finn on, that and the fact his cousin never wavered from the path McPhail set for them.

Janie found Will the most confusing of her companions. At once he was as driven as McPhail, his true disciple and protégé, a reflection of him in body and spirit, motivated only to right the wrongs in the world, and then he was a puppy dog romping about her. She could chide, scold, ignore, and shoo him away. He would limp off with his tail between his legs but a moment later be only too happy to follow her about and be her best friend. He treated her like a surrogate for his lost cousin-sister, worrying over her moods, her state of mind, and trying to rescue her from unseen dangers, but Janie could sense other feelings brewing under the surface. She saw it in the way he looked at her across the fire at night, the sidelong glances he gave her when they walked or rode side by side, and the bristles he threw up if she spoke to Finn in too familiar a fashion.

Janie could understand the dark drive. McPhail inspired a passion to set the world right, and Janie had been through enough darkness to understand the thirst for revenge. She could tolerate the protectiveness and, for now, be the stand-in for Kali if needed. She did not want the other attentions.

Those looks reminded her too much of Avery Johnson, the grocer's son. Whenever she went shopping in town, Avery had smiled at her and given her those same warm looks. He had joked with her and brushed her hand lightly when handing her the cloth or spices she had come to purchase. He asked when she would be in town next. He was the first boy to look at her as more than the poor daughter of the town drunk.

On one of the visits to town, Arthur had seen Avery's attentions and Janie's blush and shy smile in response. By that time, Janie had become accustomed to her father's nighttime attentions and learned not to cry until later, after it was over, and he had fallen into his drunken stupor. That night had been different. While Janie rode in the wagon with a blissful smile, Arthur's temper simmered all the way to the farm; and marinated with his hip flask, it roared into flame at home. He had beaten her, called her a slut and a harlot, and as he had his way with her, kept asking if she wished Avery was doing this to her. He screamed at her and hit her to force her to say yes. Then he had laughed at her and told her she would never be good enough for the likes of someone like Avery Johnson. He told her she would never be better than the filthy whore she was.

Janie did not know if Avery heard about the black and blue eyes she wore the next morning, but after that, she made it a point to avoid Avery's eyes and looks and his presence whenever possible. She had avoided the rest of the men and boys in town too.

Will Covington and Avery Johnson looked nothing alike. Avery had dark hair, almost as dark as Janie's, hazel eyes, and a crooked nose all atop a wiry frame. Will had light brown hair that glowed with red highlights in the sun, blue-grey eyes, and a lean athletic body. The look Janie saw in those blue-grey eyes across the fire at night was the same one she had seen in the hazel ones across the counter. Janie did not want those looks, but a part of her kept looking for them, nonetheless; and if for no other reason than to irk him and bring out those jealous bristles, she would sit next to Finn or laugh a little too loudly at his jokes. Sometimes she was unclear if that was meant to push Will away or tantalize him further.

And so Janie continued to ride with them. She had told Will she had debts of her own to collect, but whom she could collect them from, she could not tell.

McPhail had warned them that Benevolence was a rough town, and from her first view of it as they crested the last hill, Janie had to agree with him. The town was located near the banks of the Lobos River. The ramshackle buildings made of rough adobe and weathered beams lay jumbled about in a hodgepodge of shapes and sizes without clear evidence of any order or vision or even a reasonable street. Some lazy god seemed to have emptied his pockets of the detritus of a day's work onto his forgotten bureau that was this backwater of the Jefferson State. The result was Benevolence. The exception to the squalor was the squared-off wooden building closest to them on the eastern edge of town with a bell tower standing above the flat roof. A walkway encircled the roof where a lone figure armed with a rifle and clothed in black stood surveying the town.

"That's going to be the Revenue Office there," McPhail said. "We still have a couple of days 'til the coach is due to set out. We'll stop by and survey the town and then head east. Try not to draw too much attention, but keep your guns handy."

As they approached the town, shouts and cheers interspersed with the sound of fists on flesh reverberated around the buildings. The source was a small crowd outside a seedy-looking saloon. Despite being only midafternoon, the smell of whiskey and stale beer drifted off the group. Two shirtless, bloodied men pounded each other in the rough center of a ragged arc of bystanders who egged the two on to greater heights of brutality.

On one side of the circle, a tall, broad woman watched the fight with mild interest. Most of her attention focused on counting handfuls of money. Behind her back loomed two large men who by their looks might have been her sons. She paused long enough in her counting to appraise the four riders as if measuring their prospects. She lingered on McPhail, lanky but weathered and hard looking, dismissed Will in an instant as too small and too green, fixed Janie with a knowing look and a slight smile, and alit on Finn for a few heartbeats longer than any of them as he was the bigger of the cousins. "Too late to bet on this round, but there'll be another fight in an hour," she called out to them. Janie guessed the woman had decided they were better suited as pigeons than barehanded fighters despite the gaze at Finn.

They stopped the horses two buildings away, at a dilapidated structure with a faded "Store" sign hanging cockeyed from the eaves. The watering trough outside was a quarter full of brackish water, but the horses dipped their noses in thirst. No sooner had the horses begun to drink than a balding man with a scraggly beard and a stained yellowing apron appeared in the doorway. "Water's for payin' customers," he said.

McPhail touched the brim of his hat and adopted the simple congenial persona he had used with the shopkeeper in Mercy and hotelier in Humility. "Aye, sir, we'll be loading right up." He turned to the cousins and his voice dropped. "Will and Finn, better stay outside and watch the horses. Check out the lay of the land, but don't wander off alone. Janie, come on in with me."

The store proprietor stood glaring at the quartet as if daring them to try and leave after watering their horses. When McPhail and Janie mounted the steps, he followed them inside.

Janie was sure his attentiveness was more to make sure they stole nothing rather than to be of service.

Inside, the store smelled dank and moldy, which was an accomplishment in the arid climate. A line of ants ran up and down a barrel of flour next to the counter while another line circled a torn sugar bag. Cracked and dusty jars of spices lined shelves behind the counter, and many appeared empty. A narrow, steep stairway split the shelves behind the counter. The dried meats hanging from a rack on the opposite side had a greenish hue in spots, but that might have been a trick of the light that filtered through the dirty front windows. The leather on the boots along one wall looked old and cracked and poorly made. The few garments seemed functional though ill-constructed with jagged seams and uneven arms or legs.

The man in the apron took up a position behind the counter with his arms folded across his chest. "Whad'ya want?"

McPhail surveyed the goods behind the counter. "Tobacco if you have any, bag of flour, and another of sugar."

Janie cringed inside at the last two. Even when she and her father had been scraping by at their lowest, she had always kept their food cleaner than what was on display here. They would have to spend the next week picking out bugs and larvae before cooking. She turned away to examine the rest of the shop while the two men haggled over prices.

"Your woman need anything?" the shopkeeper asked.

"My niece, not my woman," McPhail answered.

The shopkeeper snorted and muttered something rude under his breath.

Janie spun around and rested a hand on one of her guns. "I'm nobody's woman."

The shopkeeper made to reply, but the rusted bell above the front door interrupted with a dull clank, and a mustachioed man in dark blue stepped into the shop. The Revenue Man regarded the scene before him. "Conrad." He nodded to the shopkeeper. "Just a reminder, revenues are due tomorrow by noon. I trust I'll see you in the morning?"

The shopkeeper swallowed, his eyes narrowed, and a forced smile touched his lips for a moment. "Of course, Mr. Wurst, I'll be by first thing in the morning."

Mr. Wurst smiled like a cat, all teeth. "Or I could just take the collection now. It would save you the trouble of walking all the way across the street. Revenues are due on the first of every third month, Conrad. We give a grace until the fifth, it is true, but seems everyone else in town has made their payments except you. Any problems we in the Revenue Office should know about?"

Conrad shook his head. "No troubles here, Mr. Wurst, but I wouldn't wanna trouble ya further. Tell you what, once I'm done with these customers here, I'll get the money together and be on over before sunset." A bead of sweat ran across the man's forehead.

"Ah, yes, your customers." The Revenue Man turned his feline smile on the lanky cowboy at the counter with nary a glance in Janie's direction. "New in town, I see. We don't have many visitors here in Benevolence. Why not, I am sure I don't know."

McPhail nodded in an amiable fashion. "Just passin' through, sir."

"And where might you be heading to?" The Revenue Man moved around the room to the counter, like a cougar circling its prey.

"On our way to Diligence." McPhail maintained his relaxed air.

"Really? Diligence is in the east. I know because I collect in Diligence. You and your party came in from the east. Seems to me, you're going the wrong direction." The catlike smile was bigger now, more like a puma's.

McPhail remained unfazed. "Overshot a bit comin' offa the

mountains back there. Runnin' a little low on supplies, and thought we'd stop by to restock."

Mr. Wurst nodded. "I see, Mr....?"

McPhail smiled broadly and put out his hand. "My apologies, sir. Mr. Daniel McAdams out of Reno."

Mr. Wurst regarded the proffered hand with disdain. "And what, pray tell, draws you all the way from Reno to Diligence?"

McPhail seemed unfazed by the rejection of his handshake and dropped it back to his side. "My boys and I are taking my niece here to her aunt on her mother's side." He dropped his voice quieter, and he glanced at Janie as if in apology for sharing her secrets with this man. "Lost her parents, she did, a few months back. Runaway wagon on the mountains and all that. Well, it ain't right for a young lady to be living with her father's brother and his boys, 'specially when her mama's family is still around."

The Revenue Man nodded. "I completely understand. Whose family does she belong to?"

"The Lopezes."

Mr. Wurst nodded. "There's a few Lopezes in Diligence. Is her aunt Selma or Catalina?"

McPhail wrinkled his brow and shook his head. "No, sir, I surely don't know any Selma or Catalina. Her name's Iñez and her husband's Humberto. They live about three miles out of Diligence on a little ranch, I'm told, but I ain't never been there myself."

The cat smile vanished. Mr. Wurst looked toward Janie. "Your aunt makes some passable cornbread. Give her my regards. Perhaps I'll stop by and say hello next quarter."

Taking her cue from McPhail's amiable and innocuous lead, Janie smiled and gave a little curtsy despite her lack of dress. "Thankee kindly, sir."

Before leaving, the Revenue Man looked at the shopkeeper

one more time. "I'll see you later this afternoon, Conrad."

By then, the shopkeeper had lost his bluster and forgotten about his opinion of McPhail and Janie's relationship as well as her hot response. Once they had completed their purchases, McPhail and Janie joined Finn and Will outside. Mr. Wurst stood in the shade of the saloon where the broad woman from earlier was counting out money into his hand. When they rode past heading east out of town the way they had arrived, Janie could feel his eyes following them.

Each step they took away from Benevolence should have brought relief, but those eyes weighed on the back of her mind. She rode up next to McPhail. "Is there really an Iñez Lopez in Diligence?"

"There used to be, at least. I bet there's no Selma or Catalina though. Revenue Man Wurst probably suspects everyone of something, but especially us."

So much for not drawing attention, Janie thought to herself.

The moon was a sliver in the sky sinking toward the western horizon on the fuzzy white trail of the Milky Way. To the east, the sun slept wrapped up in its blankets and snoring away behind the distant Mescala Mountains. In the near distance, coyotes yapped to each other about where to find the tastiest morsels this fine night. A weak, lonesome breeze stirred the dust in the streets of Benevolence where the drunks and fighters had long since collapsed into an alcoholic or traumatic stupor.

The quartet entered the town from the west under cover of the maze of structures. They tied their horses near an empty, rundown stable and made their way on foot toward the Revenue Office.

With a boost from a water barrel, Finn scrambled to the top of the saloon that sat across from the office itself. Even though he was hidden from her vantage, Janie knew he was lying there on the roof with his rifle aimed at the lone guard across the way. A rifle shot in the dead of the night would be as good as a shout of alarm or the peal of the bell from the roof, but at least no bullets would follow from above if Finn saw trouble and took the first shot.

When the guard turned south in his circuit of the roof, McPhail dashed across the open space to the north side of the building and began making his way around to the back side of the building and the rear door. He was going to rely on his night vision and dexterity to make his way inside through the minefield of cast-off junk that surrounded that entrance.

After the guard's next circuit, if all went according to plan, Will and Janie would approach the front of the building. They would enter through the large barn doors that concealed the loaded coach or failing that, try the main front doors.

Back in their hideout, atop the world, in the sun, it had been Janie's suggestion to assault the Revenue Office itself. Now in the dead of night, facing the dark building and an unknown number of opponents, the hubris of the idea weighed on her chest. The other three had agreed, but if anything went wrong, Janie would still bear the guilt of suggesting this foolish idea in the first place.

Will talked about dying in a blaze of glory, and Janie wondered if that would be tonight. It might be up to her to prevent that. He was a bit of an annoying puppy dog at times, but at least he was a cute puppy dog. Will and McPhail might be faster than her, but she was a better shot than Will when it came down to it, and she could out-shoot McPhail as often as not, she imagined. Tonight, she would make sure every shot counted.

The guard completed his circuit and stopped to look out

across the town. Will and Janie tried to shrink farther back into the shadows of the general store. On the roof, a match flared as the guard lit a cigarette. He leaned on the railing and puffed grey smoke into the night air.

Will growled in frustration, and Janie laid a hand on his arm. He gave her a quick smile that dropped back into a scowl as he turned away from her. McPhail would be trying the back door while they sat here unable to help.

Three puffs later, the guard began his circuit again.

Will and Janie nodded to each other and dashed across the open space. Janie winced at the soft thud Will made when he skidded to a stop against the building next to the double doors. She strained her ears for any sounds from within but heard none. She nodded to him, and Will reached out and lifted the latch. The far door swung open with a low squeal, but again, no response came from inside. The white grin of Will's teeth shown in the darkness, and he ducked inside with Janie on his heels.

Once she was inside, Janie tugged the big door shut behind them, shutting out even the starlight. They waited a few seconds in silence, but even as their eyes adjusted, they could make out only vague black outlines of the coach, harnesses, and crates. Will started edging to the left where the entrance to the main building must lie. Janie moved to the right to try and see what else lay inside the coach shed.

The distinctive sound of a pistol cocking came from her left, and she whirled that way.

"Don't move," a cool voice cooed from the direction Will had gone. Janie could just make out two merging shadows. "If you don't want your partner's insides decorating our shed, y'all just be still." The voice sounded familiar. "Now let's see what we have here." The rear figure of the two uncovered a blackout lantern and flooded the room with light.

Janie blinked and averted her eyes for a second, but kept

her gun trained toward the voice. The light threw the shed and the coach into relief as well as the shadow of another figure behind the coach. She had two opponents, one of whom had Will at gunpoint.

She looked back toward Will and just behind him recognized Revenue Man Wurst in his navy blue uniform holding a tarnished silver revolver against Will's temple.

"Well, well, well, if it isn't Miss Lopez from Conrad's store." Wurst had on his cat smile again. "I should have paid more attention to you that day than I did to old tall and ugly. When I got back here, I finally recognized you: Janie De Casas of Mercy. You're wanted in the deaths of six sworn Agents." He laughed. "Once I realized that, I knew you'd be back, and I do believe I have one of your accomplices here with me. I suppose the other two must be lurking about somewhere. Don't worry though, I have friends to handle them."

Janie shrugged. "What now?"

Will's face was pale but set as emotionless as stone. He gave her the slightest of nods.

Wurst's teeth gleamed in the yellow light of the lantern. "You'll be setting your guns down, and then we'll go about finding your other two friends."

Janie held her gun steady. *Where's McPhail?*

As if in answer to her thoughts, gunshots rang out behind Wurst in the building proper.

"That mus—" Wurst never finished his thought because Janie shot him right through those gleaming teeth.

A part of her brain worried that Wurst's death spasm would trigger his gun and finish off Will at the same time. That would be a pity, but Janie had no time to contemplate her puppy's fate.

She threw herself forward in front of the coach and spun to her right as she fell. At the same time, the figure lurking at the back of the coach came around the side firing. His bullets lanced through the air where she had been standing. Behind her, Will was swearing. At least he was not dead yet. She hit the ground and fired beneath the coach into the lurking assailant's legs. Her first shot ricocheted off a wheel spoke, but the second one found its mark and the shooter went down. He wore the black of an Agent. Janie dispatched him with three more shots that emptied her pistol.

Rolling over, Janie jumped back to her feet to face across the shed toward Will. Against his normal nature, he continued to swear and swipe blood from the side of his face and shoulder. Deeper in the Revenue Office, shots continued to explode, and outside the sound of a rifle joined the fray.

"We need to go. McPhail needs our help." Janie hurried over to Will, reloading her pistol as she came.

Will shook his head to clear it. "Right. Let's go." He regained his composure and stepped toward the door.

Janie hesitated. "Wait. One more thing." She scooped up the lantern and tossed it at the coach. For a moment, the room plunged into darkness, but then the flames spread along the oil and up the sides of the coach, and soon the wood started to catch. She joined Will at the door. "That way, if it's already loaded, we accomplished our mission."

He bobbed his head. "Let's concentrate on getting out of here alive. I'll go high, you go low."

Janie nodded.

Will kicked the door open, and they went through, guns ready.

A counter split the room into unequal halves, leaving a slim foyer in front and a wide area with two desks behind. The two Agents and three Revenue Men in the room had not decided where the threat was most likely to enter. Two looked to the back door, the one across the counter guarded the front door, and two others behind the counter faced the door Will and Janie came through. Their boss, Wurst, and an Agent had been in the coach shed, though, and so the two facing Janie and Will hesitated a moment hoping not to shoot one of their own. That hesitation cost them.

Janie moved to the right, firing at the Agent and Revenue Man guarding the passage to the back door. Gunshots went off to her left, and Will grunted, but she had no time to look his way. The Agent's gun spat fire and a wasp buzzed past her left ear. Janie's guns answered, and the Agent crumpled, holding his gut, and slumped into his partner. The blow threw off the Revenue Man's aim and his shot went high into the ceiling before Janie's next two shots found him.

"Clear," Will yelled. Kicking dropped guns to the side, he came to join her a few feet from the rear door of the room. No more sounds came from deeper in the building, but outside rifle shots still split the night at intervals. Smoke wafted in from the coach shed.

"We should have made a plan for this." Will looked around. "Somehow I pictured one big room, and we'd just see each other or be dead."

Janie had to roll her eyes at that. "Spread out some and get down by that desk." Taking a few steps away, she knelt down behind the opposite desk and leveled a pistol at the back doorway, and gestured for Will to do the same. If all was going according to plan, Finn still had the front door in his sights and would be protecting their backs. "If you're still back there, McPhail, how'd my parents die when I was from Denver?" she yelled.

Almost five seconds passed before a familiar gruff voice called out to them. "Avalanche. Everyone's asleep back here. I'm coming out." The door swung open, and the tall cowboy limped out, holding his thigh. He looked his two disciples up and down and jerked his chin at Will. "That your blood?"

"Thanks to Janie, no, it isn't." Will looked at McPhail's thigh. "But that looks like yours."

McPhail waved it off. "Got plenty left in me. I see you already lit the fire. Good work. Better signal to Finn."

The three went to the front door, and Will stuck his fingers in his mouth to whistle a crescendo ending in two quick tweets. They waited until they heard Finn's "all clear" response of three quick tweets in return before slipping outside.

They met up with Finn as he scrambled down from the roof. "You had a few visitors from across the street, but they didn't get far," Finn said. He pointed north. "Two of 'em hightailed it that way once they saw the smoke. I think I winged one though."

"We got all of them inside." McPhail motioned them faster. "Keep your eyes open, though. Never know when someone else will come looking for a reward." They kept their guns drawn as they wove back through the town. Perhaps gunfights in the night were a common occurrence in Benevolence because although a few doors creaked when they passed or faces peered through windows, the denizens of Benevolence remained ensconced in their homes while McPhail and his band regained their horses.

McPhail groaned when he tossed his bad leg over his horse. "Head west," he said.

"Until we find some shelter," Will said. "Then we need to have a look at that leg."

"My leg'll keep. Right now we need to ride."

❦ *FORTITUDE* ❧

By the time the sun soared above the distant Mescala Mountains, the grey-black smoke above Benevolence had drifted away in the morning breeze, the fire having burned itself out in the early hours of the morning. The ground between them and the town was broken by gently rolling hills, and at the crest of the last hill, they saw no signs of pursuit.

McPhail was his same grim self, but the morning light revealed a new pallor. The bandage on his thigh was stained a red-brown color, but the wound beneath had ceased seeping.

They paused on the leeward side of a hill in the relative shade to rest their horses. Finn climbed back up the hill with his rifle to watch for anyone trailing them. McPhail rebuffed Will's offer to help dress his wound. Will assumed the cowboy did not want the rest to know how serious the wound was, so he and Janie went to care for the horses and broke out rations for breakfast.

Will removed the final saddle bags to lighten the horses' load and let the last one go to browse on the nearby grasses and brush. He dropped the bag on the ground with the rest next to Janie and shifted back and forth from foot to foot. "Thank you for back there."

Janie was squatting down as she went through one of the food bags and had to cock her head back to look him in the eye. "For shooting the right one? Don't worry about it. We're even now." She turned back to her task. "I'm glad I didn't miss."

Will dropped down on his haunches and touched her hand. "I'm glad too. Thank you."

"Don't touch me." She pulled her hand away from him and glared. "I said you're welcome."

Will sat back a little and bit his lower lip. "Actually, you didn't until then." He tapped the right side of his head with the heel of his hand. "But I'm not sure I can hear much out of this ear yet."

Janie's eyes narrowed, and her glare intensified.

Laughing, Will held up his hands in apology. "Not that I'm complaining. I'd be hearing a lot worse with a bullet in there."

Her look softened as she went back to her task. "They're not great for your complexion either. Just ask Wurst."

Will looked down at the blood stains on his shirt and felt the dried blood in his hair. "At the next stream, I need a bath."

Janie made as if to hold her nose and fanned the air. "That you do. Stay downwind until then."

He laughed first, and she joined him.

When they stopped, Will found himself staring at her again. "We made a good team back there."

"If by team, you mean I did a good job of saving you while you did a good job of being bushwhacked, then yes, we made a good team." She tried to keep a scowl but could feel the traitorous smile breaking across her lips.

Will chuckled. "Fair enough. After that though, we worked well together. So you're ahead five to two for now, but you didn't see me in Chastity. Just ask McPhail. I did much better then."

"You're only as good as your last firefight," a gruff voice said. McPhail limped over and lowered himself to sit on a nearby rock. "You got bushwhacked, and I got hit, but in the end, we all made it out of there, and they didn't." Having exhausted his cigar supply, he pulled out his tobacco pouch and began rolling a cigarette.

Janie and Will exchanged a look that suggested their little party was over.

"Wurst recognized me," Janie said. "Knew my name and everything."

McPhail nodded. "Might have known all of us. There was a wanted poster in the back with your sketch alongside an old one of me, and it said we had two accomplices. I'm thinking after last night, they'll be increasing the reward. We'll start seeing those posters pop up in all sorts of towns soon."

"Wonderful," Will muttered. "I'll take some food up to Finn." He grabbed a biscuit and some jerky and started up the hill to his cousin.

Janie called after him. "Don't let anyone sneak up on you."

He turned around to look at her. "Only in the dark." He held her gaze for two seconds, but she did not offer a reply. Neither was quite sure if that was a joke or an invitation.

After a few hours' rest, they set off westward again toward the distant Santo Domingo Mountains. The Santo Domingos were the little brothers of the Mescalas. In the dead of winter, snow capped their peaks; but while the Mescalas might keep isolated pockets of snow and a few small glaciers through the winter, by late fall, all would have melted off the Santo Domingos.

Crossing them would be gentler than crossing even the mountains around Tranquility. This eastern side of the mountains was dry compared to the western slopes where most of their water poured down into the Grand River still far away and out of sight. A few streams did trickle down the eastward slopes toward the Lobos River, and so they had fresh water.

The air over the plains between the mountain ranges heated quickly as the sun climbed into the sky. They stopped to rest and water the horses where they could.

Despite his bad leg, McPhail took his usual lead. Finn hung back as rear guard. No matter how many Agents and Revenue Men they had killed in Benevolence, Finn found it hard to believe there was no one left to mount a search. He would keep the other three within easy sight when he could, sometimes drifting along their back trail by a mile or more, but he spied no signs of pursuit.

Those times of solitude helped, or so he thought. He thought back to Mr. Franklin's words. The trail boss had warned them coming back to Jefferson was a bad idea, but Will had not wanted to listen, and Finn would not desert his cousin.

Of course, back then, there still had been Kali to consider. Now she was gone too. Finn wondered if it would have been better never to have found out what happened to his sister. If they had headed north to work the ranches or gone west to mine for gold, he knew he would have felt guilty, but at least then he could have pretended his sister was alive and well, living out her life working a farm with a good man for a husband. He would have dreamed of coming back someday riding a fancy stagecoach and decked out in the latest fashions after striking it rich in North Cali. He would have brought nice new clothes for his little sister, toys for his nieces and nephews, and maybe even something for his brother-in-law if the man was treating his sister right. On his arm, he would have brought his own woman, perhaps some big city socialite who had fallen for his down-to-earth charms.

None of that was going to happen now. They were killers and fugitives, rebels against the government. Maybe only McPhail and Janie graced the wanted posters, but he and Will would follow soon.

There was a chance, before last night anyway, that they could have given it all up. Once Governor Hogg heard about what they had done, there would be nowhere safe to hide. If Finn could have gotten Will by himself earlier, if he could have found a way to put his feelings and thoughts into real words, he could have persuaded Will to leave McPhail and Jefferson and never come back. Words tended to fail Finn though. He was no orator, no great debater. In his mind, the words shone sharp and clear, but they came out confused and dim, garbled and weak. Will had always been able to talk circles around Finn. Even Kali could trip up her big brother.

All of that and Will was in love with Janie. Finn had known Will all his life. Being so close in age, they were almost like twins. He could see the way Will looked at Janie, the way he rushed to help her, the way he tailed after her. Sure, he would drift back and talk to Finn or sit by the campfire with him, or even hunt with him, but whenever Janie was near, half of Will's attention was on her, and even when Finn got Will off away from her, more than half his comments somehow related to her.

Finn recognized he was jealous. Not jealous because he wanted Janie for himself; she was pretty and all, but to Finn only pretty in a detached, intellectual sort of way. He was jealous of the increasing portion of Will's time and attention that she took up. Finn was pretty sure she did not love Will back, not yet anyway, but when she smiled, she smiled for Will. Oh sure, Finn could get her to laugh at some silly joke, but whenever she did, she would glance over to see if Will had noticed

she was laughing with Finn. The laughs were for Will's benefit, to make him jealous and reel him in or make him angry
and push him away. Finn was still working that part out, but
he had a feeling Janie was too.

Maybe Janie was the key to getting the old Will back. If Will
fell far enough under Janie's sway, maybe she could pry him
away from McPhail. Then the three of them could ride off together. Finn would be happy, and maybe Will and Janie could
manage to be happy together too, and it would all work out.
He feared that Janie might be just as set on bloodshed and self-
destruction as McPhail and Will. If that was true, whomever
Will followed would lead them all to an early grave.

They crossed the Santo Domingos without incident and followed a well-worn trail through one of the passes and down
into the valley where the Grand River ran. As its name suggested, the Grand River was impressive. On the way south to
Benevolence, they had crossed the tributaries of the Grand
River with relative ease. The river gained strength as it ran
past San Alonso, now to their north, and especially after it
turned south to run between the Santo Domingos on its eastern bank and the Elephant Mountains on its western bank.
South of San Alonso, it swelled wide enough that a town could
sit between its banks at their widest and deep enough that only
the tops of the buildings would have broken the surface.

The Elephant Mountains were a long chain of mountains
weathered down to rounded peaks that some imaginative ex-
plorer had felt looked like the backs of a string of elephants
walking trunk to tail. They stood taller than the Santo Domingos, carried more snow in the winter, and did the heavy work
of flooding the Grand River over capacity in the spring.

With all of that water volume in the river, crossing on horseback was out of the question, but their ultimate destination still lay somewhere to the west. To that end, McPhail directed them to the town of Fortitude, and the ferry the town existed to support.

While the town may have existed to support the ferry, the relationship appeared unbalanced. The first buildings they encountered were deserted with windows blanketed in heavy layers of dirt or broken out. Doors hung ajar on rusty hinges. Roofs sagged under the weight of time. Weeds and grass had begun to reclaim the streets. The only promising structure was a small shed near the dock on the banks of the river. Sunlight could still peer through the windows. Though worn, the door still stood intact. Cheery puffs of smoke drifted from the chimney, and broken stanzas of "Oh Susanna" replaced with off-color lyrics floated from an open window, but no one came to greet them when they rode up.

Will looked at his companions and got only an eye roll from Janie, a shrug from Finn, and a stoic stare from McPhail. "Hello," Will called. "Anybody home?"

At the moment, the voice ran up another octave into a long keen of chorus and drowned out Will's call.

Janie snickered.

Will swung off his horse and approached the shed. The clomp of his boots on the stairs came just before the next verse which cut off with a yelp from inside. Before he could reach the door, a shaggy-haired man stuck his head out the window. "Visitors," he squealed and then ducked back inside. About ten seconds of shuffling and banging ensued, and then the front door swung open and the man emerged pulling up his suspenders.

"Well, lookee here." He snapped the suspenders against his chest and put his hands on his hips. "You're the first visitors I've had this week." Then his face clouded. "I ain't got no money though. Nothin' worth killin' for anyway. I'm just the lonely ferryman, is all."

"We ain't here to rob you or kill you," McPhail said. "We're just looking to cross the river."

The shaggy man brightened at that. "Well, then you've come to the right man, pardner. Like I said, I'm the ferryman, at your service." He swung into a deep bow, so much so that his long locks almost brushed the ground. "Marvin's me name; crossin' rivers is me game." His smile revealed a few brown teeth mixed with black holes where other teeth had given up the ghost.

Even McPhail's lip twitched in a half smile at Marvin's exuberance.

"The ferryman needs to live too. San Alonso don't give old Marvin the support it used to, though still, they do come to collect their due. I can take all of you across and your horses, but we need to talk about what Marvin gets beside the glorious sun and the working of his muscles."

McPhail opened a pouch on his hip to produce more of the money purloined in Chastity. "We're honest, and we can pay."

Will backed down the steps to let Marvin pass. "So what happened to the rest of the town?"

Marvin gave a theatrical shrug. "Done packed up and blew away. Ain't too many people coming through for the ferry nowadays. They built a big bridge up near San Alonso, and then the coach road moved up that away too and all of a sudden, no one needed a ferry down here. Once no one need a ferry, no one need Fortitude and so poof." He blew out quick through pursed, lips like blowing the seeds from a dandelion. "Everyone scatter."

By then Marvin was out on the dock opening the gate to the ferry, a large flat square with fenced in sides, large enough to hold a good-sized coach pulled by four horses. On the upstream side of the ferry, several guide poles reached up high overhead topped by loops. A rusted, braided steel cable ran through the loops and extended from shore to shore. At the midway point of the ferry, engulfing the cable, sat a wooden structure with a large wheel in the center.

Marvin turned and grinned. "All aboard."

One by one, they led their horses onto the ferry. The deck bobbed in the current and even more so with the shifting added weight. All the horses hesitated to board, and Finn's almost balked completely. It took five minutes or more of cajoling and handfuls of sugar cubes to persuade the horse to join his companions.

Once aboard Marvin closed the gates, unlashed the moorings, gave the dock a push with a pole, and then went to turn the wheel. The wheel attached to gears hidden in the wooden frame that gripped the cable and pulled the ferry along. The ferry creaked and groaned at first, but then began to inch away from the docks with each crank of the wheel.

Finn joined Marvin. Between the two of them, the ferry soon bobbed in the current and trundled along the cable.

"So why did you stay when everyone else left?" Finn asked between deep puffs from the effort of cranking the wheel.

"My daddy was the ferryman afore me." Marvin grinned wide again with those brown teeth. Up close, Finn realized, they were even more unappealing, but Marvin's enthusiasm mitigated his other failings. "I still ferry a few locals and the odd traveler like yourselves. What else am I to do if I am not a ferryman like me pappy?"

When Marvin deposited them on the far side of the river, he accepted McPhail's fare for the ferry ride but squawked when McPhail extended another folded stack of bills as a tip.

"Think of it as appreciation for pleasant company, Marvin, and also a little payment for some information for a traveler who has been absent from our fair state for many years.

Where does the new coach road run?"

Out of the window of his office, Governor Hogg watched the wagons roll up and down the streets of his city, neat and orderly. All things in their place. San Alonso ticked along like the fine Swiss grandfather clock that tocked away behind him, not a cog out of place, not a second too fast or a second too slow. The rest of his state seemed another matter. At least four cogs seemed to be rolling about out of place and perhaps a fifth rattled around his office.

"You're sure McPhail and De Casas were in Benevolence, Agent Garland?"

"Yes, sir. Several townsfolk were glad to give them up. Revenue Man Williams, who made it out, said Wurst even set up a welcoming committee for them."

Despite not turning to look, Governor Hogg knew the man stood straight as a pine, straining every inch of his being toward the ceiling. Hogg could hear the tension in Garland's voice. He let that tension sit and contemplated. "McPhail's a loner, no family, no easy pressure points. De Casas's family is dead, and she seems to have no friends left in Mercy. What about the boys?" Hogg rubbed at his chin and watched the wagons. "Did they come back from the Federation with McPhail or did he find them here?"

Hogg spun around to face Garland and the ever-present Head Agent Warren. "We need leverage on the boys. Dick, find out who they are, who their families are. Once we know, we apply pressure."

Dick Warren gave a little nod.

Agent Garland continued to stare at a spot in the upper corner of the window even when Hogg addressed him. "Seward, get back out there and track them down. I'm starting to care less and less if De Casas makes it back here alive."

That did bring a faint smile to Agent Garland's lips.

They traveled north, following the Grand River and skirting the foothills of the Elephants. About two-thirds of the way to the new San Alonso bridge, they came upon the coach road after it crossed Gorseman's Pass alongside one of the many tributaries the Elephants donated to the Grand River. The road continued north, but they turned west and mounted to the pass.

The road itself was broad enough for a coach to pass, but if two coaches met heading in opposite directions, passing each other would present a challenge. Being so new, it was in good repair, but most days brought no more than one or two travelers in either direction.

They made camp near the top of the pass where they could observe both sides of the mountain and waited. If their stolen papers were correct, if no changes in plan had come up, if their time estimates were correct, and if the coach took this route as opposed to the longer northern route, the gold-laden coach from North Cali ought to be passing through within a week, two at the most.

They waited.

Time passed.

Will and Finn hunted.

Sometimes Janie joined them.

McPhail healed.

They kept out of sight of travelers.

They practiced with their guns.

They planned for the arrival of the coach.

By the end of the first week, they were healed and relaxed

and ready.

Two days later, boredom and wanderlust crept in.

Four days later, they spotted four horses pulling an armored coach with a driver and guard riding atop the carriage. Two more mounted guards rode escort. Everyone knew the plan. They neatened their camp, saddled their horses, and started down to take up position on the road.

Once the coach began to ascend the mountain, one rider rode in front of the coach and the other behind. They took their time ascending to Gorseman's Pass so as not to tire the horses. The day's journey ahead would still be long. The nearest coach stop lay well over the pass and then north along the Grand River, which would take them until well after sunset.

Janie and Will watched the coach pass from the cover of a copse of trees. Once it started to round the corner, they mounted and came out onto the road after it in time to hear the cry of "Whoa" when the coach came face to face with McPhail and Finn, who blocked the road ahead.

Neither Will nor Janie heard the exchange that took place, but they did hear the cocking of guns and then the eruption of gunfire. The guard on their side drew his gun and started to move around the coach when it surged forward. Will and Janie spurred their horses in pursuit.

Chaos reigned around the corner. McPhail was struggling, locked hand to hand with the lead guard, both still in the saddle. Finn was on the ground off his horse, but rising, bruised but otherwise appearing unhurt. One body, the guard from the coach itself, lay face down not far from Finn's feet. The coach was already hurtling down the road as its horses picked up speed on the downslope. The second mounted guard leveled his pistol at Finn, but Will reacted first and shot him in the back.

"Stop the coach," McPhail yelled as he and his opponent continued to grapple.

While Will had pulled up to take in the scene. Janie had not. She and her mount continued chasing the fleeing coach, and Will had to urge his horse forward to catch up.

Janie's horse was not built for speed or a long chase, and Will closed the distance, but her mare was fast enough to make ground on the coach, fully laden with gold as it was when it came upon an up-slope on the undulating road.

From inside the coach, another guard opened a rear panel and began firing back at the pair of bandits. With the bouncing of the coach, his aim proved poor. Both Will and Janie fired back, but their bullets only dug into the wood of the coach.

Now Will passed Janie and closed to the side of the coach. One of his shots drove the guard away from the window long enough for him to reach the back corner of the coach and grab on. He pushed off from his horse, and for a few moments, his boots kicked out inches away from the wheel before he was able to scramble to the top.

No sooner had he done so, than bullets came through the roof inches from his face. The guard inside was shooting through the roof at him. Will rolled forward as more shots came.

By then, Janie caught up to the coach. With the guard inside distracted, she sprang from her horse to the coach, but instead of scrambling to the top, she grabbed onto the back and shot twice through the window.

No more bullets came back at her or Will.

Saved from the danger below, Will looked to the front of the coach. The driver lay slumped to the side in his seat, shot dead by either McPhail or Finn. The horses were not being driven but ran panic-stricken on their own.

The coach reached the peak of the up-slope and started heading down a steep grade.

Janie crawled up on top to join Will and took in their situation. "Uh-oh."

They looked at each other. Their own horses had stopped running the moment Will and Janie had dismounted. The reins to the coach horses dragged down somewhere beneath the coach. To their right, a rough rock wall bordered the road. To their left, the mountainside dropped away into a rushing river. Ahead, the horses barreled toward a tight left turn.

"Jump?" he asked.

Janie looked from Will to the road ahead and the river below and back again. She was pale but determined. "Jump. At the corner."

They crouched together, gripping each other's forearms and counting the distance ahead.

Shouts came from behind them. Will stole a look back to see Finn and McPhail galloping after them down the hill, too far away to help. Maybe if the coach made the turn, they would be all right. The horses would soon run out of steam and slow their stampede.

"Will," Janie yelled to him above the thundering of the hooves and grinding of wheels on the rutted ground.

He looked back. They were at the corner. The lead horses started to make the turn, but they were going too fast, and the coach did not want to follow. It lurched up on two left wheels, tossing its passengers toward the drop. Janie and Will leapt together just before the coach turned on its side.

They hung there in the air, suspended above the drop and the water below, and then they fell.

Fed by melting snow further up the mountain, the river was ice cold. The force of hitting the water knocked the air from Will's lungs and then the passage from warm air to near freezing water constricted his chest even more, refusing to let him breathe. In the end, that was fortunate in those first few seconds as the spasm in his chest prevented him from inhaling a lungful of water when he plunged beneath the surface. The current spun and buffeted and held him down. When his head broke the surface and he took his first gasping mouthful of air, McPhail and Finn and the coach had receded to small dolls in the distance.

As the current swept him around a corner, he whirled about trying to find Janie. She splashed a few horse lengths ahead of him. He started to call out to her, but just then she dropped from sight down a small rocky fall in the river and a second later Will followed her.

Again the water pulled him under and left him sputtering when it released him.

"Will." Janie's voice came from behind him which turned out to be downriver because the water had spun him about again.

They kicked toward each other. Their fingers brushed in the water and spun apart. The water was too swift and even after only being submerged for a few minutes, numbness from the cold slowed his fingers' grasp.

A rock smashed against his leg making him cry out and swallow more snowmelt. Spray blinded him for a moment, but then a hand grabbed his jacket. For a moment, he felt the canvas might tear, but it held, and his flailing arms found Janie's.

The river ran straight for a pace, and they strengthened their hold on each other, but the current was too strong for them to make headway to shore. Ahead, another series of drops and rapids loomed.

"Feet first," he yelled above the coming roar.

Janie did not waste energy speaking, only nodded.

They clung together the rest of the way down the mountain, bouncing off rocks but never being able to find purchase for more than a second before the current would carry them on. Several times they lost their hold on each other and had to fight to come back together. Twice Will lost sight of Janie beneath the water and each time feared she was drowned; both times she managed to resurface, but each time her paddles looked feebler. Janie's strength was flagging faster in the cold than Will's own.

Neither could judge how far the river swept them, but finally, the banks stretched apart, and the water slowed and leveled, and the current deposited them along a gentle curve covered in rough pebbles and stones toward the foot of the mountains. They dragged themselves up the shore, bruised and waterlogged and shivering. The sun hung above the mountain peaks but was descending fast, and the weak rays did little to warm them while the late afternoon breeze tried to chill them more.

Janie hacked and coughed and gagged until she threw up what looked like a gallon of river water and then collapsed on her side.

Will groaned and pushed himself up onto all fours, then walked his hands up his thighs to get to a sitting position. "Come on, Janie," he said. "Gotta move." He crawled closer and shook her shoulder which quivered under his hand, but after that, she did not move. Leaning down, he listened to her breathing coming shallow and rapid. This time he yelled her name and shook her harder. "Janie, come on. Wake up." He pulled her limp torso up and pounded her back. "Janie."

Again Janie coughed and hacked and spit up more water, but this time she took a deep gasp of air afterward and opened her eyes. "I'm okay," she wheezed.

"No, you aren't. We have to get you up and moving." Will struggled to his feet and tried to haul her up after him. It took three attempts, but the third time, Janie woke enough to help push herself upright. She slipped an arm around his waist and let him lead her up the riverbank away from the shore.

Not far away they found some boulders that had soaked up the sun's heat and basked in the fading light of day. Will lowered her down against the boulder. "Better take your jacket off. It's just gonna make you colder," Will told her while he stripped off his sopping coat.

Janie grunted in response. She leaned forward with her head between her knees but did not move to take off the wet clothes.

"I'll find some firewood." Will headed back down to the river where he collected some driftwood washed up on the shore. Closer to where he had left Janie, he collected some twigs and dry grass which he dumped down in front of her. His guns had survived the trip downriver in their holsters, though whether the bullets would work was another matter. More importantly, his pouch with flint and steel had also survived the journey.

Numb and cold, his hands fumbled for several minutes before Will was able to produce the necessary sparks to feed into his ball of dried grass. Several more minutes of patient blowing turned smoke into small red tongues of flame. "Almost there." He glanced over to Janie who sat upright now, but her eyes remained glassy and unfocused. Another shiver rocked her body. Shadows crept over them. A few rays of sun still lanced up over the mountains in the west, but to the east, the sky was already purple.

Will went back to feeding his fire, urging it to grow quicker. An errant gust of wind almost extinguished the nascent flames and sent shudders through Will as well. After adding a little more grass, twigs began to catch fire, and after the twigs, the dried driftwood soon followed.

With the fire caught strong enough, Will went over to Janie. "Come on. Let's get you closer and warm you up." Her skin was ice under his hands, but then his was not much better. With the fire dancing before her, Janie shook some of the cobwebs from her head and scooted closer. She even let him peel off her wet jacket.

Words tumbled from Will's mouth in a babble as he tried to keep Janie alert while he gathered more fuel to keep the fire going. "Finn and Pa and I got caught like this once back home. Course it was late fall then and colder than it is now. We got caught in a rainstorm, not a river either, but at least it wasn't snow, and we were soaked to the bone with night rolling in. It took forever to find anything dry enough to even start burning, and even after that when we'd feed in new wood that was damp, the fire would sputter and almost go out. We could have frozen out there that night. That's when I learned you need to get out of the wet clothes as much as possible. They just make you colder. We were all huddled together under blankets in our drawers shivering all night in this little hollow against some rocks. Fortunately, the rain had stopped mostly, but all night we kept getting these little showers, and it was too cold to sleep.

"You and I shouldn't be that bad off because it's spring, and we're not in the mountains anymore, and so it won't get that cold I don't think. We aren't likely to freeze to death, but it's going to be uncomfortable. Finn and McPhail will be looking for us. Hopefully, they'll bring the blankets. If we keep the fire going, it should keep us warm enough and in the dark, it should help them find us.

"Course coming down the mountain might get too rough for them in the dark. At least if they see the fire, they'll know we're not dead. Fires can attract other people though. We'll need to dry out the guns too. I think the ammo will work, but hopefully, we won't need to find out. At least this time, we know no one's chasing us."

With the supply of nearby firewood collected, Will dropped

down beside Janie. She was holding her hands out to the fire. It was warm and large and burning merrily now, but her boots were still on, and she was still shivering. Will pried off his soaked boots and then went to work on hers. Shuffling about their little camp had gotten his circulation going some, but he was still cold and could see Janie's purple lips against porcelain skin in the light of the dancing flames. The heat from the fire was welcome but seemed meager in the growing dark.

"Come on, Janie. We have to get you warmed up." He scooted closer and put his arms around her, but she recoiled from him.

"Don't." Her voice wavered, hoarse and weak.

He went to embrace her again. "You're freezing."

This time her voice came loud and harsh. "No." Her eyes flared with more fury than Will had ever seen in her.

They sat there staring into each other's eyes, his shocked and hers enraged at first but then coming back into focus and softening.

She closed her eyes for a moment as if trying to blink away tears. "Please, Will, don't." She sighed. "Here." She shifted position to just behind him and wrapped her arms around him and rested her chin on his shoulder. "I'll be okay like this, I promise."

"Let's turn a little." Will shifted to point more of her body toward the fire.

They sat like that, side by side, staring into the fire. The chills still ran through them both, but Will could feel hers lessening. Her arms around him felt good, as did her breath, now more even and strong, on the side of his cheek. He could not see her face from this position, but he thought he felt a new dampness on her cheek near his neck, but it might just have been the water still drying in his own hair. She sniffed once.

"I know I never met her, but I can understand your cousin." Janie's words so close to his ear and so unexpected startled him out of his thoughts and made him flinch. She kept talking, little louder than the crackling of the fire, but so close to his ear, her words came strong and clear. "Do you know why they were going to hang me?"

Will shook his head a fraction, afraid that any words from him would derail what she wanted to say in this moment.

"I killed my father." Her voice broke, but she pushed on. "I loved him. He took care of Ma and me as best he could, and after she died, we did our best to take care of each other." Will was convinced those were tears on his neck now. "But I hated him too. He would drink and beat me when he got angry. When I got older, he made me lay with him like a woman."

Will tried to turn in her arms to face her, but she held him firm.

"I thought about doing what your cousin did. I almost did it myself, but I never could get up the courage. I kept thinking about what would happen to him if I wasn't around anymore to take care of him." She sniffled and gave a cross between a laugh and a cry. "Can you believe that? I was worried about him. I knew Ma loved him, and I didn't think she would forgive me if I abandoned him or if I could forgive myself. Isn't that stupid?"

A definite trail of tears ran into his damp shirt collar with a strange mixture of warmth and cold all at once.

"So instead of killing myself and abandoning my father who I loved, I decided to kill him. Does that make any sense either?" She shook her head against him, and the shaking that ran through her body was no longer from the cold.

Since she would not let him face her or hold her, Will took her hands in his own and squeezed.

"He came home drunk one night just like any other night. I don't even know what he was yelling about, but I just thought about how he just spent all the money on drink, and how he hit my mother for no reason when I was little, and how he hit me now for no reason either, and all those other things he made me do. It just made me mad, and so I picked up one of the guns and shot him right in the face when he came through the door just like I did to that guy Wurst, and then I went over and kept shooting until there were no more bullets left, and he stopped moving."

Janie sobbed, and her arms loosened around Will's waist. He had no idea what to say, but he turned to her and folded his arms around her and held her head to his shoulder and let her cry.

"I deserved it," she said. "If I'd been a better daughter, he wouldn't have had to yell or hit or do those things to me. That's not true, but it feels just as true as it doesn't. I hated him, and he was evil and deserved to die, but he was my Da, and I killed him, and so I deserve to be hanged. That's not right either, but also it is too."

"Oh, Janie," Will said. He held her and let her cry. He whispered meaningless words into her ear that tried to convey so much meaning at the same time. Before he could stop himself, he kissed her cheek on those salty tears streaming down her face. He continued to brush those tears with his lips as her sobs ebbed.

She pulled far enough away to regard him with those dark brown eyes. Then she closed them and leaned forward and kissed him on the lips, a soft brush of hers against his, just the slightest pressure. Janie leaned back and shook her head. "I'm no good for love or you, Will. I want to have you hold me, but sometimes when you get close, I see my Da. I can't be with anyone. I'm broken like Kali was."

"No, you're not," he said.

Janie laid a finger on his lips to shush him. "Please don't say anything. I'll let you hold me for now." She lay down on her side facing the fire with her head in Will's lap. He wrapped one arm around her upper body and slipped the other underneath to cradle her head in his arm. They huddled like that, watching the fire burn and the stars come out in the sky until she fell asleep. Will remained awake for a long time afterward. Sometime in the night, he fed the last of the wood into the fire and lay down next to her in the dancing shadows. She woke enough to snuggle into the warmth of his arms against the cold of the night, but off and on in her sleep she would twitch and moan and cry against the demons in her dreams. When that woke him, Will would whisper more gentle words into her ear and try and hold her until the nightmares passed.

∾ CONVIVIALITY ∾

The next morning, Finn and McPhail found Will and Janie asleep in each other's arms, lying next to the remains of their fire.

Somewhere in his dreams, Will became aware of the sound of horses' hooves and someone calling his name, but he only roused when a rough hand grabbed his shoulder. "They aren't dead, are they?" Finn's anxious voice echoed far behind that hand.

Will groaned. His muscles, cold, bruised, and aching from their swim in the river, contracted in protest.

"They're not dead yet, but damn close. Get some firewood, I'll get the blankets." That was McPhail's voice.

Will opened his eyes and winced when he pushed himself to a sit. Despite the cold and the pain, he grinned at Janie when she opened her eyes. "We survived."

She smiled back at him and allowed him to pull her to a sitting position. "Thanks to you, Will. Looks like I owe you again."

"No, friends take care of each other."

"Is that what we are?"

Before Will could answer, McPhail was back throwing blankets over them. "You're still too cold. Lucky you made it. Next time get all the way out of the wet clothes. Better to be naked and alive than wet and dead with your modesty intact. If it had been colder last night, you both might have frozen even with the fire."

When Janie caught Will's eye, he felt the blush on his cheeks that warmed more when she pulled him close under the blankets. "Come on. He's right. We're still cold."

She was correct. Now that he was awake, he could feel the coolness of her skin and the spontaneous shivers they both still shared.

McPhail relit the fire, and Finn dumped off more wood. "I thought you two were goners when you fell in," Finn said. "Coming 'round the bend last night back up there, we spotted your fire." He gestured back up the mountain. "By that point, we were off the road, and it was getting too dark, but at least we knew you'd made it."

With efficiency born of years living off the land, McPhail had the fire burning high within minutes. Finn broke out the food, and McPhail warmed water and coffee grounds.

"What happened after we fell?" Janie had her hands wrapped around the warmth of the tin coffee cup, but she still leaned into Will whose arm encircled her waist under the blankets.

"Well, once the coach went over, the horses couldn't pull it anymore, and they had to stop." Biscuit crumbs spewed from Finn's mouth as he jammed in breakfast between explanations. "The coach was kind of just hanging over the edge. Problem was when the gold shifted the whole thing went sliding down the cliff after you and started to take the horses with it." Finn jerked his head toward the Ranger. "McPhail and I got the first two horses unhitched in time, but the other two went over with it. One died in the fall, and we had to put the other down." He looked sad for a moment, but then brightened and grinned at Janie. "At least you get your pick of the new horses. That old mare of yours can be our pack horse from now on, or we can sell her."

For the first time, Janie looked over to where the horses grazed and realized there were now eight with the addition of the two coach horses and the guards' horses. The four new ones stood off in a cluster, forming their own little herd, but the members of each group would nuzzle and sniff at the other from time to time. At least they were not fighting.

"What about the gold?" Will had already finished his coffee and chewed on some jerky.

McPhail grunted. "Still in the coach, half submerged in the river. We'll have to go back later and see what we can do about it before anyone else comes along. That and take care of the bodies."

Will paled a bit at that. He had killed more than his share of men in the past few months, but the bodies had always been someone else's responsibility. He had been too busy running away. Now he would have to see the consequences of his bullets up close. He made eye contact with Finn. The waxen look on his cousin's face told Will that Finn must feel the same.

The sun sat high above them before Will and Janie had warmed and replenished their energy stores. They took time to clean their wounds and apply salve to their numerous cuts and scrapes from their journey down the river.

Will was amazed at how far the river had swept them without killing them. The trek back up the mountain to the site of the ruined coach and the ambush took more than an hour, but finding both sites proved simple enough. They just had to follow the vultures descending from the sky.

They started at the site of the ambush, which seemed appropriate. Near the copse of trees that had provided cover to

Will and Janie, they found a flat area with loose enough dirt. Janie and McPhail started to dig while Will and Finn retrieved the bodies.

In an attempt at some form of atonement, Will crossed himself and said a prayer over the body of the guard he had shot in the back. The man had never suspected Will was behind him, never had a chance to surrender, never had a chance to plead for his life, never had a chance to send a last message back to whatever family he came from, and all of that was Will's fault. The man was just doing his duty, guarding a gold shipment. There was no crime in that, even if the shipment was destined for a man Will hated. It was Will, Finn, Janie, and McPhail who had instigated the fight. Yes, Will had shot to save Finn's life, but if they had never waylaid the coach, then this man need not have died. Those thoughts weighed on him throughout the remainder of the day.

The insects had found the bodies. Will's stomach turned when it dawned on him that the tear on the man's face was likely not from the fall from his horse but from one of the buzzards that circled up above them and dove down toward the site of the overturned coach. In death, the man was heavier than anything Will had tried to lift. It took both he and Finn to drape each body over the back of a horse to transport it to the gravesite. Even on the horse, the bodies tried to slide off, and the cousins had to walk back on either side of the horse lest they would have to hoist the body up a second time.

Once all three men lay spread out side by side in the ground, the four companions bowed their heads. McPhail spoke. "Lord, these men died bravely doing their duty and defending their lives and their companions. I did not know them, but they seemed men of honor. Please see it in your wisdom and mercy to watch over their souls in your great prairies in the sky. Amen."

"Amen," chorused the other three.

They covered the bodies in dirt and rock. Janie marked the graves with small cairns, and Finn lashed sticks together into crosses to stand among the rocks.

It was late afternoon with less than half their duty complete.

With a cacophony of squawking complaints, the buzzards scattered to neighboring trees when they arrived at the scene of the coach crash.

There was no hope of moving the horses. They would have to leave them where they fell. The body of the coach driver had disappeared with no blood trail or boot prints. His body must have fallen into the river and washed away.

The coach lay on its side halfway in the river. If the door had been barred from inside, the brace had fallen out in the crash. It took McPhail inside the coach and Will and Finn on the side-now-top of the coach to hoist out the final guard. His body was puffy and waterlogged and looked much like Will and Janie ought to have looked after falling into the river.

This time Will and Janie dug the grave on the shore of the river while McPhail and Finn unloaded coins and bars of gold and packed them in bags on the sides of the horses. Above them, the buzzards squawked continuing complaints over the interruption of their dinner.

The sun crept behind the mountain peaks by the time they finished their duties and led the horses back up the mountain to the camp that had been their home for two weeks. Somehow, it no longer felt like home.

The gold would be too heavy and too obvious to carry away with them. In McPhail's mind, the importance was in preventing it from passing to Hogg and his government. They buried the gold that night in the camp.

Up until now, their camp setup had followed a habitual routine. McPhail would lay out his bedroll to one side of the cook fire. Finn and Will would lay out theirs some distance away next to each other. Janie would stake out her sleep spot another third or so of the way around the circle. In these warmer months with less need of the fire's warmth, their bodies resembled three spokes jutting out from the hub of a wheel.

Janie changed that routine the night they buried the dead and the gold.

McPhail, Finn, and Will laid out their bedrolls in typical fashion. Without any comment, Janie rolled out her blankets about an arm's width from Will. Finn raised his eyebrows at Will when he saw that but said nothing.

The chorus of goodnights circulated about the campfire.

"Goodnight, McPhail. Goodnight, Finn." The slightest of pauses broke Janie's cadence followed by the slightest change in tone. "Goodnight, Will."

That tone sent little shivers up and down Will's spine that had nothing to do with being cold. "Goodnight, Janie." In the dancing firelight, he could see her face framed by her black hair and her dark eyes staring back at him. She was lying on her side with her hand protruding from beneath her blanket. Afraid he was misinterpreting her gesture but determined to try, Will reached out his hand to hers. Their fingers touched and then interlaced. Janie squeezed his hand and smiled at him before she closed her eyes. Will did the same, and they drifted off to sleep, joined at the fingers.

The next morning, drained from the events of the last two days, they descended the eastern side of the Elephants. Janie rode a big stallion that had belonged to one of the guards. They led her mare and the other three horses behind them. Near the bottom of the mountains, they passed another caravan of travelers, an extended family. The two bands greeted each other and exchanged pleasantries before continuing in opposite directions.

The party rode north along the Elephants. They avoided the first two towns they came to and camped in the wilderness far from prying eyes. As the miles lengthened, the heaviness of caring for the bodies of their victims drained from Will. Since the night on the shore of the river, his growing closeness with Janie buoyed him and distracted him from the dark thoughts. For the first time in months, thoughts of revenge for his adopted family drifted to the back of his mind.

Janie still had walls, a truth Will accepted, but for him, the walls loomed less. In some ways, he still needed good climbing gear, plenty of grit and determination, and an afternoon devoted to climbing, but they were lower.

She no longer sighed or rolled her eyes or ignored him when he rode with her. That was a major improvement in and of itself. In fact, Will realized Janie rode with him more often than not. He tested it a few times by drifting back or ahead to talk with Finn or McPhail. At first, she would let him go with the same level of indifference she had shown before their swim in the river, but more often than not, within a few minutes he would find her by his side again.

Despite the thawing of their relations, Janie's moods still plagued her. Will no longer received the glares or recoils, but sometimes he could see her stiffen when he approached, or she would give him a sad shake of the head. He learned at those times not to push; she needed her space. At meals, if she wanted company, she would make room for him next to her on a log or a rock or might even come to sit next to him of her own accord, but if not, she created a sort of bubble around herself with body language that kept the other three at bay. At night, Janie always slept closer to Will than she had before, but sometimes only an arm's length away, sometimes two.

Within Janie, the pull of looking for and wanting closeness

continued to battle against the push of habits and memories and pain. For now, at least, the pull had the upper hand, but memory and pain were wily and fought dirty.

Will could see the look in her eye when a memory had snuck up on her, joining past to present. He could see her inner struggle in the stiffening of her shoulders, the closing of her eyes, the shivers, and the deep sighs. At those times, he paused and waited. When her eyes opened, he could read whether the pull or the push had won. When pull triumphed, a small smile might grace her lips, and he would continue talking or moving with her. When the push prevailed, he would give her an encouraging smile accompanied by a little shrug and drift off until she let him know she was ready for his company. It became a dance between them, predicated on the smallest of cues, and the dance exhilarated Will in ways beyond his ability to discern.

Four nights after burying the dead and the gold, as the sun set, they arrived in the town of Conviviality. McPhail told them that he thought they were far enough off the coach's path that no one might recognize the four extra horses or suspect them of any wrongdoing. The town was large enough that travelers might blend in without drawing too much attention.

After he made his pronouncement and started ahead Janie motioned Will and Finn closer. "And it's the first town we've passed so far where Hogg has significant holdings." She nodded at McPhail's back. "He might be carrying the ledger, but I remember the town names."

"Good to know how much he trusts us," Finn muttered.

Will sighed. "Keep your guns handy, don't unpack, and don't get too comfortable."

He started to urge his horse forward, but Janie stopped him. "If there are more wanted posters out there, one of the governor's towns is bound to have some."

And according to McPhail, a recent drawing of Janie graced the poster. McPhail's was old, and Will and Finn remained faceless accomplices.

"Well, there's another cheery thought. I'm gonna sleep real well tonight." Finn spurred his horse after their leader.

Janie and Will looked at each other for a time. "Tuck your hair under your hat and keep it pulled down over your face. We'll get you indoors and out of sight as soon as possible."

"He's using us, Will."

Will shrugged. "We're all looking for payback from the same person. I'm using him to get me there." Janie saw the flint inside Will, reflected in his eyes for the first time in the weeks since Benevolence. He was thinking about the Hennessys, the father he had never met, and the mother who had died when Will could barely form sentences. Then like the tide coming in, the softness she had become accustomed to rolled in and the flint sank beneath the surface. "We'll look out for each other, Janie. You, me, and Finn will stick together no matter what. We won't let anyone take you."

Janie smiled back at his hollow words. Finn would stick with Will, that was true, and he would stick with Janie as long as Will did. Maybe Will really would stick by her. Over the past few weeks, a part of her had grown to believe that he would, if she managed not to push him away, that was; but when the bullets started flying, there would be no guarantees for any of them. "Yeah, we'll stick together."

McPhail reined in his mount at the first building they came to, a tavern with rooms upstairs. The streets remained busy with knots of people out on the town in the relative coolness of the summer night. He left the other three to stable and care for the horses while he went to secure rooms.

Janie tried to keep to the shadows and lose herself among the horses, but her heart beat out an accelerating tattoo with each passing second. The air thickened in her chest with each breath. Revenue Man Wurst's all too knowing smile danced in the back of her mind. If someone recognized her, if the Agents captured her again, there would be no Sheriff Daniels to watch over her and keep them on good behavior while she sat helpless in a cell. She could feel the rough hemp rope on her skin, the moment of weightlessness when the trap door opened, and the tightening around her neck. Her eyes darted back and forth, but no one seemed to take much notice of the trio unsaddling the horses.

A hand thudded down on her right shoulder, and Janie whirled away from the grip and dropped a hand to her holster. It was Will.

He laid a gentle hand on each shoulder. "You're okay. Just take some nice deep breaths. Everything's okay." His voice, calm and even, fought the panic pounding in her ears.

How had he known what she was thinking? Why was he shaking her? Then she realized Will was not shaking her; she was trembling like she had upon emerging from the cold of the river.

"You're okay, Janie. Finn and I are here. Nothing's going to happen to you."

Janie forced several deep breaths and closed her eyes. Her face burned in the dark and flushed more at the weakness she felt inside and for what she needed to ask of him. "Don't leave me tonight, Will. I don't think I can be alone."

In the dark, his expression was inscrutable, but when he spoke his voice caught. "I'll stay with you. Don't worry."

"Thank you." She gave him a quick hug, pulled him tight for the span of perhaps two heartbeats and pushed away. It was the first time she had hugged him since the night by the river and the first time she had done more than brush against him in passing since holding his hand while they fell asleep the night after.

"All right, we've got two rooms, all they have left. Stables and tack room are around back." McPhail strode down the porch steps. When he got closer, he lowered his voice. "I told them we'll take dinner in our rooms. After that, we need to talk."

Will looked at the cowboy. "Yes, we do."

The two men, the older and the younger, held each other's gaze. "Aye, we will." The cowboy nodded and took the reins of his horse.

Will turned to look for Janie, but she had slipped away among the horses.

The two rooms lay adjacent to each other and were small, with a double bed and table in each. They crammed into one of them and sat cross-legged on the floor. The meal consisted of a savory beef and vegetable stew with peas and beans, soft carrots, potatoes, and onions, and fresh bread with beer to wash it all down. Compared to their most recent trail food of dried beef, hard biscuits, moldering cheese, and sediment-laden stream water, the meal tasted of heaven.

The meal took Janie back to a time when she was young. It had been during one of her father's dry times on a warm summer night much like this one, years before Maria Montello De Casas fell ill. Her mother had spent the day simmering stew in the large pot over the stove and baking fresh bread in the oven, and in the twilight, the family of three sat around the table laughing and filling their bellies. Janie could not remember a single raised voice. There was no yelling, no thrown dishes, no tears, and no bruises in the morning. They had played hide and seek in their small house, and before bed, in his rough, halting voice, her father had read her the story of Noah and his ark. He had kissed her on the cheek and called her his sugar-blossom before that term of endearment had any negative connotations, and then her mother had kissed her too, still smelling of those warm kitchen aromas. Her parents had stood in her doorway, framed by the lamplight from the front room, Maria leaning her head on Arthur's shoulder, Arthur with his arm around Maria, and they both watched their daughter snuggling in her covers, gripping a stuffed bunny rabbit. Janie had watched them through the cracks between her lids and saw them kiss each other with an otherwise bygone tenderness. It was one of the happiest memories from Janie's childhood and coming now as it did eased some of the tension running through her.

"Whooee." Finn pushed away his empty plate. "I was famished there and didn't even know it. It's amazing how good real cooking is."

"Well, you could try a little harder helping out at dinners." Will tossed a piece of bread into his cousin's open mouth.

Finn chomped the morsel and swallowed. "Yeah, but that would involve effort. Hey, McPhail, did you ever learn to cook in the Rangers?"

McPhail shook his head. "Food is just energy for the body. Doesn't need to be pretty, just sustaining."

Janie rolled her eyes at Will. "That certainly explains some things."

"I guess maybe it is time we had some explaining." The jovial look on Will's face vanished, and that flint glinted in his eyes as he stared at McPhail.

McPhail returned the stare in spades, but the corner of his lip turned up in a small smirk. "None of you are stupid. There was nothing we needed in the last two towns, but we have business with Governor Hogg here in Conviviality. According to the ledger we found, the money from Hogg's businesses in town is deposited in the bank he owns here on the last day of the month and then sent off via stage to San Alonso on the first. Tomorrow is the final day of June. We mean to appropriate those funds tomorrow evening with as little bloodshed as possible."

"And when were you going to let us in on the plan?" Will continued giving a flint-eyed scowl to their leader.

"Now. Like I said, you're not stupid, Will. You know what we're about. We hit Hogg where it hurts, and we keep it up until we take down his empire."

"We're a team. We need to know the plan."

"And I'm the leader of the team. I tell you the plan when you need to know and when your eyes are on the goal." McPhail's eyes darted to Janie and then back to Will. "I'll do whatever it takes for us to accomplish it."

If Will recognized the reproach in that flicker of the eyes or the veiled threat, he chose to ignore it. "I know the goal as well as anyone. I saw what happened to Kali. We'll end Hogg's reign. What about the wanted posters?"

McPhail shrugged. "Didn't see any here, but they'll be at the bank, post office, sheriff's office, and the Agents' Office."

Janie flinched at the mention of the Agents.

"There were two Agents in the saloon downstairs when I came in. Neither of them took any notice of me. I was watching for it. That's why I said we'd eat in our rooms though. You'll remember we came up the backstairs from the stables. They don't even know we're here." McPhail's eyes never left Will's, cold iron against flint. "I'd still suggest no one sleeps alone to-night." Here he did look at Janie as if he expected her to challenge the proclamation. When she did not, he turned back to Will. "Tomorrow, Janie keeps indoors. I'll take care of selling the extra horses, we know you and Finn are no good at haggling, and you two get the lay of the land. No one knows who you are. We'll hit the bank just as it closes."

"I guess you have it all worked out then." Will threw a stony glare back at his mentor, identical to the one he received.

"Always." McPhail stood up as did Will. "Finn and I will take the other room. Bar the door, and don't leave the window open, but no one knows we're here."

"Good precaution since we're all so safe."

"No one's safe as long as men like Alistair Hogg are allowed free rein. Let's go, Finn." The last look he gave his protégé before he left the room contained a measure of paternal pride mixed with a healthy cup of admonition.

Finn sighed and dragged himself to his feet. "Thanks, Will. I really appreciate that. He's gonna be a real pleasure to hang out with tonight." He shook his head and looked at Janie. "Be glad you don't have a pig-headed little brother or cousin to stir up trouble for you."

"Yours seems to be doing a good enough job for both of us." Janie hugged her legs to her chest and rocked against the bed. "You better get going. If he comes back, one of them might draw."

Finn nodded. "Goodnight, Janie. Goodnight, Will." In another time and place, Finn might have given his cousin a wink and a grin on leaving him unchaperoned in a room with a young lady, but tonight Finn's mirth had fled.

Will caught Finn's arm before he exited. "Someone had to say something."

Finn held up his hands in submission. "Never said he didn't deserve it."

"He always knows more than he lets on," Will persisted.

"Again, I am not disagreeing. Just maybe, don't poke the bear again for a while." Finn waved off whatever Will was going to say next and closed the door.

With no one else left to face, Will turned to Janie. "Was I wrong?"

Janie shook her head. "No, Will, you weren't wrong."

The sad look she wore drained away Will's anger. He looked over her head to the bed she leaned against. The last time he had been alone in a room with a woman, Kali sat on the bed. He shook himself to clear away the image the thought conjured and started gathering the plates and bowls to stack on the small table.

With that task completed, he meandered back and forth in a small arc until Janie caught his hand. "Thank you for staying, for saying you'll keep me safe."

Will recognized the look in those dark eyes. She was forcing herself to make eye contact, to thank him, to hold his hand even though her demons were screaming at her to run and hide, or worse yet, reach for one of the guns she wore on her belt.

She shivered. "You take the bed. I'll take the floor."

"No." His voice was not as cold as it had been when challenging McPhail, but it was firm.

She misunderstood, and tears welled to the brim of her eyes. "Will, you know I can't. Don't ask me to."

He hunkered down next to her and took her hands in his. He smiled. "I'm supposed to be watching over you." He nodded to the door. "I'll sleep across the doorway. Anyone trying to get in here has to go through me. You take the bed."

Relief flooded her face. "Thank you. I don't deserve you."

"Sure you do. Someday, I hope I'll find out what I did in a past life to deserve the chance to meet you." He squeezed her hands one more time before letting them go and moving to prepare his bed.

The wooden floor was about as soft as sleeping on the hard-packed earth of the last few nights, but at least no rocks dug into his back. Will tucked the edge of his blanket into the crack beneath the door to block the draft from the hallway. He laid out the rosewood-handled guns on the floor next to him and his boots at the foot of his bedroll.

Janie tossed him one of the hard, flat, cotton-filled pillows from the bed. She did not offer a hand to hold, but she did lie with her head at the foot of the bed so they could see each other and whisper to each other in the night. She hung her gun belt on the stump of a bedpost nearest her.

Whether the Agents had noticed the party or not, McPhail was correct that the night passed without interruption.

"I gotta say, I think you missed your chance. You didn't even kiss her?" Finn and Will were kicking up dust along the main street of Conviviality in the heat of the late morning. Two carriages passed each other in opposite directions. A grey mongrel yapped at both coaches but spun in circles in the middle of the street, undecided which one to chase. They passed a ranch hand sitting with his legs up on a barrel outside a barber shop.

Will paused to look at his reflection in the glass and then at his cousin. "Maybe we should get haircuts. Ma would not be proud of how long our hair's getting."

"I thought something had already happened between you two after the river. I mean, you two were all wrapped up together when we found you, and then all of a sudden she's bedding down next to you." Finn nudged his cousin with an elbow. "Let me tell you, that's a great way to keep yourself warm in the night. You really should try it."

Will looked back at his reflection and rubbed the roughness along his chin. "Yeah, I'm getting a haircut." He reached for the door and entered with Finn on his heels. The barber occupied the sole barber chair, but he stood when the doorbell above his door jangled. "Haircut and a shave, please," Will told the man who ushered him into the chair.

"How could you spend the whole night sharing a bed and not even try to kiss her?" Finn was dogged this morning if nothing else. Of course, it was the first time in days the cousins had been far enough out of earshot of McPhail and Janie to talk.

"I told you, I slept on the floor." Will kept giving Finn side-long glances while the barber set to work on Will's tangled waves of hair.

Finn threw up his hands in disgust and plopped down on a bench by the window. "Why did you do that? That was the perfect opportunity. I saw her last night. She was begging you to stay with her."

"She was scared, Finn. I told her I'd keep her safe."

"Could have kept her just as safe in the bed as on the floor. I'd have told her I needed to hold her real tight, so she didn't fall out of bed."

Will rolled his eyes. "And that is why she wanted me with her, not you."

Finn snorted. "You ask me, I'd say when a woman asks you to stay with them all night, they're looking for more than a doorstop."

"Again, likely the reason why she wanted me and not you."

"Yeah, but she does want you, Will. If you don't act on it, she's gonna go looking elsewhere."

Will shook his head only to be scolded but the barber. "Keep still lessen' you wanna lose an ear, sonny."

"Sorry," Will said and sat still. He fumed to himself for a minute before speaking. "Look, Finn, Janie's been through some really tough times. You don't understand her. I think I do. It's going to take time."

"Well, all I'm saying is time flies. Don't let her lead you around on a leash. Sometimes you gotta grow up and be a man, Will Covington. Grab the bull by the horns and all that."

Will sighed and decided to change tactics. "Do you remember the practice dummy?"

"What practice dummy?" Out of the corner of his eye, Will could see Finn's confused expression at the non sequitur. Half a second later, his eyes widened as realization bloomed. "Oh."

"Don't mess with Janie. That's what I learned. We go as

slow as she wants and no faster."

The door jangled again and two men in black stepped into the room. "Mornin' Montgomery." The first one through the door nodded at the barber.

"Mornin' Agent Pryor, Agent Reynolds. Little early for you monthly, ain't it?"

"Gonna be goin' outta town to San Alonso. Thought we'd come early, rather than late. Mrs. Pryor likes me well-kempt."

The second Agent guffawed. "That ain't all she likes, I hear. You know she makes him bathe at least once a week? How's a man supposed ta keep healthy if he scrapes off all his skin so often?"

When the Agents entered, Finn grabbed up a yellowed broadsheet of state news off the table and Will affixed his eyes to his reflection in the mirror.

The barber chuckled with the Agents. "Well, I must say, Mrs. Montgomery does prefer I scrub the grime off every now and again too. Can't say I blame her much. I do apologize, Agents, if I'd a known you was comin' in I would have cleared my calendar, but as you can see, these two young men beat you to it."

"Only one," Finn squeaked. He cleared his throat and continued in a more normal but strained voice to Will's ear. "Just my cousin, Mr. Montgomery. I'm doing all right, and I'd hate to keep the Agents waiting."

"Well now, that's right kind of you, my friend. Nice to see some respect around here from the young ones." The Agent sat down on the bench next to Finn and leaned back. "I'm Agent Pryor, and this here's Agent Reynolds. You boys must be new here in town."

Finn looked a panic, and so Will picked up the slack. "Yes, sir. Just came in last night. Been on the road quite a while and thought we'd rest up a day before moving on. Bed's a lot nicer place to sleep than the ground."

The barber's cluck of amusement made Will start to rerun their previous conversation in his mind. How much had they said in front of the man?

"Oh, I can agree with that. Course, beds can make a man soft. Good to be out on the trail now and again to toughen you up." Agent Pryor nodded, laced his fingers behind his head, and put his feet up on a stool. "Just you two boys on your own?"

Bile rose in Will's throat. "No, sir, traveling with our pa and sis—a, uh, family friend."

"Are you two brothers?" Agent Pryor turned to Finn. "Didn't you just call him your cousin?" He looked back at his partner. "Didn't this one just say they was cousins?"

A bead of sweat appeared on Will's forehead. "Yes, sir, you did hear correct. My ma and pa died when I was young, and my aunt and uncle took me in. Finn's like a brother to me, but we're really just cousins." The truth flowed easier than a lie.

"Where are you and your cousin, your uncle and this friend, who I'd guess ain't a sister, traveling to?"

Will swore inside his head. This man was quick. What did McPhail always say? "Diligence."

"Diligence? Why'd you wanna go there?"

"Work, sir."

Now both Agents guffawed. "Work in Diligence? Boy, you ain't gonna find any work in that crappy little town. They are the laziest sons of bitches you ever will find. Ain't no one there does more'n scrape on by and look for handouts. Whooee, that's gonna be a long trip all to be disappointed." Agent Pryor slapped his knee and laughed some more.

Will just sat wishing the barber would hurry along and finish. He wanted to jump out of the chair right then and run out but knew that would only make matters worse. He had to sit and let the laughter die down.

Now Agent Pryor leaned forward to peer at Will. "Those

are some nice guns you got there. Look a bit much for a boy like you."

"Thank you, sir. I am a man grown though this past year, and they suit me fine."

The growing tension within the room seemed to have dawned on Mr. Montgomery. He made two more quick snips. "There you are, young man." He whipped the drape off Will and backed up. By this time, both he and Will had forgotten the shave.

"You can handle those big guns now, can you?" Agent Pryor's voice had lost its joviality and descended into a sneer.

Will stood up from the chair, and Agent Pryor joined him. The Agent was good six inches taller than Will, but he faced the man unblinking. "Yes, sir, I can handle these guns just fine, like my daddy before me." He turned to the barber and handed over the money. "Thank you much, sir. You did a right fine job. Please keep the tip." He looked to Finn. "Let's go, Finn, and let the Agents have their turn."

Agent Reynolds stood barring the way, but with a nod, Agent Pryor signaled to let them pass.

Will's hand touched the knob when Pryor's voice stopped him. "What's your name, boy?"

"Will Covington, sir." Without turning, Will opened the door. Finn pressed close behind him, eager to get out of the small barber shop.

"I'll be keeping an eye on you, Will Covington, and you Cousin Finn. Don't you be causin' any trouble in my town. You hear me?"

"Yes, sir. We won't cause any trouble at all." And then he and Finn were out on the street walking toward the post office and the bank beyond. The door to the barber shop did not bang shut behind them, and Will could feel Agent Pryor's eyes boring into his back.

"So much for low profile," Finn muttered.

Will grunted in resignation.

McPhail was off looking for a horse buyer, Will and Finn were looking over the bank, and Janie was stuck in the hotel room. Even with the window open, the air hung close, and since it overlooked the stables, the meager ventilation did nothing to improve the aroma of the room, and whiling away the hours alone did nothing to help her tension.

Out the window, across from the stables and corral, a small church stood behind the hotel. Growing up, her mother had taken her to church every Sunday. Those trips ended the day they laid Maria to rest under the old pinyon tree on their farm. Janie was out the door and halfway down the back stairs before she realized she had made the decision to go. Will and the others might fret if they came back while she was gone, but expecting her to stay locked up all day was absurd. At the foot of the stairs, she did take a moment to wrap her long hair up under her hat and pulled the brim down low over her face.

Outside, she saw Henry, the hotel owner's son who doubled as the stable boy, lugging a bale of hay across the yard. The horses, who had been clustered in the shade of the building, started to amble toward the fresh food. Engaged as he was with the hay bale, he failed to notice Janie slip past him and cross the street.

The church doors, heavy and weathered, swung on their hinges with the barest of squeaks. Inside felt cool with the rays of the sun off her. The open room held two rows of six pews each facing a simple altar and pulpit. Two tall thin stained glass windows flanked a crucifix hanging above the altar. The morning sun would strike those two windows and fill the room with color. To the right stood a small confessional, and a door led out past it to another part of the church.

Janie crossed herself and walked down the center aisle.

She stopped at the second pew from the altar and sat down on the left side in front of the pulpit. She stared up at the crucifix and time faded. She thought about her mother and all the times they had come to church together, sans father. The kneeling and standing, bowing her head in prayer, singing the hymns loud and clear, the priest and his beguiling sermons she could not understand at the time except the admonishments against sin.

Janie had not understood sin well then, but she suspected she now fit decidedly in the sinner category. Her mother had died before Janie reached the age of confirmation and taken her first communion, and Janie's father had never brought her back for either. God remained absent from her thoughts during the intervening years, and that sounded sinful. She did not know how God would judge her role in the carnal knowledge with her father, but she doubted He would approve of killing him. She thought that was one of those top ten sins the priest had railed against. She had done more killing since then, and lied and stolen. She did not even know what day of the week it was anymore, and so was not observing the Sabbath. Over the past few weeks, conflicted sinful thoughts about Will assailed her, which kept getting mixed up with memories of her father.

Yes, in the last few months she had made a good run at all of those top ten prohibitions, and yet here she sat, drawn to this small church so much like the one in Mercy, sitting here and contemplating... what? God? Justice? Right and wrong?

Janie heard the shuffling footsteps when they approached her flank. "Can I help you, dear?" asked a soft voice.

Janie turned and looked into the face of a nun. A few dark hairs mixed with grey protruded from her wimple, and her face had the beginnings of crow's feet around her eyes and mouth. Her face seemed the kind that endeavored to smile and put people at ease. Janie opened her mouth to say she did not need any help, but instead, "I don't know" tumbled forth.

The nun smiled at that. "Now that is an honest answer. Most people say 'no' when they really mean 'yes,' and those that do say 'yes' sometimes have their own ideas about what help they need, and the Lord may have different thoughts indeed. May I sit down?"

Janie scooted over, and the nun sat down next to her.

"I'm Sister Maria. May I ask your name?" She extended a hand.

Janie's voice caught in her throat, but she managed to take the warm hand in hers. Sister Maria was likely a few years older than Janie's mother would have been, but the coincidence of the name called forth all sorts of spurious but somehow vital similarities: the hair color; the soft brown eyes, lighter than Janie's; the height just a shade taller than Janie; the slim build beneath her habit; the smile lines around her mouth. "I'm Janie."

"Pleased to meet you, Janie. Are you here to pray?"

Janie shook her head and everything started to spill. "It's been too long. I don't think I know how to pray anymore. I haven't been to church since my mother died. I was just thinking about all my sins since then. I don't know if God would even listen to me if I could pray."

"Oh, child, the Lord is always listening, especially to us sinners."

Janie shot her a sideways glance, and Sister Maria laughed. "We all have our sins, Janie, even nuns and priests." She patted Janie's hand. "I don't know what sins you have, but if you are here thinking on them, then the Lord is listening to you."

"Even if I'm not praying?"

"My dear, praying isn't about folding your hands or using fancy words. If the words are coming from your heart and soul and you believe them, then I'd say 'Amen' to it. From the look on your face, I'd say you were speaking from your soul there."

Janie gave a crooked smile. "Belief might be the hard part." She looked back up at the crucifix. "How does He judge our sins? Sometimes it seems any choice you make is a sin. I've seen people doing terrible things in this world. It seems like if you stand up to stop them, well, that might involve fighting and even killing, which is definitely a sin, but if you stand by and don't help, that seems like a sin too. How do you know which sin is worse?"

"That's a very deep question, Janie, one that I don't have all the answers to. I believe, though, that the Lord put us all here to look after one another. Cain didn't believe he was his brother's keeper, but that we are. Helping someone doesn't always have to involve fighting and bloodshed, mind you, but the devil has his minions about in the world seducing man away from the path of righteousness. Protecting those who can't protect themselves is never a sin to my mind."

"How can you be sure though?"

"You have to look into your heart and the good pure soul you were born with. We all carry the mark of original sin, but underneath that lies the soul God gave you. If you are being true to that soul, then it will guide you away from sin and into the light of the Lord."

"What if that soul's been damaged? There's been a lot of darkness in my life, a lot of darkness done to me. I'm not sure my soul is pure anymore. How can it guide me to the right path then?"

"Oh, Janie, no one can ever damage that soul God gave you. Sometimes life can bury it down deep, cover it up, but nothing anyone does to you can ever put out that light. Not even anything you can do can damage that pure soul underneath. You just have to do the heavy work of digging it back out, uncovering it, and allow it to shine again."

The two women sat together gazing up at the cross and the stained glass. After a time, Janie stood to leave. "Thank you, Sister Maria. I appreciate your help. I think I was supposed to come here. You remind me of my mother. She was a good, strong woman, and I miss her."

Sister Maria stood with her and patted her hands. "I'm glad I could be of service to you. Maybe your mother told you to come here and told me there might be a need of me in church today. I think that might be true."

Janie walked across the street and passed the stables with her head down, thinking about Sister Maria and her words. The stableboy was gone, and the horses had found what little shade the nearby trees and eaves of the stable offered. She opened the back door and went to ascend the stairs when voices from the front room caught her attention. It was midday now, but the saloon was quiet.

A gruff voice spoke first. "So there were four of them who took rooms last night? Did any of them look like this?" Papers rustled.

Another voice answered. Janie assumed it belonged to the hotel proprietor. "Hmm, only really saw the older one well. Looked a bit like this drawing of the young man, but the cowboy last night was a lot older'n that."

"That could be. This here sketch's maybe twenty years old, I'm told. What about the woman?"

"Like I said, I didn't see a woman with them. Just the cowboy last night. Said there were four of 'em needed rooms. I only had the two available, and he said that was fine. This mornin' the older one and two younger ones come downstairs and headed off. Ain't seen 'em since."

"They gone for good?"

"Oh no siree, the older one was looking to sell some of

their horses. They rode in with eight horses but only been needin' five of 'em. I told him to go see Patch Ramos. Patch's always looking for good horses. He set out this mornin'. Can barely have ridden there and back by now."

"So they're still in town? You sure of that?"

"Well, I told you, at least one of 'ems out at the Ramos place, but my boy Henry just came back in from feeding and watering their horses, so I'd guess they're still around."

"And you never saw the fourth one. Could have been a woman, a young lady?"

"Like I said, I only seen the older one up close and the two boys in passing. Could be a lady, I presume." The voice paused a moment. "You know, my boy Henry helped 'em stable the horses last night. He might've seen the fourth." Now the voice turned to a yell. "Hey Henry, git in here!"

Janie shrank from the stairway, but the footsteps came from out of the kitchen away from her. "Yes, Pa?"

"Those four that came in last night, was one o' dem a woman?"

"Yes, sir, Pa. A might' pretty one, I reckon."

The gruff voice spoke up. "Did she look like this here drawing, boy?"

There was another brief pause and a rustling of paper. "Yeah, that's her all right, 'cept she don't look so mean in person."

"And where is she now, boy?"

"Well, sir, when I was out seein' to the horses, I seen her lookin' out the winder of her room. That t'wasn't more'n an hour ago. I ain't seen her since, but I'd guess she'd still be upstairs."

"Upstairs right now?"

"Yup."

The murmuring of low conversation came from around the corner. Then the first man asked the hotelier, "What rooms are they in?"

"Four and five, top of the stairs and halfway down to the back."

At that point, Janie decided it was time to leave. She shuffled backward on tiptoes and when she turned to the back door saw McPhail striding across the yard. She slipped outside and held a finger to her lips to silence the scolding rising in his throat. Once she shut the door behind her, she ran over to whisper to him. "At least two Agents are inside. They know we're here, and they're searching our rooms."

McPhail's eyes darted from the back door to the windows upstairs. He grabbed Janie's arm and pulled her against the hotel out of sight of the overhead windows and started moving toward the tack room and stable. "Hope you didn't leave anything important in your room. Let's saddle up the horses. We need to find Finn and Will before they come back here and run into the Agents. Looks like we'll be making an early withdrawal."

Will and Finn finished their rounds of Conviviality and the bank around noon. The morning rush of representatives of various businesses died down as the lunch hour approached. Neither Will nor Finn could tell how much business was typical and how much belonged to Governor Hogg's monthly tithe.

Will felt a little guilty for leaving Janie cooped up in their room while he and Finn leaned on the railing in front of the general store enjoying the warmth of the spring sun. Finn nudged Will's elbow. "Don't look now, but our buddies Pryor and Reynolds have company."

Despite Finn's warning, Will glanced down the street. Another Agent was hurrying up the street to Agents Pryor and

Reynolds, who stood outside the Agents' Office, surveying the town. "Time to mosey along back to the hotel."

They started off down the street away from the bank and across the street from the Agents' Office. As they passed the next alleyway, Will caught movement out of the corner of his eye and spied Janie and McPhail astride their horses riding along the back street toward the bank with Finn and Will's horses in tow

Janie saw the cousins at the same time. "Will, Finn, over here."

At that moment, another voice from across the street called out too. "Hold it right there, Will Covington."

Will's heart sank. His eyes locked onto Janie's, and they mirrored his own fear.

Beyond Janie, McPhail's face wore only determination. "We're finishing the mission. Take care of business and keep them busy." He clucked his tongue and urged his horse off at a trot.

Janie looked helpless for a moment but followed their leader.

"You were right, Finn. I should have kissed her again." He watched Janie until she passed beyond the edge of the building. He hated that fear might be the last look she ever saw from him, but there was no helping that now.

Finn almost choked. "What do you mean again? I thought you never kissed her."

"Will Covington and Cousin Finn, I am talking to you. Turn around," the voice yelled.

Will laughed a little and shrugged. "Well, she kissed me actually. Back by the river. Sorry, I forgot to mention it." He looked at Finn. "This really happening?"

"Seems like it."

"Blaze of glory?"

"Blaze of glory."

The cousins turned to face the Agents. Agent Pryor had stepped off the porch in front of the office about twenty yards away. Agent Reynolds and the new Agent flanked out on his wings. Traffic on the street pulled to a halt except for one rider who got caught in the middle for a moment and spurred his horse into a gallop to escape the line of fire. Pedestrians scrambled back to clear a path, but while some ducked in the nearest building, many more merely pulled back and tried to find a good vantage point.

With Janie out of sight and after the laugh with Finn, the pit in Will's stomach seemed to fill and his vision cleared. "Something I can do for you, Agent Pryor?"

"Seems you two boys are up to causing trouble in my town. As known associates of Janie De Casas and David McPhail, I am placing you under arrest, Will Covington and Cousin Finn."

"Why is she getting top billing now? We rescued her," Finn muttered. Then he yelled back to the Agents. "By the way, it's Finn Hennessy, not Cousin Finn."

Will snorted. "Sorry Agent Pryor, but Finn and I have other plans for the day and won't be joining you."

Agent Pryor stalked a few paces closer, and Finn drifted off to Will's left. The Agent glared at them and smirked. "You should know, the poster says dead or alive, boy."

Will shrugged.

"Guess we're gonna see how good you are with those big guns of yours." Agent Pryor flexed his fingers by his side.

"Your funeral," Will replied.

Agent Pryor's right hand darted to his gun and drew.

Will's mind seemed to float out of his body to observe the proceedings with a kind of detachment. Agent Pryor must be what McPhail considered one of the real Agents, a direct member of Governor Hogg's famed posse. The man was fast and drew first, but it turned out Will was faster, and where the

Agent continued to raise his gun to shoulder height before firing, Will fired from the hip just like McPhail had drilled him. His shot took Agent Pryor on an upward trajectory in the left shoulder. The impact spun the Agent, and his shot missed Will wide to the right.

To his left, Finn and the new Agent exchanged shots, but Will's attention was drawn to Agent Reynolds on his right. The man had waited for his leader, expecting him to score the kill, but was now left scrambling for his gun. Will leveled his gun at the man and waited for a pair of heartbeats, but the Agent drew anyway, and Will fired once each into his belly and chest as the Agent's barrel cleared leather.

More shots came from the left, and Will's tunnel vision widened. Finn was swearing, and his opponent lay sprawled in the dirt, but then Will spied the source of Finn's agitation. Two new men with gold stars on their chests, indicating sheriff and deputy, were running out of a building two doors down, the sheriff armed with a rifle and the deputy with a pistol. Across the street, the door to the Agents' Office swung open and another man in black came out shooting.

"To me," Will yelled to Finn and began firing across the street. He flinched down and retreated toward the sidewalk.

Now the gawkers started to scream and run for cover themselves, which only added to the confusion of bodies flying amid the bullets.

Will dropped down behind a couple of barrels outside the general store and reloaded. Finn arrived just as he was finishing, closely followed by the crack of a rifle bullet biting into wood. Will snapped off two shots in the direction of the sheriff to hold him off.

"I think I winged the deputy," Finn panted. Another rifle crack. "But that sheriff's a tough buzzard. Too many people anyway. Can't get a clear shot."

"Well, they don't seem to care about that." Will leaned

around the street side of the barrel and fired toward the Agent who was trying to flank them on the opposite side of the street. The man went down yelling and clutching at his leg. Will pulled back just as another shot bit into the barrel. "Sheriff's got company or the deputy's back up again."

"What do we do?"

"Keep shooting."

"Thanks. Then what?"

Will looked down the street. "Keep backing up toward the bank. That's where McPhail and Janie are headed."

"Yeah, since we're doing so well here ourselves, I'm sure they'll be eager for our help."

"Hey, as long as we're still breathing, we're doing great. Loaded?"

"Yup."

"Let's go then."

They stood up from behind the barrels and started firing. Their opponents were multiplying with the addition of another Agent from across the street and two helpful townsfolk who did not like to see their town shot up by ruffians. In the end, that just made for more targets from which to choose.

The bank was situated at the end of Conviviality's main street. It faced another saloon across the way while a blacksmith occupied the space across the small side street before Conviviality gave way to the desert. The first shots rang out while Janie and McPhail hitched the horses at the side of the building.

McPhail tossed a saddlebag to Janie and threw another over his shoulder. "I give the orders and do crowd control. Back me up and get the money."

Janie hurried to follow him but avoided looking down the

street toward the showdown. As long as the firefight continued, one of the cousins must be alive, and Will had promised to look after her, and those two facts meant he must still be alive. Strange that only a few weeks ago, she had shot a man right over Will's shoulder and only vaguely hoped she had not killed Will in the process, and now what she wanted to do was run down the street to join him in victory or death because the thought of a world without Will Covington seemed too much for her to bear. Instead, she did her duty while Will did his and, guns drawn, followed McPhail into the bank.

Two men had come out the front doors to see what the commotion was about, and McPhail pushed past them with Janie on his heels. Inside, the bank was painted white with a worn, dusty red carpet on the floor. A teller sat behind the counter and was speaking with a customer. Two other employees were in the back of the room sorting stacks of paper and money on a table with an open safe behind them. Two other customers waited in the lobby area.

All but the teller and his customer were turned toward the front of the building listening to the shots from down the street, but then everyone looked at McPhail when he put a bullet in the ceiling. "Everyone on the floor. We're here to make a withdrawal on behalf of our esteemed governor."

A ruddy-faced man, one of the waiting customers, began to bluster at the intrusion. "What in the hell do you thin—"

With nary a glance in the man's direction, McPhail fired left-handed and sent the hat flying off the man's head.

The man screamed and put both hands to the thin red streak running through his hair above his left temple where the bullet had grazed his scalp while taking the hat.

"The next one goes between your eyes," McPhail said. "Everyone in front of the counter on the ground now. Everyone behind the counter get out here and then on the ground." This time, he received full compliance. "Janie, do the honors. I do believe that table back there is covered in our governor's ill-gotten proceeds."

She grabbed McPhail's saddle bag along with the one she had carried in and vaulted over the counter while the tellers and bank manager shuffled out the other way. Even inside the bank, she could still hear the sounds of the gunfight. Was it getting closer? With one set of saddle bags full, she began on the next set. "The safe too?"

"No, just Governor Hogg's account. Wouldn't want to inconvenience anyone else."

"Then we are done here."

So were the gunshots outside.

McPhail knelt beside the bank manager. "When Governor Hogg or his Agents come around asking what happened here today, you tell him that Territory Ranger David McPhail was here and sends his regards. You got that?"

"Y-y-yes." The man was trembling and staring at some point in space behind his interlocutor.

"What's my name again?"

"D-d-david McPh-ph-phail."

"Perfect. Don't you forget it." The lanky cowboy stood. "I'd suggest everyone just stay here on the floor for a little while longer. Wouldn't want anyone to accidentally catch any stray bullets now." He looked at Janie. "Let's go."

She hefted the two sets of saddlebags and headed out the door he held open for her. She wondered if he was guarding her back or waiting to see if someone outside would decide to start shooting again and would rather it be at her.

McPhail gave one last glaring sweep of the room. He tipped the brim of his hat to the ruddy man with the bleeding head and followed Janie outside.

Bodies lay scattered about in the middle of the street and a few people had begun to peer from buildings, but the only two active figures on the street were Will and Finn. Finn jogged ahead while Will ran a sideways gallop with one gun pointed behind him in case anyone else decided to be the hero of Conviviality.

"Let's move," McPhail ordered and headed around the corner.

Finn followed but stopped and turned to watch his cousin and Janie.

Janie just stood there until Will was on top of her. His hair hung down wet with sweat. He had a scrape across his chin and dirt smudges on his face. His breathing was heavy. His eyes glittered pale blue in the afternoon sun and oh so very alive.

"You cut your hair," she said.

He smiled into her dark brown eyes. "I may get in trouble for this, but I promised myself I would." He reached an arm around her waist to pull her close, but she beat him to it by grabbing each side of his face and pulling him into the kiss. His world dissolved into her lips on his.

Finn cleared his throat. "Sorry to interrupt, but I don't think we have much time."

Janie released Will. "He's right." She turned and ran around the corner to the horses.

Will managed to shake his head clear and follow her. As he went past, Finn gave him an ear-to-ear grin and pounded him on the back.

❦ *ABSOLUTION* ❧

Of their increasingly repetitive escapes from each town they visited, Chastity had likely been the worst with the gunfight just to get out of the town and then the chase through the night with what seemed like the entire population out searching for them, or so it had seemed to Will at the time. At least that escape had occurred under the cover of darkness, making concealment easier. They had fled Mercy in broad daylight which left them exposed, but fortunately the pursuit had been halfhearted.

The flight from Conviviality lay somewhere in between the two, but closer to the Chastity side of the scale. While they mounted, the ruddy man from the bank tried to take a potshot at McPhail, but the Ranger was already ahorse and watching for trouble. The pugnacious fellow did little more than step around the corner, bellowing and brandishing a gold-plated revolver, before McPhail brought him down.

After that, they had ridden a mile or more out of town before the real pursuit began. In killing or incapacitating the town's sheriff, deputy, and five Agents, Will and Finn had destroyed the town's leadership and eliminated the men most able to mount an effective pursuit. The two men at the head of the posse wore the Agents' black, but from the distance, the rest seemed to be composed of regular townsfolk volunteered or drafted into the role of avenging their fellows.

The sun pounded down on them from on high, and the band's horses huffed and sweated as they ran in the heat. "They're pushing their horses pretty hard. That'll burn 'em out sooner. We need to pace ourselves." McPhail reined in his horse to slow their flight a bit. "We keep making for the hills and hopefully lose them or wear them out. If not, we find high ground to make a stand."

What ensued was a slow but dogged chase across the desert plains. As predicted, the posse had to slow their pace or kill their horses, but they continued to harass the quartet throughout the afternoon. Although they had not supplied themselves for such a hasty exit, McPhail and his wards did have food and water for themselves which kept up their stamina, while the posse behind them seemed to have neither and flagged as the day drew on.

In midafternoon, they descended into a small arroyo with a tiny pool and creek at the bottom where they paused to water the horses. Realizing that their quarry had stopped, the posse spurred their horses into a gallop to try and close the distance. McPhail had them remount and head out again. The posse did get close enough to send off a few ineffective rounds that fell well short of their targets, but at least one man pushed his horse too far, and the animal collapsed just short of the arroyo. The posse was then forced to stop, and although not as well watered as McPhail would have liked, he was able to increase the distance from their pursuers and lose them from sight for an hour or so as they entered the low hills leading up to the Elephants.

The chase continued into the night of the new moon.

Having last seen the posse more than an hour before and plagued by darkness, brambles, and fatigue, McPhail called a halt in a tree-filled hollow between two hills. They picketed the horses for the night. Feeling the most rested of the group, Janie took first watch, and the other three bedded down for some sleep wrapped in saddle blankets they had appropriated as bedrolls against the chill of the night.

Despite the emotional low after the adrenaline high from the gunfight and the weariness from their flight, Will tossed and turned in his blankets for what felt like hours while Finn let out low snorts into the night.

When Janie woke him, Will was not even sure he had slept, but the shifting of the stars in the sky belied that. For a disorienting moment, he thought she was climbing under the blanket with him, but she was not coming to join him. "They're here," she whispered before moving on to Finn.

McPhail pantomimed to all three, and they started moving in the darkness.

Janie was right. Less than five minutes later, dark figures filtered down one of the hills and spread out in an arc around the hollow and their camp. The man in the center of the group raised his left hand above his head and brought it down in a chopping motion. At the signal, the eight men in the group opened fire into the bedrolls. The horses cried, bucked, and whinnied in fear at the roar of the guns and tugged at their tethers, but none of the bullets came their way. The pistol and shotgun blasts tapered off as each man finished emptying his weapon into the unsuspecting figures.

"Did we get 'em?" someone asked.

"Abe, go check 'em out," the leader ordered.

A single figure, presumably Abe, edged forward to the blankets closest to him and nudged it with his foot. The only resistance he found was cloth and pine needles. He looked up to his boss. "They ain't here."

From the trees above, McPhail's voice echoed in the night. "Rangers to arms!" With that, the cowboy dropped to the ground with both pistols drawn.

In response to the cry, Janie stood up from behind a boulder twenty yards up the little valley.

Finn came to his knees out of a clump of high grass about twenty-five yards in the opposite direction.

Will came up from behind a thorn bush behind and to Finn's right.

The fight, such as it was, ended in seconds. Having already exhausted their bullets into what they believed to be sleeping outlaws, even the two Agents in the group never returned a shot.

"Will, Finn," McPhail called to them and gestured up the hill in the direction their pursuers had come.

The original posse was ten strong. Even with the loss of one earlier in the day at the arroyo, that left at least one man, perhaps guarding the horses.

The two young men hurried up the hill, reloading their guns as they went. Away to the south, they found the posse's camp with a lone figure standing armed with a shotgun not far from the posse's tethered horses. While Finn approached from the front, Will circled around the far side to come at the guard from behind.

"Who's that there? Is that you, MacFarlin?" The guard raised the shotgun in Finn's general direction.

Finn waved a hand and kept coming.

"If that's you, Abe, you better speak up." The man's voice warbled now with raw nerves.

Will stepped up from behind and cocked his pistol at the base of the man's skull. "Why don't you lower that gun of yours nice and slow."

The man's Adam's apple bobbed in the dark, and he lowered the gun.

Keeping his gun hand steady, Will took the shotgun with his other hand and tossed it to the side in the grass. "Any other guns we need to worry about?"

The man shook his head. "Look, I don't have anything against you. I'm just a store clerk. It was the Agents White and Karstairs who grabbed us and told us we needed to come after you. I got a wife and three kids to support back home. Please let me go. I won't tell anyone what I seen." Sweat poured from his brow and tears pooled in the corners of his eyes.

By now Finn had arrived and stood eyeing the man. "Oh yes, you will tell people what you've seen here. You get on your horse and start riding back to Conviviality. You can bring back friends tomorrow for all the bodies, and you tell them it was the Hennessy Gang that did this. You warn 'em all to stay clear. Do you hear me?"

"Yes, sir. Yes, I do. Don't mess with the Hennessy Gang."

Finn smiled. "That's right, friend. Let's get you a horse and get you heading home. I don't ever want to lay eyes on you again. Do you understand?"

"Yes, sir, Mr. Hennessy. You won't never see me again."

Finn nodded at Will who removed his gun from the man's neck. "Go on now."

The clerk did not need another prompting. He ran over to the nearest horse, mounted, and rode off in the opposite direction.

Finn watched him go but turned when he felt Will's eyes on him. "What?"

"You think that was a good idea? The Hennessy Gang?"

"Hey, I'm tired of you and Janie and McPhail getting the top billing all the time. It's time the Hennessys got some credit around here."

"Ma and Pa would be so proud."

Finn laughed. "Yeah, I bet they would."

"I was being sarcastic."

"That's a low form of humor, you know."

"Let's leave the horses. Come on." Will trudged past Finn. By the time they got back to the camp, Janie and McPhail had salvaged what was left of their gear.

"You found them?" McPhail asked when they returned.

"Over the rise. Just one of them."

"I didn't hear a gunshot."

Will stared back expressionless. "No, you didn't." He brushed past McPhail toward his horse.

"It's not a good idea to leave an enemy at your back, Covington," McPhail said.

"We didn't leave an enemy at our back. We sent a scared clerk home to his family," Will answered.

The Ranger kept up his steely stare. "If you show kindness to the wrong person, it will come back to bite you."

Will threw the saddle blanket over his horse and went to heft his saddle up after it. "We didn't."

The remainder of the time, they broke camp in silence. McPhail mounted last and turned his horse north. Finn followed next and Will and Janie brought up the rear. No one had anything else to say until orange and red streaks gilded the eastern horizon.

They rode north all morning into the tablelands, the large mesas interspersed among desert plains and mixed grasslands. The mesas extended around the corner the Elephants made as they headed east, and McPhail and his band followed them in a slow, steady march. They dismounted and walked their horses in the heat of the late morning to give the animals a break until they found some sparse shade in the overhang of one of the mesas with a small watering hole for the horses.

For Janie, walking had been better for keeping awake after the sleepless night, but when they stopped, she collapsed on one of the bullet-ridden blankets and fell asleep. Will leaned back on a rock near her and pulled his hat down over his eyes but was only able to find a light doze, which was broken by Finn's periodic snores and the acrid smell of McPhail's hand-rolled cigarettes.

An hour later, McPhail roused them. "Time to move along. We still have a ways to go before nightfall."

"Where are we headed?" Finn cracked his neck when he stood up.

"There's a pueblo another three hours ride or so from here. I should be able to get us a place to shelter for a night or two while we plan our next move."

Janie stood up and stretched. "As long as they don't have wanted posters or Agents."

"Hogg doesn't care much for any of the tribes." McPhail spat to the side. "He's marginalized them, taken their lands, and isolated most of them. You won't find any friends of Hogg in the villages, and you won't have to worry about wanted posters."

About two and a half hours later, they spotted the first signs of smoke from cook fires emanating from one of the mesas in the distance. Green surrounded the base of the mesa and tapered off to the north along the course of a stream running off the Elephants to the south. As they got closer, they could make out the square and rectangular shapes of adobe buildings climbing up the steep side of the mesa and crowning its top. At the base of the mesa, crops grew in the tilled rich soil near the river with small irrigation channels running between the parcels of land.

A group of men met them well before they reached the village. They wore a mixture of what Will thought of as traditional tribal wear of rough woven cloth and buckskin breeches mixed with textiles that came from the anglicized towns of the area. Two men carried rifles and the rest pistols. They did not ride horses, but one man near the front held the leads of six large dogs that made the horses shy at their smell and low growls.

The leader of the group hailed them in English, but McPhail answered in the local language. As near as Will could tell, his accent caused a few snickers in the back of the group, but the leader seemed pleased with the response. The two went back and forth for a time before the leader turned and gestured for them to follow.

McPhail turned to his charges. "We walk from here, but we have a place to stay."

Will dismounted with the rest. "You know their language?"

"I can speak three of the local languages passable enough, and understand enough of two others to get by if need be."

"How do you know this tribe?"

The four walked on, leading their horses, with the tribesmen falling into flanking positions. The man with the dogs let them pull him back to the village faster than the rest, and they yapped all the way home.

"I told you, the Rangers were friends with most of the tribes. We needed their knowledge of the landscape, and being on friendly terms helped to broker peace between them and the settlers early on. I was good friends with the chief's second son once upon a time." McPhail pointed to the leader of their welcoming committee. "That man is his nephew. He remembers hearing about the Rangers, and his uncle has talked about me in the past. He's taking us to his uncle's house."

The villagers did not have many horses, but the ones they

did stayed in a corral at the bottom of the mesa, and that was where the band left their horses for the night. The village did have dogs in abundance. The frisky younger ones bounded about to greet the visitors only to go tearing off to chase one another up the narrow streets while the more mature ones lifted a head to sniff in the direction of the newcomers; but since they offered neither food nor resistance to their masters, the dogs let them pass unmolested.

Up close, the buildings were even more impressive than from a distance. Adobe square and rectangular buildings with flat roofs terraced up the steep slope of the mesa with narrow stairways forming serpentine roads that led to the top. Will could see how defensible the town was with the steep climb and the narrow streets. On the top of the mesa, several of the buildings stretched to four stories high, fighting with their fellows to reach closest to the stars, taller than any buildings Will had ever seen. All the buildings had a look of age and permanence. They had been standing perhaps for centuries and planned to go on doing so for centuries more.

McPhail's friend, Atsa, lived in a three-story structure on the top of the mesa with his extended family of daughters and sons and grandchildren. The home itself belonged to his wife, Doli, she having inherited it from her mother, and who would in turn pass it down to her oldest daughter in the future.

The two men greeted each other as old friends, and Will, Finn, and Janie were ushered in and treated as the offspring of the honored friend and guest. Atsa's family threw extra meat and vegetables into the cooking pots and began baking more cornmeal dough for dinner. The unfamiliar aromas were enticing to Will and intoxicating. "We've been eating like kings the last couple of days."

When the meal was ready, they gathered to eat on one of the broad terraced roofs of the home while the stars came out and the Milky Way danced across the sky.

Most of the villagers spoke some English and certainly spoke it better than any of the three Rangers-in-training could speak the native language, but the majority of the conversation took place in the villagers' tongue and bypassed the three. In his exhaustion, that did not concern Will. His belly was filling with nourishment, and he felt at home, as if with family and friends. Finn sat on his left, wolfing down food, while Janie sat close on his right with their knees touching as they sat cross-legged on the floor.

Doli, being the matriarch and final arbiter in the family, rearranged the living quarters to give the younger three a small room on the second floor while McPhail received a room of honor to himself on the third story. If anyone in the family resented the displacement the guests caused, Will could not sense it.

As dinner wound down, Janie stood up and excused herself to go lie down. Will gave her a wistful smile and watched her disappear into their room after sending him a demure backward glance. He was tired himself, and thought about following her, but decided it would be best to wait. Finn seemed to have gotten a second wind with the food in his belly and was regaling the young man next to them with a hunting story from a few years ago. He kept turning to Will and elbowing him to ask for corroboration.

A few minutes passed, and Janie came back out. She walked over to Will and held out her hand to him with an impatient expression. Will gave her a quizzical look but took her hand and let her draw him to his feet. Exasperation turned to a smile, and she began pulling him after her with deliberate backward steps.

Will heard Finn snort and knew his cousin was laughing with his new friend. There might have been a hoot or two from the dinner party, but Will hoped that was about something else. He felt his blush, but he only had eyes for Janie.

Now that she knew she had his attention, Janie turned to lead him to their room. She held aside the curtain hanging over the doorway and ushered him inside before slipping in behind him. They both had to duck slightly as they passed through the doorway. The curtain fell across the opening, blotting out the light of the fires.

Inside, the space was partitioned in two by a beaded hanging rug. The room must belong to a small family with one large pallet on the left side of the room and two smaller ones on the right. An oil lamp near the large pallet illuminated the room in an orange glow.

Will found he and Janie were standing close to each other. She had taken both of his hands in hers. Under the surface of those dark brown eyes, he could still sense the battle churning within her, but he could also see her determination to carry through with her decision.

Neither spoke. She leaned toward him, and he met her halfway for the kiss. Her mouth was warm and moist against his. He could still taste the hints of the sweet masa from dinner on her lips. Underneath the smell of sweat and horse they both shared, he could smell the sweet aroma of her breath and body. Above, there was the soft compliance of her lips on his, her passion for him radiating out, equal to his own for her, but when he stepped close to her body, below, he could feel the tension and rigidity of the conflicts within her. After what may have been an eternity or an instant, she broke the kiss and shifted back so she could focus on his eyes.

"I can't do everything you want me to do." Her voice sounded timid at first, an odd tone coming from Janie, but gained strength as she spoke. "But yesterday, I thought you might die, and I realized I don't want to be without you. It's been building for a while and's only gotten worse since the river. I'd like it if I could just hold you tonight and have you hold me. You make me feel safe."

At that moment, her face was so beautiful, flickering under the lamp light, a mixture of pride and sorrow and worry and hope all mixed up as one. "Anything you want. Anything you need. I love you, Janie."

"I know," she said, and led him over to the bed.

They took off jackets and boots and dusty outer layers. He extinguished the lamp, and they curled up together under the blankets, lost in each other's arms and gentle kisses and nuzzles until Janie nestled into his shoulder, and they fell asleep in an embrace.

Will woke multiple times that night, each time convinced that his last waking had been a dream, but each time, he found himself lying next to Janie, the warmth of her body pressing against him. Over the previous months, he never would have described Janie as cuddly, but that night she snuggled up against him and clung to him. Her demons slept in peace, and so did she.

Once the sun peeked above the horizon, the village began to stir with the barking of dogs, the crow of the roosters, and the sounds of people beginning to cook breakfast. Since no snores had interrupted his sleep, Will already knew the answer, but he still lifted the curtain to confirm that Finn had not joined them last night.

"He grabbed a blanket in the middle of the night and left." Janie's eyes were open and looking at him with tenderness. "Thank you. I haven't slept so well in a long time." She kissed him.

"Me neither." That was a white lie, but it was true that he had never been so happy to climb into bed in a long time.

"We should probably go find him and McPhail."

Finn had camped out with Bidziil, the young man he had been talking with when Janie absconded with Will. After the pair slipped away, Finn and his newfound friend imbibed a bit too much of the local brew. That helped to put Finn in a bit of a frisky mood, and he made a pass at Bidziil's sister, Nascha, which came across more comical than offensive. Still, Finn and Bidziil had to camp out on the roof by themselves, Finn to cool down, and his friend to keep an eye on the honored guest.

As usual, McPhail had fared better with a comfortable room to himself and was well rested. They found him on the next terrace up, enjoying breakfast with Atsa and Doli. "Glad you three finally made it up," he said in greeting.

Even though Finn was the one to have caused the scene last night, Will still felt McPhail gave all of them a look of reproach. Janie squeezed Will's hand and gave him an eye roll when he looked in her direction.

As the breakfast wore on, Will soon felt he had nowhere to look but his plate. McPhail kept up a low-grade glower whenever Will looked his way, as if Will had disappointed the Ranger in some deep manner. When Will looked toward Finn, all he got was a wide grin and elbows in the ribs. Atsa and Doli would smile and nod in Will's direction, and if his plate looked partway empty, Doli would wave over one of her granddaughters to ladle out more, but Will's lack of language skills left conversation with them out of the question. That only left looking toward Janie, and although Will would have been happy to stare giddily in her direction all day, that only seemed to make matters worse with his companions. In any case, the reserved Janie had reared her head. He could still see the warmth behind those eyes, but she kept a few handbreadths between them, and her body language was stiff. As the breakfast wore on, Will began to feel the body language was more for show than to keep him away.

After breakfast, McPhail called a conference in his room.

The money from their bank robbery filled a saddle bag in the corner, but across the floor, he had strewn stacks of other papers, letters, and dispatches that ought to have been on their way to San Alonso with the money for Governor Hogg.

"Our next stop is Absolution. It's the end of the line for the railroad over the Mescalas and the closest stop to San Alonso that the railroad gets. A shipment of ammunition and arms from the Federation is arriving in less than a week. From there, a wagon train will take it to San Alonso." McPhail looked at his Rangers. "We're taking out the warehouse in Absolution."

Will raised his eyebrows. "Like blow it up?"

McPhail nodded. "With all the gunpowder, shouldn't take more'n a stick of dynamite well placed for the whole place to go up."

Finn whistled. "That'll be some fireworks. They may see them all the way down in San Alonso."

"That they may." McPhail's lip curled in a tight smile. "About a week later, it'll be Revenue Day again. The eastern Revenue Office is in Triumph, and that'll be our next target."

"They'll be expecting trouble, you know." Janie drew her knees up. "Wurst realized something was up and laid a trap last time. Hogg won't be stupid enough to let it happen again."

"It didn't make any difference last time. It won't make a difference this time. You're all Rangers now, well trained and tested by battle." Pride shone from McPhail's eyes but with a crazed note to it. Janie did not think he truly saw what was before him. "In the old days, you all would have been inducted already. I've never been one to stand on long ceremonies. I've been all that's left of the Rangers for years and we always chose our own in the past. Well, now I've got three new Rangers to join me."

He stood up. "You get one more day of rest here. Tomorrow morning we head out for Absolution."

The three newly blessed Rangers spent the remainder of the day helping around the household and village, farming in the fields down below, molding new adobe bricks, and carrying the dried ones up the mesa.

When they saw him trudging past dragging a load of bricks, Nascha and her friends giggled at Finn, but one of them, the tallest and darkest, blew him a kiss and a wink. Finn smiled and winked back, but when he came back around after dropping off his load, the young ladies had disappeared. At the dinner that night, the tall dark girl joined them. Her name was Sahkyo, and she gave Finn lingering looks all night, much to Nascha's delight.

After dinner, Sahkyo and Finn sat together on the edge of the roof. Her English was excellent, and she tried to teach him the names of the stars in her language and told him the tribal stories of the constellations. Janie and Will joined them for a while before retiring to their room. An hour or so later, Will heard Finn come stumbling into his pallet. Even in the dark, Will recognized the dreamy look in his cousin's eyes. Finn was smitten.

The next morning, the quartet set out after breakfast. Their hosts had refilled their saddlebags with vegetables and fruits and dried meats and new blankets. Finn kept turning around to look back until the tall figure of Sahkyo disappeared into the shadows of the mesa.

"When we're all done with this, I'm going back for her, Will," Finn said when there was no one left to see behind them. "Don't let me forget."

Will laughed. He found it hard to imagine asking Finn to remind him to go back for Janie if their positions were reversed, but he kept that thought to himself.

At camp that night, they reverted to the equilateral triangle of old, but now Janie and Will formed one of the legs together under the same blankets.

"He doesn't approve," Janie whispered into Will's ear.

"I never asked for it," Will whispered back before kissing her.

For the end of the rail line, Absolution was a small town nestled at the base of the Mescala Mountain range on the shore of a muddy lake. The railway over the Mescalas was small and not designed to carry heavy freight or many cars up the steep grade, but it could serve to transport small loads of people and cargo. The rail yard had enough room to shunt cars onto two different side tracks and a loop turnaround back to the main line. The rail station abutted a small warehouse. The rest of the town consisted of multiple homes, a general store, a saloon, a church, and a telegraph office with one line heading west toward San Alonso and another running parallel to the railroad tracks.

This time, the quartet did not enter the town. They approached Absolution along the mountains from the north a day before the train's scheduled arrival and pitched camp in the pine trees above the town, where they could watch the comings and goings and monitor the tracks.

By the next morning, wagons and coaches began arriving with families and workmen. Most came with empty wagons ready to pick up passengers from the inbound train, but a few came with luggage and trunks for their outbound journey. Within a short space of time, the small quiet town became a bustling hive of activity.

Three hours after dawn, a train whistle echoed down the

hills and puffs of steam began to sprout above the trees, accompanied by little chuffs of sound. Down in the town, the crowds coalesced on the station as the train came around the final bend and descended the last slope into Absolution. It was a small train consisting of an engine, tender, two passenger cars, a baggage car, two box cars, and a caboose. The engine pulled to a stop at the station with a monstrous roar and billows of steam that turned the entire scene to mist from Will and Janie's vantage point.

They sat together in the spiked shadows of a pine tree atop a rocky ledge that overlooked the town. They watched the passengers disembark into the arms of family and loved ones and porters unload the luggage cars. Once the majority of the civilians cleared away and the engineers and coal men headed off to lunch, a second group of men descended on the two box cars and began the heavy but delicate work of unloading the gunpowder and munitions from the last car. These they moved into the warehouse next to the station. That process took almost two hours. After that, they loaded a few other parcels and crates into the lead boxcar. By midafternoon, they had completed the process.

During that hour or two, the new arrivals scattered to the winds, and the town settled back into relative sedateness before a new procession of coaches and wagons appeared. The passengers loaded onto the train. The railmen refilled the train's tender with water and coal. With a shrill blast of its whistle and puffs of steam, the engine began its slow roll around the loop of track and headed back up the mountains and out of sight as the sun began its descent into the distant horizon.

On that horizon, Will spotted the dust plumes off the incoming wagon train. Hogg's wagons were arriving to move the munitions to San Alonso in the morning. "Looks like we move tonight."

In the dead of the night, the half moon shone down on the little town of Absolution as McPhail, Will, Janie, and Finn entered the rail yard.

The wagon train had pulled into town in time for a rousing party in the saloon. This was not Temperance or Chastity, though, and so the extracurricular activities were limited to drink and some gambling, which the men managed to exhaust in good order. With no other entertainment on hand and the looming job of moving combustible materials in the morning, the men retired at a reasonable hour to their wagons for the night.

The wagons stood near the rail station on the town side. McPhail approached from the rail side where a coal car in need of repair sat on a side track. They secured their horses in its lee. Janie drew the job of lookout, and the three men stole across the yard to the warehouse. Although earlier in the evening two men had been standing watch in the rail yard, the pair seemed to have turned in for the night themselves.

The door stood unbarred. McPhail looked to see that Will and Finn both had guns drawn, and Finn still carried their shuttered lantern. He nodded to the boys, eased the door open, and slipped inside. Will and Finn waited on either side of the door for McPhail's low all-clear whistle before following him and pulling the door shut tight behind them.

The warehouse had no windows, and the three stood in darkness for a moment before Finn lifted the shutter on the lantern a finger breadth. A ray of yellow light stabbed out into the room and tracked side to side with Finn's arm. "They came prepared," he whispered.

On one side stood twenty large barrels of gunpowder. Next to them were crates of bullets and cannon shells. Along the opposite wall sat twelve crates of dynamite and blasting equipment.

McPhail tossed an empty saddle bag to Will. "Load up on

bullets." He pointed to Finn. "Take the tops off the barrels and move three of them to the center. I'll check out the dynamite."

Finn set the lantern on a low shelf away from the gunpowder and dynamite. Will had already levered the cover off one of the crates of bullets. He handed the crowbar to Finn and began to load bandoliers of bullets into the saddle bags until they weighed him down.

By the time Will finished, Finn had lugged two barrels to the center of the room and was glad of Will's assistance with the third. They were working on prying lids from the remaining barrels when a series of accelerating hoots cut through the night. Janie was signaling trouble.

Finn almost tripped in his haste to douse the lantern.

All three men crouched in the dark with guns drawn.

Outside the door, boot falls clunked on the wood. Two voices murmured to each other in the night. A match struck against the doorframe, and soon the acrid smell of smoke drifted through the cracks in the sides of the door. The truant guards had returned and seemed ready to camp out for the night.

Minutes ticked by and still, the conversation continued.

If their preparations had been complete, they might have been able to surprise the guards and set off the munitions, but they were not ready and a gunshot or ill-timed shout would wake the men in the wagons. Will did not relish the idea of another shoot-out if they could avoid it.

Fifteen minutes later, a new set of boot falls echoed on the decking. The voices outside changed, sounding challenging at first, but then one let out a chuckle. "Well, well, young lady, are you lost?"

"Just out for a walk. No harm in that, is there?" Janie's voice had a lilt Will had not heard before. Her footsteps stopped with the guards just outside the door.

"Awful late for a young lady to be out all by herself."

Will edged closer to the door trying to keep his tread light, but the guards' attentions seemed too distracted to notice any sounds from inside the warehouse.

"I guess maybe I got lonely and thought I'd go looking for some company."

Will bristled. Had she ever used that coquettish tone with him?

"Would y'all have another of those cigarettes for a lonely young lady?"

Another deep chortle reverberated through the wood. "Yeah, right here. Damien, you got a light for the lady?"

Another match struck against the wood of the door, but a wet thump and a gurgle drowned out the pop of the igniting flame.

"Huh?" the second voice said, but then died into a wheeze with more wet thuds and the louder sound of a body hitting the door outside.

Will put a shoulder to the door, which resisted him for a second before the weight fell away and the door swung open.

Outside, one man lay on the walkway, twitching and clutching at his neck while it oozed a thick dark liquid into the planks. The other man lay facedown at the base of the doorway halfway off the wooden platform in the dirt and his own darkening pool. Janie leapt back. In her hand, she gripped a bloody hunting knife. "You better hurry," she rasped. "I don't know if anyone will come looking for these two or not."

She wiped off the knife blade on the back of the second guard's coat. While Finn and McPhail finished their tasks, she and Will dragged the two bodies inside the warehouse. At least someone else strolling past would not see the two lying in the dirt, and the blood would not be obvious in the dark unless they got close.

It took another fifteen or twenty minutes to arrange everything to McPhail's specifications. In the end, he measured out lengths of fuse, paused to look at the ceiling in thought, and then measured out a few more lengths. With a few quick twists, those deft fingers attached the fuse to a blasting cap on a stick of dynamite at the base of the tower of explosives.

McPhail began playing it out behind them as they backed out of the warehouse. "Once I light this, we need to get on the horses and head straight out into the plains. Best to keep the coal car between us as much as possible when it blows." All three stared back wide-eyed but nodded. "Go untie the horses and mount up. Signal me when you're ready."

They turned and ran to the coal car and their horses. No one stirred in all of Absolution save the Ranger and his apprentices. Astride his own horse, Will led McPhail's to the edge of the coal car and waved. He could feel Janie and Finn's presence behind him watching too. He saw the flare of the matchstick in McPhail's hand and a second spit when the matchstick touched the fuse. A sizzling pop sounded across the open space and the flame began dancing up the long black string in the dark. McPhail was already running full tilt toward them. "Ride, you fools!" he bellowed at them.

Will heard Janie and Finn turn their horses and gallop away, and he turned his own horse but held his ground and the lead to McPhail's mount until the Ranger reached him.

"Go," McPhail ordered again.

Will dug in his heels, and his horse raced off after Finn and Janie.

He tried to count the seconds in his head but was past eighty and counting too fast if McPhail's math was correct. He risked a glance back and saw nothing but the building silhouetted in the light of the moon. He looked forward to see where he was going and saw Janie looking back toward him. Red flashed in her dark eyes followed by a brighter flash that lit up Janie, Finn, and the countryside around them and cast Will's shadow like a tall dark ghost far out ahead of them. Then the sound arrived and hit them with such a force that for a moment Will felt as though the hand of God had reached down to scoop him from the earth. His horse cried and stumbled but kept its feet and tried to run even faster. The heat hit them next like lying too close to the fire for a brief instant, and then it followed them like a warm summer breeze wafting past.

When he steadied himself enough to look back, a tower of flame and black smoke reached up to the sky and blotted out the stars. Embers rained down all around the rail station and even a few out where they rode.

"Head east into the mountains." McPhail angled his horse, still heading away from Absolution, but now directed into the Mescalas.

The morning light found Will, Janie, and Finn up in the pine forests gazing back at their night's work. McPhail had taken a brief look, grunted, and went back to camp. The other three could not tear themselves away.

The warehouse and station had disintegrated, that much they had known last night. The distance made it hard to be sure, but it appeared that the crater left in their wake had consumed large sections of the track. The coal car had rolled over on its side and now lay far from the torn side track. The wagon train lay decimated: smashed, burned, and scattered; but again, they had expected that much given how close they had lain to the station. What they had not expected was that all of Absolution was gone. Every last building and home had either been flattened by the blast, burned to the ground, or both. No matter how long they watched, nothing stirred in Absolution, nothing made a sound save the crows and the vultures.

"We destroyed a whole town." Finn's voice was husky with

emotion.

Janie squeezed Will tight and buried her face in his chest. She did not sob, but Will could feel the damp of her tears through his shirt. He hugged her back. A shiver ran up and down his spine. "Those weren't Agents or Revenue Men there. Those were families."

"I think we killed them all, Will. We killed them all. There's no going back after this. We're damned." Finn crouched down with his face in his hands.

The three stayed that way for a long time.

Once he was able to rouse them, McPhail led the somber procession south along game trails for the rest of the day.

At camp that night, Will and Janie excused themselves and wandered farther up the mountain. Thirty minutes later they sat on a log together watching the sunset when the crack of pine needles and the crunch of rocks and dirt under boots announced Finn's bull-like plod to find them.

"At least we know when he's coming," Janie said.

Will laughed a little. "I think he does it on purpose in case we're indisposed in some way."

Janie gave him a look.

"I've tried to tell him, but he doesn't listen." Will tried pleading first, but her challenging look did not waver. Will cocked his head to the side and switched to accusatory. "You're the one who dragged me into your bed, and we sleep under the same covers every night now."

Janie blew a lock of hair out of her face. "I didn't have to do much dragging."

As Finn scrambled up the last slope, he waved to them. "There you are." When he got closer, he dropped his voice so that it would not carry back down to camp. "We need to talk."

Will and Janie nodded and scooted down to make room for Finn on the log. He shook his head though, and began pacing back and forth while running his hands through his hair. "We need to stop this. We have to get out. It just keeps getting worse. Taking on the Agents and the Revenue Men was one thing. Stealing Hogg's money was fine, but now we're killing people who aren't even involved."

He looked up at the couple and could see their slight nods. "You didn't see at the coach, and maybe they weren't going to surrender anyway and maybe they drew first, but I swear *he* started shooting first." Finn continued pacing. "Then in Conviviality, Agent Pryor started it, so fine, but then we ended up shooting up the sheriff and his deputy and a bunch of innocent townsfolk."

Will interrupted. "But they were shooting at us, Finn. We didn't have a choice."

"If we hadn't been trying to rob the bank, nobody would have come after us." Finn stopped pacing and stood facing them with his arms crossed.

"Actually, they're after us for the whole Benevolence thing."

Finn threw up his hands. "Fine. What about all those people in that town back there? What did any of them do to us? I didn't see anyone trying to chase us down there."

Will and Janie exchanged an uncomfortable look. Will sighed. He was talking to Finn but looking at Janie. "It was an accident. We didn't know how big the explosion would be." His voice was plaintive and unsure.

Janie ran a hand across his cheek.

Finn knelt in front of them. "What's the next mistake going to be?" He and Will stared at each other. "Look, we can still go. We can get on our horses and ride north and just keep going. We can go all the way to Montana or farther if we want, or head out to San Francisco and see the ocean."

At the suggestion of fleeing, the flint-eyed Will flared up. "What about Ma and Pa? What about Kali? If we leave now, Hogg gets away with it."

Finn shook his head in frustration and looked at the ground for several seconds to collect his thoughts. "We've hurt Hogg already, and we've hurt a lot of other people along the way." He sighed and looked back up. "What about you and Janie, Will? You two deserve a life together." Finn looked to Janie, pleading with his eyes. "You've been good for Will. You've helped him come back from where he was after... everything. When he's with you, he's like the old Will I grew up with. He's been good for you too, I think."

Janie and Will turned to look at each other, to search each other's eyes for an answer. Janie gave a slow blink and shrugged her shoulders a fraction. "Your choice," she whispered.

Will looked from Janie to Finn and then back again. Whatever he said, they would follow him no matter how they felt. Somehow, despite being the youngest of the three, he was their leader. He thought about his adopted ma and pa. He thought about Kali. He thought about all the Kalis of the world out there hurt by Hogg and men like him. He thought about Janie and how much he loved her and how good it felt to hold her in his arms. He thought about the damage done to her by one of Hogg's trusted men. The words tumbled over each other in his brain and caught in his throat, but when he looked into Janie's eyes, he found the strength to speak. "We'll go with him to Triumph. We promised. We owe it to Ma and Pa and Kali and all the families like ours. One last blow to Hogg, and then we'll head north. We'll start a new life together then, all three of us."

Janie was thinking about Sister Maria and what her own soul wanted her to do. She smiled at Will. She would follow him anywhere.

Finn sighed. "Okay. One more job, and then we're done. I'll hold you to it." He stood up and walked back to camp.

Behind a tree ten yards away, McPhail nodded in satisfaction and slipped away like a cat on silent paws.

∽ *TRIUMPH* ∾

Governor Hogg sat at the head of a slim table in the conference room off his main office in the capitol building in the center of San Alonso. He peered over his steepled fingers while his lieutenants argued amongst themselves and made up excuse after excuse for their failures. Although he had long ago stopped listening to their blather, his eyes still darted back and forth from one speaker to the next. While his eyes played their game, his mind focused on the map of the Jefferson State hanging on the wall at the far end of the table and all the reports that had come across his desk in the last several months.

"This is Murdock's fault." Governor Hogg's flat voice cut across the current argument. All the other voices fell silent and turned to look at their leader. "Murdock or DuBois, the Revenue Man from Tranquility, did this. Yes, more likely DuBois stirred up the trouble, but Murdock was always ham-handed."

Governor Hogg stood and strode across the room to the map. "Thanks to Agent Garland and Mrs. Weatherwax, we know David McPhail is leading this merry little band. McPhail was a Ranger, it's why he holds such a grudge against me and why no one here has been able to kill him." He stared at his lieutenants, lingering on Agent Garland, daring them to say otherwise. When no one spoke up, he turned back to the map. "Nine or ten months ago, DuBois put a squeeze on the Hennessys in Tranquility for back taxes. George Hennessy was also a former Ranger but sensibly and quietly in retirement. DuBois called in Agent Murdock as muscle, and that idiot was not one for subtlety. He burned down the Hennessy farm and in the process got himself and three of his posse killed. Hennessy had two boys, now young men, and the posse claimed they died in the fire, which was a lie to save their sorry skins."

Hogg tapped the map over the Tranquility Valley. "Now no one hears hide nor hair of either boy until almost two months later when a neighbor looking for a reward claims to have seen them in the company of an older gentleman. So, the boys did not die in the fire, but they disappear, maybe into the mountains, but more likely working somewhere, a cattle drive or railroad work, maybe. During that time, they manage to hook up with McPhail. Maybe their old man told them to track down his old friend with his dying words, who knows. In any case, they come back home not looking for their parents, because they know they're dead, but looking for their sister, who is also missing."

Now Hogg tapped over the mountains on the black dot representing Chastity. "A few days later, there is a shoot-out in one of my establishments in Chastity, the Broken Mare. Two dozen men are killed, including the manager of the establishment and one prostitute." Hogg looked back at his lieutenants. "Can anyone guess the name of the prostitute?" He raised his eyebrows and held out his hands, but no answer came. "No one?"

Hogg shook his head. "Hennessy. She was one Kalirose Hennessy, arrived just over a month before, delivered up by whatever moron took over for Murdock after he got himself killed." He stared at the map again. "Three men, well, one man and two boys really, kill more than a score of armed men and escape with a large amount of my money. In the process, they believe that I, Alistair Hogg, turned their sister into a whore. Do you think that endeared me to the boys? I sincerely doubt it."

Back to the map, he pointed to a much smaller dot at the edge of the plains. "A few days later, in the company of two unidentified young men, McPhail appears and rescues one Janie De Casas from the noose despite Agent Garland's valiant efforts." Governor Hogg rolled his eyes to the ceiling on the last words of that sentence. He shook his head at Seward. "Arthur De Casas was a right bastard, which is why he was no longer a member of my posse if you remember. Rumor has it he had been banging his daughter six ways to Sunday for years. Stringing up the poor thing for relieving him of his manhood was about as stupid as DuBois and Murdock leaning hard on George Hennessy. You would have been better off giving her a pat on the back and her own Agent's black and a badge."

Hogg threw out his hands to the table. "And there we have it. David McPhail now has a band of like-minded and very deadly disciples: Finn and Will Hennessy and Janie De Casas." Now he began jabbing points on the map in rapid succession. "Humility: my summer home burns to the ground, and Mrs. Weatherwax is menaced by the gang to give over my papers left there by loyal Horace. Benevolence: our southern Revenue Office is robbed and our representatives killed. Gorseman's Pass: a significant gold shipment is waylaid and lost. Conviviality: a bank robbery where only the money destined for San Alonso disappears, carried out, we're told, by the Hennessy Gang. And finally, a train load of munitions from the Federation explodes and levels the town of Absolution. I do not believe that is a coincidence. McPhail must have been there."

Governor Hogg leaned on the end of the table. "David McPhail and his wild boys are laughing at us, at *me*, and my trusted advisors have done nothing."

The four men around the table swallowed hard and avoided their leader's eyes.

Hogg straightened back up. "Fortunately, you have me." He pointed back to the map. "They are circling us, getting closer to San Alonso. It's a death spiral they intend to end here on my doorstep." He surveyed his lieutenants. Weatherwax had gone pale. Horace was not a fighter and never would be. Garland looked grim.

One final time, Hogg turned to stare at the map. "I have some lucrative establishments in Justice, there is an important silver mine just outside of Faith, and the eastern Revenue Office is in Triumph." He stabbed at the map. "Their next target will be Triumph." Hogg saw Garland's face wrinkle up in confusion. "Oh, the other targets are tempting, but it's the closest likely target to their last known location," Hogg shrugged. "Agent Garland, assemble a welcoming committee. Take as many men as you see fit. Cover all three if you need to, but I tell you their target is Triumph. When they get there, put them in the ground or don't come back."

Triumph was more organized than Benevolence with straight, rectangular streets branching off the central hub of the city, its tall church and steeple. From the top of that steeple, Foster Callaghan on midday watch duty spotted the quartet of horse riders as they crossed the plain. Foster placed the spyglass to his eye, brought them into focus, and swore. He hurried down the stairs and across the street to the telegraph office and his boss, Agent Seward Garland. "Four riders, coming from the east, sir, about two miles out."

Agent Garland regarded the man. "And?"

The watchman paused to catch his breath. "Three men, one woman, sir. The older one looks like McPhail."

"Well, I'll be damned," Garland muttered. "The governor was right." He swatted the man next to him. "Send a wire to Justice and Faith. I want the rest of the posse on the way here, pronto. Then send a wire to San Alonso and let the governor know we've spotted McPhail and his gang." Garland stood up from his chair and adjusted his gun belt. "Callaghan, tell the rest of the boys to get in position, but nobody better fire until I give the word."

"Yes, sir." Foster threw a salute and ran across the street to the saloon where the rest of Agent Garland's posse had elected to spend their day.

The hairs on the back of Will's neck prickled the closer they rode to Triumph. The feeling only worsened when they started down the center street toward the church. For the size of the town and the time of the day, it seemed asleep. No, not asleep, more like watchful or poised, like a rattler preparing to strike but without the warning sound. A man in a straw hat rocked in a chair outside the general store and made a point of not looking at them as they passed. On the opposite side of the street, another denizen walked in shuffling steps in the same direction they traveled, but paused to stare at the windows.

From McPhail's posture, Will could tell he felt the same tension. When he looked in Janie's direction, her face was taut and her eyes darted from side to side and up to the rooftops. She gave Will a tight smile and continued scanning the area. Even jolly Finn seemed to be catching the mood by the time they stopped their horses at the saloon.

McPhail looked at Will and Janie, and with a jerk of his head directed them across the street toward the post office.

To Will's knowledge, they had no business there, but he understood the message that they needed to spread out. Coming to Triumph was a mistake, a trap. Janie had been right. He could feel it down to the heels of his boots. He wanted to squeeze Janie's hand or give her a quick hug to buoy her spirits and his, but instead, they drifted apart to make less of a target and kept their hands near their guns.

They had crossed halfway when the batwing doors to the saloon behind them swung open, and a man in black stepped out. "Welcome to Triumph, McPhail, Ms. De Casas, and the Hennessy boys. Your little run of troublemaking is at an end."

Will turned to look at the man who spoke. He seemed familiar, but Will could not place him, but the paling of Janie's face clued him in. It was Agent Seward Garland, last seen in Mercy those many months ago. At the sound of the Agent's voice, more figures stepped from doorways up and down the street, including two on the rooftops. All wore black.

The men on the roofs had rifles in their arms, but otherwise, no one had drawn a gun. That could not last long.

McPhail stood relaxed at the bottom of the steps leading up to the saloon. He puffed the cigarette in his mouth a few times. "So we meet again, Seward. Been a long time coming to this."

"You'll lay down your weapons now, David, and we'll take you and your gang into custody. Governor Hogg promises a fair trial before a jury of your peers, just like the law states." Agent Garland rested his right hand on the gun in his belt. "If not, things will go poorly for you."

McPhail chuckled. He took a long pull on his cigarette. "That would be a trial to see. As far as I know, all my peers died at Fort Vigilant." He plucked the cigarette from his mouth with his left hand and flicked it aside. Garland's eyes darted to follow the movement, and in that instant, McPhail drew and fired from the hip.

Garland was crafty too. Even though his eyes could not resist the ruse, his brain recognized it for what it was, and he threw himself to the right. McPhail's bullet clipped him in the left side of his abdomen, but the pain was a distant yelp. He drew his own gun while falling and fired toward McPhail, but missed.

Foster Callaghan stood on the roof of the post office across from the saloon and saw it all happen in a flash. McPhail drew and Garland went down and chaos erupted. Everyone drew and started firing. Callaghan raised his rifle, but a bullet from the woman drove him back from the edge, and he ducked down.

In the street below, Will whirled when Garland went down. The Agent at the post office already had his gun halfway out of its holster. Will dove quicker than Garland, and the man's shot missed him. He turned the dive into a roll back to his feet while drawing his own guns and caught the Agent before he could track to Will's new position.

A few yards away, Janie had both guns drawn. One of her shots drove back the man on the roof, and another one hit an Agent stationed near the post office. Looking for cover, she ran to a stack of barrels on the near side of the street. Will followed suit and took cover beside a wagon.

Back across the street, Finn ducked underneath the hitching rail to come up on the walkway firing to his left at the Agents there. To his right, Garland had scrambled into the saloon, leaving a trail of blood, while McPhail exchanged gunfire with the Agents to his right.

Bullets coming from the post office bit into the wood of the wagon above Will's head. He leaned around the edge to fire at his assailant, and the wood exploded next to his shoulder where his head had just been followed by the echo of a rifle crack. He had forgotten about the Agent on the roof across the street. He swung back to the rifleman in time to hear to quick pair of pistol shots. The rifleman grabbed his stomach and toppled off the roof to the street near the horses. Down the block, Janie gave him a nod and a smile and returned to firing at the men coming out of the buildings.

Will snapped off a pair of shots into the post office, but the third hammer fall landed on an empty chamber. He ducked back to reload. Two doors down toward the church, another pair of Agents came out firing and drove Will back for a moment. Staying by the wagon was no longer an option as more men emerged on Finn and McPhail's side of the street. Sooner or later, the crossfire would get him.

He poked one gun hand around the edge of the wagon and fired to make the Agents think twice, and then he charged around the wagon, firing both guns. The man in the post office tried to track him, but Will's shot got there first. The two Agents down the way fired wildly, but they only hit the wagon behind him. Will's aim was truer, and he gained the raised walkway. Now he could shelter from shots from the other side of the street among some crates.

On the opposite side of the street, Finn punctuated his gunshots with wild shouting and swearing. In contrast, McPhail remained quiet save for the rhythmic tempo of his shots and the methodical tramp of his boots as he moved through the melee oblivious to the bullets whizzing his way. Between a space in the crates, Will saw him stride through the batwing doors into the saloon with all the appearance of a gentleman going in for a quiet drink save for the raised pistols in either hand. Shots rang out from inside, but Will did not have time to dwell on McPhail.

Straw Hat from the general store joined two other men in black to advance on Janie. The gunfire from the three was enough to keep her pinned down behind her barrels. Will looked to his right and found no more opponents in that direction. Hoping that his back truly was clear but also knowing where his heart and duty lay, he jumped up and started running and firing at the trio.

He clipped one of the men in black and spun him around. Straw Hat readjusted his aim first and began returning Will's fire. One bullet yanked at the left side of his shirt and another burned past his shoulder. Will kept firing, and the second man in black went down.

With her attackers distracted, Janie popped up over the barrels and shot Straw Hat. Though hit, the first man in black was not down. He swung his gun around at Janie and fired.

Will's heart leapt to his throat at the sound of her cry as she fell from view. He screamed her name and unloaded the rest of his bullets into the wounded Agent.

Heedless of everything else, Will continued to run past the post office, searching for any signs of Janie behind the barrels. As he passed the doorway, a big body came through the doors swinging the barrel of a shotgun across Will's gut. He doubled up with a grunt, and his arms reflexively came down around the barrel as it knocked the air from his lungs. The next instant his arms and belly shook and burned as the man pulled the trigger.

The buckshot blew a hole in the wood of the walkway, but not in Will. Little good that did him though, because he fell to his side still gasping for breath from the blow to his solar plexus and the barrel slipped from his grasp. Will's vision blurred around the figure hulking over him. The shotgun cocked, but the sound was distant in his ears. The barrel swung toward his face as the color seeped back into Will's world.

Three more reports sounded, and the figure pitched backward through the doors with crimson spots blooming on his chest and neck. Will twisted his head to see Janie up and alive. She winked at him over the smoking barrels of her guns and then turned her attention up the street where more attackers had emerged.

Will rolled to the side of the post office and tried to catch his breath while reloading his guns. The coast seemed clear behind him, but ahead gunmen still leaned from doorways or sheltered by crates, posts, and railings. Before going past the post office again, Will slipped in the doorway to assure no more Agents lurked inside.

Back outside, another of the gunmen was down, but three more kept firing toward Will and Janie. Across the street, Finn and McPhail still battled their own adversaries. Janie ducked back behind the barrels to reload. Will leaned out and shot along the walkway to keep the other gunmen at bay. When he saw she was done reloading, Will called to her, "Cover me."

Janie nodded, and at the next pause of the incoming shots, she sprang to her feet and began firing both pistols. The three gunmen ducked back, and Will sprinted from cover. He counted Janie's shots in his head and made it ten yards before her fusillade expired. Her barrage had taken out one of the Agents and given Will the time he needed to close the distance. As her shots ended, both remaining men looked out to return fire, but already on top of them, Will brought the fight to an end.

He crouched there near the final gunman's stack of crates and listened as the last of the gunfire died. Twenty seconds of silence fell over the town of Triumph.

Will peered above the crates. Across the street, Finn and McPhail stood in the lee of the opposite buildings. Bodies littered the street, but no one else moved. Down by the barrels, Janie stood up and took a cautious look around. Her eyes found Will's and a giddy grin of relief spilled across her face. She walked around the barrels into the street and up toward him, and he stepped down, ready to run into her arms.

Up above, Foster Callaghan lifted his head at the silence. Had they won? They must have. Seward Garland was one of Hogg's top Agents and Garland's personal posse had never lost a fight. Not that they had been in many fights, but they were Agents and twenty of them had lain in wait here in Triumph for the past three days. Foster peeked over the ledge, and his jaw fell open. Two of the devils still stood in the shadows across the street, and the woman was just below him and looking ahead to where the fourth must be out of Foster's line of sight. His palms were slick with sweat, but anger finally overcame his fear. He stood up with his rifle and aimed.

Across the street, Finn saw the rifleman stand up on the roof. Words caught in his throat. He raised both pistols.

McPhail was faster than Finn, but only caught the movement from the corner of his eye and so was half a heartbeat slower. His arm moved upward like a leaded weight dragged through a thick sea of honey. No one was faster than David McPhail, but this time, he did not know if he would be fast enough to prevent the last Agent's shot.

Will could see none of that. He saw only Janie. Her smile stretched from cheek to cheek. Her teeth sparkled in the sunshine. Her eyes shone with pure joy. Joy at surviving. Joy at being alive. Joy that she was only steps away from Will. Joy that she would throw her arms around his neck and feel his arms encircle her. Joy at the kisses she would bestow on him.

She came toward him with a little jump. "We did it!"

Neither she nor Will heard the crack of the rifle. Will saw her arms go up in the air in an exaggerated Hallelujah. The joy in her eyes turned to shock and then pain. She fell forward into his knees, and when he went down to catch her, warm wetness on her back coated his hands.

Somewhere in another world, McPhail and Finn were shooting again. Another body was falling to the ground. Will's world shrank to those dark brown eyes staring into his. He could see the confusion and the pleading in them as the lids slipped down to hide them from view.

Janie's breath came ragged. Her eyes twitched beneath lids that refused to open. She lay limp in Will's arms up on the wooden walkway where they had moved her out of the dirt. McPhail had packed her wound with bandages to staunch the bleeding. That had caused her to moan and cry out, but at least the bleeding had slowed. They all knew that bleeding inside likely had not.

Will was lost. Tears streamed down his cheeks, and he rocked back and forth like a metronome whispering her name over and over on each beat.

McPhail pulled Finn aside. "We need to leave. No one here will come after us, they're too scared, but Garland told me he'd already wired Justice and Faith. More men are on the way."

Finn looked at his cousin. "He won't leave her."

"We won't leave her." McPhail pointed to the wagon down the street. "Get the horses and harness it up. We'll take her in that."

"She won't make it, will she?"

McPhail shook his head.

"Can't we do anything else?"

"I could cauterize the wound. That might stop the bleeding outside but not inside. She dies soon of blood loss or days later of infection and gangrene. I've seen both. The first can be peaceful. The second isn't."

Finn looked back at his cousin and Janie. When he turned back to McPhail, his face was hard. "I told them we should have left days ago. I should have made them."

"Maybe you should have." McPhail turned and headed up the block.

It did not take long for Finn to harness two horses to the wagon and pull it close to where Janie lay. McPhail went into the general store and appropriated armfuls of blankets, more bandages, and some food. They made a bed for her in the back of the wagon. It took several minutes to get Will to process what they needed to do. He refused to let her go, and all three of them lifted her with as much care as possible and laid her in the back of the wagon. Will held her head in his lap and resumed rocking her. His tears spotted her cheeks like raindrops.

Finn laid his rifle next to him on the box seat before taking up the reins. McPhail tethered the other two horses together and led them and the wagon northeast, out of Triumph.

Will's world was shattered. He counted Janie's breaths. He felt each fading throb of her heart. He watched her face pale with each beat. He spoke to her until his throat dried and his voice became hoarse, but he kept talking to her, insuring her that she was not alone, that he was there, holding her, caring for her, and that he would never let her go.

An hour later, her eyes fluttered open. They blinked in the sun and roved back and forth as if searching for something.

"I'm here, Janie. It's me, Will. I'm here. I have you."

Those dark brown eyes came into focus on his face and a smile touched her lips. She tried to speak but managed a croak. Will poured small aliquots of water into her mouth, and she swallowed.

"I can't feel my legs, Will."

He nodded. "It's okay. I'm here, Janie. I have you. I'll never let you go."

She tried to smile again. "I know." But the smile faltered. "I'm scared, Will."

He swallowed and blinked back tears. "I'm scared too, but

I'm here with you. We're together. It will be okay."

She laughed. "No, it won't, Will. I'm dying."

He cried harder now. "No, don't say that. I won't let you."

Her shaking hand reached up to stroke his cheek. "You can't stop me. Neither can I." Her tears were mixing with his falling on her face. "Kiss me."

Will leaned into her, and the warmth of her lips touched him for one final time. He held that kiss for as long as he could until she pulled away.

"I love you, Will. I never said it, but I love you."

"I know. I've always known. I love you too, Janie."

"You helped me heal. Because of you, I'm whole again. Please just hold me. I need to feel your arms on me. Don't let me go." Her voice grew weaker, and her eyelids fluttered.

Will was sobbing. "I won't, Janie. I won't let you go."

"Thank you." Her eyelids refused to stay open. "I love you."

Those last words floated away in the wind, but Will heard them and held onto them, echoing in his mind over and over.

Her eyes twitched beneath the lids, but they did not open. Her lips hung ajar on that last syllable. Her breath calmed and slowed as if she were at peace. It took two more hours before she breathed her last, but those beautiful deep dark brown eyes did not open again, and no more words passed through those pale red lips.

Will sat in the back of the wagon with Janie and held her for the rest of their journey. He slept there with her at night trying to will warmth back into her cold stiff form. He cried until no more liquid remained in his body, until his tear glands must have shriveled to nothing, and then he cried some more. Finn had to force him to take sips of water and small bites of food, but how could he eat or drink when the only person in the world who mattered would never eat or drink with him again? A void opened within him and swallowed him whole.

They brought her to Mount de Dios. They all knew it was where Janie had been happiest. They had to leave the wagon at the entrance to the weaving pass. They wrapped her body in a shroud of blankets, and her stallion with Will astride pulled her on a travois all the way up to their hideout.

Will chose the spot where they buried her on a grassy overlook with the world spread out below them. Small pale purple wildflowers sprouted nearby, and it was close enough to the spring that she could have heard it burble in the quiet of the mountains.

At first, he refused to let Finn and McPhail dig her grave but relented when his exhaustion became apparent even to him. He laid her in the grave himself and snipped a lock of her long black hair. He tied it with a piece of twine and tucked it in his shirt pocket. He kissed her cold, unyielding lips one last time. Before covering her face with the blanket, he sprinkled handfuls of the purple flowers in her hair and around her face so she would have their sweet smell to keep her company. Then he covered her body with the dirt careful handful by careful handful. This he insisted on doing himself until he had covered her with all the gentleness that he could in that first layer of embracing earth.

The three of them finished the job together and covered the broken ground with stones the color of the sunset.

McPhail said words that Will could not hear.

He said his own words to her in his heart.

Finn knelt next to Will with his arm around him as the sun went down. After a time, he left but returned to wrap blankets around his cousin.

Will slept there by her grave that night.

To Finn's and even McPhail's surprise, Will joined them at

breakfast. He ate mechanically but fully, as if eating was a necessary but distasteful job in the pursuit of a loftier goal; and in a sense, it was.

When they finished, Finn started gathering the plates to wash. "So what do we do now?"

McPhail leaned back and pulled out one of his cigarettes. "Well, I think it's best if we lay low for a while, but I think our next job..."

"We're going to San Alonso." Those were the first words Will had spoken aloud to either of them since burying Janie.

Finn shivered at the sight of Will's eyes. He did not recognize what he saw there, and it scared him. Despite the magnitude increase in intensity, Janie would have recognized the flint-eyed Will staring back.

"There are debts to pay in San Alonso, and we're collecting." Will stood up. "Get packed and saddle up. It's Judgement Day."

⌒ SAN ALONSO ⌒

Alistair Hogg leaned back in his chair at the head of the table and rubbed his temples. They were back in the conference room with Horace Weatherwax, his secretary and advisor; Ovidio Nazario of the Revenue Office; Dick Warren, the Head Agent; and Rob Nelson, taking the deceased Seward Garland's place as second in command. At the far end of the table, Rob shifted from foot to foot like a preschooler needing to pee or a Catholic schoolboy brought before the mother superior for punishment.

"So they're all dead? All twenty Agents including Agent Garland perished in Triumph?" Hogg opened his eyes enough to see the young Agent's nod and closed them again. "And those twenty Agents only managed to kill one of McPhail's band, Janie De Casas?"

"Yes, sir, Governor sir, but she might not be dead. She was wounded, and they took her away in a wagon."

Rob's dancing about grated on Hogg's nerves, but he breathed in deep and pushed those feelings down. "Oh, if she's not dead yet, she will be soon." Hogg shook his head and leaned forward. He massaged the back of his neck and thought. He let the uncomfortable silence linger on until even Warren and Nazario had begun to squirm in their seats. Weatherwax had been squirming almost as early as Nelson had, but Alistair had not brought the man to San Alonso for his bravery.

Hogg looked back up to survey his lieutenants. "So, we have the worst of all possible outcomes here."

Warren cleared his throat. "At least they managed to get one of McPhail's gang. There's so few of them, one down makes a big difference."

Hogg closed his eyes a moment to suppress his rage. These were good enough men, but none of them, with the possible exception of Weatherwax, could think enough moves ahead, and Weatherwax's strength was politics, not battle tactics or personal psychology. "Not true. Kill McPhail, and the band falls apart. The other three probably run off to North Cali or one of the northern states, and the problem is solved. Kill one of the boys, and they're weaker like you say and maybe De Casas and the remaining brother run away together. Kill the woman, and now they're much worse."

Warren, Nazario, and Nelson all looked confused. Only Weatherwax seemed to have a light on upstairs, but it was a feeble candle at the moment.

Hogg sighed again and cursed the ill luck that had raised up these four men as his cream of the crop. "Janie De Casas would have been either a lover of one of the boys or the surrogate for their lost sister, Kalirose. My men have not only killed the boys' parents and debauched their sister, but they have now killed their sister again or their lover, or maybe both. At least one of the boys is on the warpath for my head and the head of anyone else near me he can get his hands on. McPhail will only fan those flames, and if the other brother isn't just as outraged, he'll still go to war to defend his brother." He looked around at his lieutenants. "That is why this is just about the worst-case scenario." He threw his arms in the air. "On the other hand, at least we can now be assured that the governor's mansion here in San Alonso is their next destination. That should give us all a little peace of mind at night."

It always amused Hogg to see just how pale Horace Weatherwax could get. If only his valet could find suit linen the same color. The other men looked grim, save for Nelson, who wore a dyspeptic grimace.

Once again it fell to Hogg to make the plans. It was his burden in life, damned to be the smartest man in the room. "So, here is what we do. First, we hang wanted posters with sketches of McPhail and the Hennessy boys on every last wall in the city. Second, we place guards on all the entrances to the city and search every wagon for them if we have to. Third, Dick, you are going to go to Tranquility and bring me back DuBois and whatever moron took over Murdock's posse. They set this crap storm in motion. I want them strung up on the capitol grounds for the crows. When those boys arrive, I want them to know Governor Hogg metes out justice wherever it is needed."

The air inside the coach clung to the nostrils and baked the occupants while the rutted road jostled them at inconsistent intervals and in irregular directions to make sleep almost impossible despite the heat's attempts to swoon them. Sweat ran in rivulets down the sides of Will's temples and soaked into the collar of his new shirt as well as up and down his back, under his armpits, and into his groin.

At the coach stop in Honesty, he climbed aboard as Joey

Hoskins on his way to visit his aunt and uncle in San Alonso and ended up in the middle seat riding backward jammed between two portly businessmen. Across from him sat a mother, father, and daughter. The girl might have been Kali's age. She sat at the window and craned her neck to catch what breeze trickled through and sped it up with an emerald fan she waved in her face. She had orange-brown hair and pale skin with freckles. Throughout the ride, she cast glances in Will's direction but that had more to do with him being the closest person to her age in the coach than anything else. A few times, she attempted to start a conversation in his direction, but combined with her mother's tuts, Will's taciturn responses killed those attempts.

San Alonso lay another hour away. If all went according to schedule, Finn would be arriving at the capital about now as a hired hand on a wagon train carrying food from the farms south of the city. McPhail should have entered this morning in the company of a group of tribesmen coming to the city to trade their wares in the market. The three planned to rendezvous in the afternoon at a saloon named the Loyal Groomsman on the seedy west side of town. By entering separately, they hoped to avoid the net of guards who watched the three main entrances to San Alonso.

Will felt naked without the rosewood revolvers on his hips, but they did not fit well with his disguise. They rode atop the coach in Will's valise. Given how much he was sweating in his suit, they might have rusted during the trip if he had worn them. That thought made him snort in laughter to himself.

The girl looked in his direction, but since he had not given her any encouragement, she sniffed and put her nose up in the air and directed it back out the window. *I'm doing you a favor,* Will thought at her. *Count yourself lucky.*

He dozed and dreamed Janie was watching him from afar. His eyes snapped open, and he jerked his head off his chest. A little drool had mixed with the sweat on his chin. The girl smirked at him but then tried to turn it into a smile one last time when she saw her mother was not looking.

The coach had rolled to a stop in what seemed like a line, but Will could not get a clear look out the window from his position. Boots crunched in the dirt as one of the coach drivers jumped down to the ground. He leaned his bearded face into the window. "Sorry, folks, but we got a bit of a wait. They've got guards watching the roads for bandits a little more closely these past two weeks. Shouldn't take too long."

The pronouncement received a few groans from the coach's occupants. Will pulled on his hat and tipped it over his eyes like he was trying to get some more shut-eye and sank further down on the seat.

The driver was correct, and in a few minutes, the coach rolled forward another short space before rocking to another stop. This repeated four more times before new voices echoed through the windows. A new man popped open one of the coach doors and leaned in. He blinked to see in the relative gloom of the coach's cabin against the blaze of the noontime sun overhead. "My apologizes, ladies and gentlemen, we just need a quick peek to be sure none of the wrong types are entering San Alonso."

The businessman nearest the door harrumphed. "Do you really think some ruffian would travel here by coach? Let us through, man. I have an important meeting to get to."

The guard tipped his hat. "Depends on the ruffian, I suppose. Governor's orders though, you see." He surveyed the six one last time. "You all have a good day and a nice stay in our fair city." He closed the door, gave a whistle, and thumped three times on the side of the coach.

With another sway and a jerk, the coach set off into the heart of San Alonso.

It took another fifteen minutes for the coach to find its way through the crowded thoroughfares of the capital city to the coach station.

Despite his suit and the weight in his heart, Will felt every inch an awed country bumpkin when he climbed down the coach steps. Six other stages sat parked at the stop with two more pulling away and another coming up from behind. Wagons, carts, horses, and bodies bustled about in every direction. The noise of it all drowned out the sound of the Grand River as it made its sweeping arc around the city. Looking about him, Will figured they could have gathered up all the other cities he had visited in the past year and dropped them down on the footprint of San Alonso and had room to spare.

Someone tossed his valise down to him. Will caught it without thinking. The girl gave him one last haughty sniff before parading off with her parents, but Will did not notice that either. He took a minute to look up to the sun and the sliver of the Elephants he could spy between the buildings to orient himself, and headed what seemed to be west.

Navigating the city took longer than he expected. The crowds remained thick. Carriages barreled up and down the streets as if intent on running down the unwary. Streets deadended into buildings or walls which forced him to turn and lose his bearings. Oh yes, and then there were all the wanted posters hanging on fences and posted in windows.

Finn's sketch was darker and more jagged but a reasonable facsimile. His description must have come from the clerk from Conviviality they had set free. Will's own portrait reminded him of looking at his reflection on the surface of running water. He could recognize himself, but it might also be anyone else. Still, he kept his hat pulled down low over his face and averted his eyes from his fellow pedestrians. That seemed to be the city's cultural norm in any case.

The hardest part was the voices. He kept hearing snippets of conversation and echoes of Janie's voice. Again and again, he twitched his head towards a woman's voice with his heart insisting she was Janie. On one block, he caught sight of a woman with black hair and a maroon dress walking away from him around a corner. Even though he knew it was not her and that the maroon dress from Humility was long gone, he hurried down the street after her because he had to be sure. The lady stopped to speak to another woman in the street, but because she spun her parasol behind her, Will had to walk past and steal a sideways glance. The woman was older than Janie, the wrong height and pregnant. The discovery relieved him and made him undeniably sad. If Janie was still out there somewhere, married and with child, at least he would have comfort in knowing she still breathed the same air, watched the same sunsets, and saw the same stars dance across the night's sky as he did.

With all the detours and misdirections, it took Will an hour to find his way to the Loyal Groomsman. Of course it was a bawdy house with a smoky interior, poor lighting, and a pianist banging on an out-of-tune piano accompanied by one of the ladies of the house whose voice was a smidge less out of tune.

Will dropped down into a chair across from Finn at a table off to the side of the room. "Really?"

Finn shrugged and took a swig from his mug. "I don't think they did a good job on my face." He shook a finger at his cousin. "You're okay, but I'm hideous."

"That's because you are." Will had finished his water flask off in the coach ride and not found a chance to refill on the walk over from the stage depot. He waved to one of the barmaids who brought over a dirty mug of warm beer along with a wink and smile. Will paid her but waved away the unspoken offer. "Why here?"

"Because it's dark and loud and no one will pay us any attention." McPhail dragged one of the chairs around to the

other side of the table and sat down so he could face the doorway. "You're being sloppy, Covington. I've been following you
for two blocks. You never looked for a tail once, and now
you've got your back to the door. If you want this to happen,
get your mind on the job."

Will took a long pull from his mug. It tasted terrible, but
he was too thirsty to care. He wanted to make a scathing re-
tort, but the old Ranger was right. If he wanted to avenge
Janie, he needed to stop being awed by a mere city built by
men and bury his pain and longing down deep. He would have
ample time to mourn her when Hogg lay in the cold earth too.
"You're right, no more moping."

McPhail stared at him, trying to take Will's measure. He
was a true Ranger. How could the son of Joseph and Samantha
Covington be anything else? But he was still young; fire tested,
yes, but young and worse yet, still love-struck. McPhail
watched Will's eyes and saw him push that loss down beneath
the flint. The pain lurked in those pale blue eyes. Directed
properly, pain could be a powerful tool.

It was a pity that Janie and Will had distracted each other
so much in the past few months to the point of almost pulling
themselves off the path of righteousness. She had been every
bit the Ranger Will was and perhaps even more so. Her loss
was a severe blow to McPhail's dreams of rebuilding the Rangers on the wreckage of Governor Hogg's empire. His decision
had happened in the space between the seconds ticking off the
clock, but David McPhail did not regret staying his finger on
the trigger for that one brief moment back in Triumph.

"We're in the belly of the beast now, but the beast doesn't
know it's swallowed us yet." The Ranger leaned into the table
and kept his voice low. No one here would care about them,
but that also meant no one here would care about selling their
secrets to the highest bidder. "Tonight we'll scout out the governor's mansion and the capitol building. We'll need to find

out what we can about Hogg's movements and decide where to strike. He'll be surrounded by guards. His top Agents will be here in San Alonso, men like Murdock, De Casas, Pryor, and Garland. We can't let them know we're here until it's time to act."

In the dark, Finn paled a bit, but Will maintained his stony countenance, assured and deadly. "We handled the others. We'll handle them."

They ordered food and more drink and talked in low murmurs until sunset.

Just before sunset, the barmaid serving them finished her shift, hung up her apron, pocketed their generous tips, and headed out into the night. She knew a woman who had a steady relationship with a cowboy who was friends with a guy who worked in the stables near the governor's mansion where the Agents kept their horses. Someone there would know an awful lot about the conditions on those reward posters hanging all over town and given that the string of relationships made them almost kissing cousins, surely he would not cheat her out of one dime of the reward money.

The gas street lamps that lit the major thoroughfares of San Alonso mesmerized Will and Finn, who had grown up with campfires and lanterns. Even sunset failed to darken the capital city of Governor Hogg's empire. Fewer people promenaded along the streets than in the daylight, but carriages still rolled past up and down the streets and enough pedestrians moved about that the company of three did not seem out of place.

McPhail knew the city better than Will and navigated them toward the capitol building with his usual alacrity. Only twice during their journey did Will think he heard Janie's voice, and only once did a head of long black hair pull his eyes away from their destination.

Gas lamps illuminated the capitol building grounds, but dark squares peered from the building itself. Those gas lamps also revealed the sobering sight of two corpses, one in blue and one in black, hanging from twin gallows off the main path to the building entrance. A sign detailing the miscreants' crimes stood in front of the gallows, but none of the company ventured close enough to read the death decrees.

A few blocks away, in contrast to the somber exterior and dark interior of the capitol building, carriages paraded up the wide driveway to the governor's mansion and light glowed from all of its windows. The annual winter ball was starting to warm up with all the upper crust of San Alonso and Jefferson State arriving for the evening's fete. Through the window of one of the passing carriages, Will saw an older woman who seemed familiar, but he could not place her face. If she saw him, she gave no sign of recognition. In turn, he failed to notice the family of three from his stagecoach ride make the turn up the governor's driveway, but the girl spied him and clamped her hand over her mouth and tugged on her mother's sleeve.

Given all the street traffic and the men in black guarding the gates to the mansion grounds, the three companions faded back into the shadows on the far side of the street and slipped down alleyways.

McPhail led them in a wide circle to the back gate where the servants and delivery men arrived, but Hogg's Agents manned that gate with the same attentiveness as the front. One was waving the delivery trucks through while another was talking to an excited young lady who seemed insistent on getting inside.

"Storming the mansion seems out of the question," Finn said after they had turned back toward the west side of town.

"Maybe if we had some party clothes, we could blend in with the crowd tonight," Will mused.

McPhail shook his head. "Those Agents were checking invitations. If we had more time, maybe, but not tonight. Tomorrow night will be quieter. We can climb the fence in the dark and take our chances."

"Those Agents had dogs with them," Finn said. "They were on leads tonight but maybe not tomorrow."

"No one ever said taking down Hogg would be easy, and no one said we'd all make it out alive." With that, the Ranger strode ahead of them into the night.

Finn opened his mouth to quip to Will about their leader's cheerful demeanor but stopped when he saw the look in Will's eyes. Will was staring daggers into McPhail's receding back, and his hand caressed his hip where the rosewood revolvers usually rode. Finn decided to keep his mouth shut.

They made their way out of the gaslit streets to the west side of the town and a series of rundown two-story buildings near the warehouse district and off the docks on the banks of the Grand River. From the mud stains and water marks, Will surmised that this section of the town was subject to floods, and the river might one day reclaim the land. Several of the buildings appeared burned out and abandoned, and the inhabited ones hovered on the brink of abandonment.

McPhail brought them to a decrepit example of the latter at the end of a small square. The space was familiar to Will and Finn as they had dropped off their paltry gear in one of the upstairs rooms before setting out on the reconnaissance mission. An old fish market occupied the ground floor with a back door opening out to a rotting dock where boats brought in their catch. Stairs behind the counter led to a small kitchen and sitting room and two bedrooms overlooking the square. Newer docks and fish markets further upstream had choked away the livelihood of the little shop, and flooding put the final nail in the coffin.

Behind McPhail and his charges, two figures watched from the shadows of an alleyway. Once the door latch snicked shut, the two men nodded to each other. One turned and hurried up the street. The second receded deep into a dark doorframe, struck a match for a smoke, and settled down to wait.

Upstairs in the fish shop, without preamble, McPhail started with the orders for the morning. "We'll need to keep a low profile in the daytime tomorrow, and we shouldn't be seen together. There are too many eyes in this city. Get some sleep." With that, he chose a room and closed the door.

Finn flopped down on a musty, rotting settee. Will stared more daggers at the closed door before beginning to pace. Too much fractious, nervous energy crackled through his system to sit or lay. His hands alternated from running through his hair and dancing about his belt until they could take it no more. He pulled his gun belt out of his valise and strapped it on. Now those hands danced over the guns, drawing them, spinning them, dropping them back into their holsters, and repeating.

After ten minutes, Finn sighed and stood up. "Come on, you need to get out of here." He grabbed his gun belt and headed downstairs with Will on his heels. At the bottom of the stairs, Finn turned left and headed out onto the small quay and dock along the river.

The smell off the river mud was a tad fresher than the aroma of rotted fish in the market, and at least the breeze wafted about enough to cleanse the nostrils from time to time. The two cousins stood together watching the water drift past under sparkling stars. The sliver of the moon hid at intervals behind thin wisps of clouds.

"Let's walk," Finn said. He turned downriver and started to weave along the space between the buildings and the riverbank. Will caught up with him, and they walked shoulder to shoulder.

"He doesn't care that she's dead," Will said into the night. "He doesn't care if any of us die."

Finn slipped his hands into his pockets and kicked at a small stone.

"I held her in my arms when she died. She was the only woman I'll ever love, and I watched her die." Will held back the tears but let that anger bubble forth. "I'll make Hogg pay for what he did to our family, but after that, McPhail and I will have a reckoning, Finn."

"I wouldn't want to be him."

They wandered like that for more than an hour, first down along the river and then turning into the city proper and wandering the streets. This time, in contrast to the earlier trudge back from the mansion, Will's tension faded, and the silence became companionable.

Few people ventured out in this section of the town at night. Without gas lamps to light the night around the houses and businesses, the upstanding citizens kept inside. The ladies of the night plied their wares where more foot traffic passed. The duo passed a few knots of men who may have been looking for trouble, but the looks on Will and Finn's faces and the guns on their hips waved off any approach.

They made their way toward the fish market. A block away, they could hear the sound of a coach rattling down the road and boots on the dirt. Finn grabbed Will and pulled him into a shadowy doorway. Dark-clad figures hurried past along the cross street ahead. Noise behind them caused them to turn, and more figures crossed along the road behind them.

Finn grabbed the handle of the door, and it turned in his hand. The two boys slipped inside and knelt behind the door as they closed it behind them. They crouched there for less than a minute before boots passed from south to north on the other side.

Will glanced around the dark building. It was some sort of market, similar to the fish market, but it seemed to still be in business. In the back, he could see a stairway. He pointed up, Finn nodded in understanding, and they scurried across the floor in a hunched crawl and headed up the stairs.

Upstairs turned out to be a storeroom, not living quarters. Windows in the back overlooked the little square and their fish market hideaway. Men in black blanketed the little square, taking up positions against buildings, in doorways, and behind barrels or crates. All of them trained their weapons on the fish market.

The coach entered the square and turned broadside to the fish market. The coach door opposite the building opened, and Will and Finn could just spy a tall lanky figure in white step from the coach. The coach shielded him from the fish market and blocked most of Will and Finn's view of him. Neither of the cousins had ever seen the man in person, but they recognized him from newspaper sketches with his slim build and long mustache. Will reached for his guns, but Finn stopped him with a hand. "Bad idea, cuz, there's too many of them, and you don't have a shot."

Will disagreed with the latter part of that assessment, but Finn was correct that the odds did not look good.

"Well, well, well, if it isn't the governor himself come to visit," a voice called from the upstairs of the fish market. McPhail was awake and aware of the ambush. Did he know Will and Finn were gone?

Hogg reached back into the carriage and pulled out a speaking trumpet. He leaned it on the top edge of the coach and spoke into the other end. "May I assume I have the pleasure of addressing former Ranger David McPhail and his band of desperadoes?"

"If you'd come out from behind that coach, I'd be happy to tell you who you're addressing," McPhail yelled back from the fish market.

Hogg chuckled. "Oh, I am not nearly the fool you may take me to be. I've heard too many good words about your handiwork. First though, as you can see, my men have you surrounded. Before we proceed further, in the interest of protecting the innocent, my men are evacuating citizens from the surrounding buildings. I do hope you do not object."

Now that Will looked, he could see the men in black were opening doors and entering all the buildings off the square. Across the way, he could see a woman clutching a baby and a man leading two small boys hurrying out their front door and off around the corner.

"Take your time. I've got all night," McPhail yelled back. Will thought the Ranger's voice might have come from a different window.

Downstairs from Will and Finn, the front door banged open. The two ducked down behind some crates. Voices called from below and boots tromped on the stairs. The light of a lantern swept over the room. "Empty," someone said, and the boots receded.

Hogg was back on his speaking trumpet. "While we're waiting, I would like to say a few words to the Hennessy boys." After a few seconds of pause for a reply, he continued unperturbed by the lack of response. "Believe it or not, boys, I do not know everything my Agents and Revenue Men are up to all the time in this beautiful state of ours. I want to emphasize that I never would have sanctioned the actions Revenue Man Du-Bois, Agent Murdock, and Murdock's replacement Agent Stark took with your family. In fact, if you have stopped by the capitol building, you may have noticed that they have learned a hard lesson about abusing their power over the citizens of our state."

Will and Finn looked at each other, remembering the bodies they had seen earlier that night.

"Also, although I do have extensive real estate and other business holdings in various cities around the state, I am not personally involved in their day-to-day operations. To wit, I wish to extend my sincerest of apologies for the deplorable treatment given to young Kalirose, may she rest in peace. The manager of the Broken Mare clearly needed a lesson on how to properly run a business and the proper way to recruit young ladies to work in said establishment. It is a job I would have had to undertake myself, but as fortune saw fit, you handled that job yourselves. For that, I must say thank you."

Will and Finn were looking at each other but no longer seeing one another. Both of them crouched near the window, eyes unfocused as they each drifted in their private memories.

Hogg paused to take a sip of water and clear his throat. "Once I learned of these crimes inflicted on your dear innocent loved ones, I have done my best to make amends in such poor ways that I can. The bodies of your parents were already laid to rest in a cemetery in Tranquility. I have made arrangements for Kalirose to be transported back to Tranquility so she may be laid to rest next to her parents with all the dignity and respect for the good Christian girl that she was."

A tear formed in the corner of Finn's eye as he thought about his sister. Will might think him cold-hearted or forgetful, but some thoughts and memories were just too sharp and needed to be pushed down.

"I hope you can both agree that I am trying to be as just and fair as I can be. I cannot undo the past deeds of those men who abused their privileged positions and sacred responsibilities as representatives of Jefferson State, but to the best of my ability I have made them pay the requisite price for their betrayal of my trust and yours."

He took another sip of water. "That being said, Finn and Will Hennessy, you too have committed crimes against Jefferson State and her citizens. There have been mitigating circumstances, and you have been led astray by a false prophet and inadequate information, but you have committed crimes. I offer you this: lay down your guns and surrender peacefully now, and as governor, I swear that you will receive a fair and just trial in front of a jury of your peers. Decline the offer, and my Agents and all the law enforcement representatives of this fine state will hunt you down like the low-life bandits you have become. You have five minutes to decide."

Hogg pulled out his pocket watch and marked the time. "Oh, and Mr. McPhail, the same offer applies to you. Lay down your weapons and surrender and you will receive a fair trial. Choose not to, and well..."

McPhail's laugh echoed in the courtyard. "It'll be a cold day in hell before I surrender to the likes of you, Hogg. I saw what happened at Fort Vigilant, and I've seen what you've done to this state since then. I will see you roasting in hell."

"So be it." Hogg waved a hand. "Kill them."

Gunfire erupted in the night. Dozens of muzzle flashes from pistols and rifles sparked like fireflies up and down the courtyard. The windows of the fish market blew apart top and bottom.

Will and Finn ducked down, but no bullets came their way. Will lifted an eye above the windowsill and watched the carnage unfold. One of the Agents darted forward from cover and tossed a lit oil lantern through one of the broken downstairs windows. A minute later, red and orange flickers of light danced about the bottom floor and tendrils of grey smoke began to curl from the windows.

Was McPhail dead already? No, a single shot came from the left upper floor window, and a man in black went down. Gunfire concentrated on that window, but the next flash came from the right window and another Agent went down.

"We have to help him," Will said. He reached for his gun, but before he could get it out of its holster, Finn's fist connected with his cheek.

The pain was unexpected and excruciating. Will had not been in a fist fight with his cousin or anyone else for years, and this blow was stronger than the one McPhail had planted on him in Chastity. He fell back to the floor, lights flashing in his eyes, and Finn leapt on top of him.

"No," Finn rasped. "We already lost Janie; I am not losing you too."

Will tried to fight back, but Finn had his arms pinned to the floor. "Let me up. They're going to kill him."

"Better him than you or me."

"No, I have to get to Hogg, for Janie."

Finn lowered his face inches from Will's. His eyes flared in anger. "Janie wouldn't want that. She'd want you to live."

"Don't you tell me what she'd want."

"She was my friend too, Will."

That and the tears in Finn's eyes stunned Will almost as much as the punch.

"I may not have loved her like you did, but she was my friend, and I know she wouldn't want you to throw your life away like this. You promised her one last job. It's over. We lost. It's time to go. Now."

Will swallowed and nodded. Finn let his weight off Will's arm, gingerly at first, ready to clamp down if his cousin made a move to continue the fight, but Will did not.

Satisfied, Finn nodded in return. "I think there's another door to this place. We should try for a boat."

"Okay." Will pulled himself back into a crouch and together they scrambled low to the stairs.

Finn was correct that a side door led away from the courtyard. They listened for a moment at the door, but the gunfire and crackling of flames drowned out the sound of any guards outside. They exited with guns drawn, but no one occupied the alleyway. To their left and straight ahead, the Grand River flowed past under the stars, indifferent to the cacophony around it.

As hoped, a rowboat bobbed in the water at the end of the alley. Finn climbed in and started to undo the moorings, and Will looked upriver toward the back of the fish market. Four men in black waited, their eyes scanning the back door and windows for any signs of escape. Black smoke filtered through the closed door and cracks in the walls. One of the men half turned and spied the two young men. "Hey, you, halt!" the man yelled. His companions turned and began raising their guns.

Preparation and speed were with Will again. He had already drawn and raised his guns in the Agents' direction, and the rosewood six-shooters began thundering and bucking in his hands. McPhail had been correct that the Agents of San Alonso were a notch better than most of the men Will had faced, but Will had grown into a trained and battle-tested Ranger. Bullets bit past him, but he stood his ground and did not falter. The other four did.

"Get in," Finn yelled from behind as the last of the four fell.

Will climbed in, and they pushed off from the shore. Will kept his guns trained on the back of the buildings, but their shoot-out seemed to have passed unnoticed by the men out front.

The current grabbed the boat as it neared the center of the river and whisked them around the bend and into the night. They watched the column of black smoke rising to block out the stars and the orange glow reflecting off the river behind them. Soon they passed beneath a wide bridge and left San Alonso, Governor Hogg, and David McPhail behind them.

⟨∿ SANCTUARY ∿⟩

Finn struggled with the oars during the first leg of their journey but soon realized that as long as he only wanted to head south, the current would do most of the work. They used the oars to keep them toward the center of the river and off sandbars or rocks. They sailed the Grand River all night and had traveled miles from San Alonso by the time morning dawned above the Santo Domingos to the east.

By morning, Will had taken over on the oars, and he directed the rowboat toward a small beach on the eastern bank of the river. Dragging the little rowboat up onto dry land took more effort than the exhausted cousins expected. They found a shaded area near some brush and boulders up the shore and collapsed for a few hours of sleep.

When they woke, they took stock of their supplies and prospects. They had their clothes, guns, and a few extra bullets. Finn had the money he had earned from transporting produce the previous day, while Will had only pocket change and a lock of black hair. They had no food, but at least the river would provide water. They had no horses. Will had been unwilling to part with his horse because he had taken to riding Janie's stallion, and so paid to stable him in Honesty, but that town lay far back upriver. Finn's horse was at the farm he had started from, but he was no longer sure if the farm was north or south, and in either case, Hogg's Agents might well be paying the farmer a visit right now if they had determined how Finn entered the city.

"We need supplies and horses. We can hunt, but we're low on ammunition, and like as not, the Agents will be out tracking us. We need money and a town to spend it in." Will leaned back against the boulder and stared at the sky.

Finn thought with him. "Well, let's see what we've tried so far: knock over a brothel, home invasion, highway robbery, bank job, train robbery." He chuckled. "Heck, we are a couple of desperadoes, cuz."

Will frowned and shook his head, but then a light turned on in his eyes, and a smile spread across his lips. "Highway robbery."

"Whoa, I was just kidding. I'd really like to try not to kill anyone for a while."

"No need to." Will pointed to the mountains a few miles down the river. "That's Gorseman's Pass down there."

A grin spread across Finn's face. "And we've got some buried treasure up on top."

They rowed downriver until they found where the river off Gorseman's Pass joined the Grand River. They beached the boat again and concealed it with cut branches and bushes before starting the trek up the mountain. It took them the full day to reach their old campsite and retrieve some of the gold coins from among the bars of gold. The sun was setting by the time they completed the return trek to their small rowboat, which lay undisturbed under the camouflage.

Their proximity to the main road made them both nervous, and so they climbed back in despite the looming dark and sailed a few more miles downriver before stopping again to make camp.

Late the next day, they met up with an old friend.

"Heddy-ho there, gentlemans. A welcome to Fortitude on this fine evening." The mop of shaggy hair bopped about in the breeze, and below that hair, the familiar embattled teeth beamed out at Will and Finn. Chapped lips pursed around those teeth and the face scrunched up in concentration. "Has Marvin a met youse afore?"

Finn climbed from the rowboat first and extended a hand. "Yes, sir, Marvin, you crossed us and some other friends a while back."

Marvin's face brightened again. "Marvin always remembers his passengers." He craned his neck to look upriver. "Your friends comin' in their own boat?"

Finn glanced back at Will who was tying up their boat. "No, Marvin, they won't be joining us."

The shaggy man nodded. "Well, all good friends meet up again someday. That's what brought you back to Fortitude. People only come here to cross the river, and I see you don't need me for that, so you must be here to see your old friend Marvin. Welcome back, old friends." With that, he grabbed up first Finn and then Will into a big bear hug. "By the way, what's your name, old friends?"

It turned out that Marvin was not alone in his little shack on the river. An itinerant preacher, Father Prescott, had arrived on a donkey not long before Will and Finn moored their boat. Given the nearing dark, he had elected to spend the night in Fortitude and share a meal and some words with the ferryman.

Father Prescott had a thin face and humorless eyes, but he sniggered under his breath when Will and Finn joined him at Marvin's crowded table. He stood and crossed himself and gave a little bow of greeting. Then he directed his eyes toward the ceiling, "I knew you had good reason to ask me to stop here this night, Lord. More of your lost lambs have found their way to my doorstep." He looked back to Will and Finn and gestured to some chairs. "Please, come and join Marvin and me for a repast and exploration of our everlasting souls."

Finn gave Will a little eye roll, but having had nothing of substance to eat for almost two days, they were too famished to decline any food, no matter the price. The meal was simple enough, consisting of beans, tortillas, and some stunted carrots pulled from Marvin's garden supplemented with some dried lamb and spices the preacher carried with him.

While the Father blessed the food and said grace, Marvin bowed his head in solemn piety, and Will and Finn bowed out of politeness. Once the amens chorused around the table, the three young men tucked in with gusto. The company inspired Marvin's appetite, and he gobbled up the food as fast as Will and Finn. Will reflected that maybe he was just afraid of losing too much of his food stores to his guests and so wanted to grab as much for himself as possible. If that was the case, Marvin never let that worry show through his grin and happy gabbling.

In contrast, Father Prescott picked at his food as if he had to pay a penance for every mouthful he consumed. "So tell me, boys, how clear is your conscience that you follow the path of the Lord?"

Marvin grinned his usual happy grin and spewed small pieces of bean and tortilla from the gaps between his teeth. "My pappy always said that ferrymen do God's work. We is like Moses taking the Israelites across the Red Sea, only we uses a boat, and Moses waved his hands and spread the waves. I thinks ferries is easier. Less mud on yer boots." He lifted a foot up to the tabletop to show off the lack of caked mud.

Father Prescott's face twitched into a small frown at that

bit of ferryman blasphemy, but instead of objecting, he focused his gaze on Will and Finn.

Will swallowed the last of his beans. He wiped his mouth with his handkerchief and leaned back in his chair. "My conscience is clear enough that I've only ever done what I needed to do. When I'm done here in this world, I'll stand before the Lord and let him judge my soul."

"Ah, the brave words of so many of the young." Father Prescott chuckled in what he must have thought of as a friendly way, but it rang hollow on the ear. "The old man is wiser and a bit more circumspect in his declarations before the Lord. Would you grow to be a wise man in the ways of the Lord? If so, I, His humble servant, am here at your service."

The preacher's words held one meaning, but the eyes and posture hid a sharper edge, Will reckoned. "I don't know, Father. Will I grow old?"

The two men stared at each other. Father Prescott let his gaze drift down to the rosewood revolvers on Will's hips. "I am a man of the cloth. The Lord's grace is my shield and His word is my sword, or I suppose my six-shooters in this age." He nodded at the cousins. "You both seem like so many other young men who have let yourselves harden despite the wonders of the Lord about you. I despair you may not grow old, Will. I wonder, have you lived long enough to see and feel the glimpses of Heaven that God offers us in this life? They give us the strength and encouragement to follow His path to everlasting life."

Will leaned forward. "And what is Heaven like then, Father? What's waiting for me there?"

"Will, why everyone who follows the path of the Lord, everyone who has gone before you waits for you there. I imagine there are broad plains aplenty to ride in the light of the Lord. But why the rush to go there so young? Have you found the joys the Lord gives us in this life, or have you forgotten them?

Have you had the bliss to sing the joy of the Lord while His life-giving rains fall around you? Have you lived long enough to feel the blessed love of the Lord through another person?"

Will's eyes stared at Father Prescott, but what they saw was Janie in that final instant with her arms flung to the sky. "I've seen love come, Father, I've seen love shot down, and I've seen love die." He stood up and left the warmth of the little shack for the cold of the night.

The next morning Finn paid Marvin with some of the gold coins for his hospitality and a small satchel of food each for him and Will. They left the rowboat to the ferryman and crossed over the Grand River with the preacher and his donkey. Despite the preacher's attempts, Will avoided conversation.

Once across the river, the preacher bowed to them. "I can tell that my company would displease you for now. I journey on to the town of Sanctuary, west along this road. It will take me a day to ride, and you two a day and a half or two afoot. You can find supplies there and maybe even some horses. If your minds have changed by then, I look forward to speaking with you more of the Lord."

Finn nodded. "Thank you, Father. We'll keep that in mind." He gave Will a sidelong glance and nudged him.

Will did not smile. "Good day, Father."

The preacher bowed again, climbed astride his donkey, and trotted off down the dusty road.

Will and Finn waited for the small dust clouds the donkey kicked up to settle before they too set off with the sun at their backs.

It took them the full two days to reach Sanctuary, another

small town, this one sitting at the southern foot of the Elephants. Much like Fortitude, when the road was better traveled it had thrived but had shrunk in size and vitality with the opening of the new coach road. Unlike Fortitude, Sanctuary managed to cling to some of its luster. It warranted a thin telegraph line that stretched northeast toward distant San Alonso. Despite the connection to the capital, the wanted poster hanging in the window of the telegraph and post office was the old one they had first encountered in Benevolence. The only difference was that someone had drawn black *X*s across Janie and McPhail's faces.

The post office joined at the hip to the ubiquitous general store. Enough travelers came up from the southwest to support the small hotel and saloon, and the local townsfolk and ranch hands and farmers supported a barber, a blacksmith, a one-room schoolhouse, a church, and even a small printing press.

Finn and Will arrived in town riding bareback on a pair of horses. A rancher a few miles outside of Sanctuary had the horses to sell, but not the saddles. By the time they arrived and took rooms in the hotel, the general store had closed for the evening, but they met the owner in the saloon that night, and he promised to outfit them with saddles and gear come the morrow. The preacher dined there too, but Will ignored him.

The sight of the black marks across Janie's face had unsettled Will, and the marks on McPhail's only confirmed what they already suspected. They were on their own.

That night, Will ordered a bottle of whiskey and chased it with one of tequila. For the first and last time since Temperance, the boys got drunk. The first time, they had washed the liquor down with laughs and good cheer among trail mates. This time, they drank the liquor to drown the pain and loss of the past year.

"To McPhail," Finn croaked as they neared the bottom of the second bottle.

"To McPhail." Will clanked his glass to Finn's on the second try and then threw it back. He gasped and his eyes watered, but he kept the spirits down.

Finn poured the last of the bottle into their glasses. "And mostly to Janie. She and I may have argued a lot, but she was the best."

"Don't talk about her." Will swirled the amber liquid around in his glass. "She was better than any of us. She didn't deserve to die."

"No, she didn't."

They drank to the bottom of their glasses. Will stared at the table and the empty glasses and bottles. "That didn't help."

Finn burped. "Don't think it ever does. Just makes you forget for a while."

"I'll never forget her." From his pocket, he produced the lock of black hair.

"Maybe we need another bottle." Finn made to stand.

Will put the lock of hair to his nose and inhaled before placing a soft kiss on the ends of the strands. "I don't want to forget her, Finn."

Finn nodded at his cousin. "I wouldn't want you to. Time to go then."

On wobbling legs, they hoisted each other up the stairs to their room.

The whole time, the preacher sat rigid in his chair, glowering at them from across the room.

Late morning brought Will and Finn back downstairs for coffee and a sparse breakfast.

"What are we going to do now?" Finn set his mug on the table.

Will wiped his mouth on his sleeve. "Get some saddles and supplies."

"And after that?"

Will just shrugged. He could tell Finn had something on

his mind but was afraid to speak. "What?"

Finn began spinning his mug between his hands. "I was thinking maybe we could go track down Mr. Franklin and see about another cattle drive to Temperance." He glanced up to gauge Will's reaction before continuing. "And maybe after Temperance, we could hop a train west and see the ocean."

To Finn's mild surprise, Will nodded. "Yeah, that's a good idea. Maybe we should."

Finn's goofy grin, misplaced somewhere along the way in the last few weeks, spread across his face. "Yeah, we should. We really should."

Despite himself, Will smiled back. "We should."

They left their horses with the farrier to shod the animals for the long trek back toward Tranquility. In the general store, they purchased the saddles and blankets they lacked as well as new bedrolls, a change of clothes, cooking gear, food, and extra ammunition. The owner raised his eyebrows at the gold coins, but he tested them to be real and accepted them without further comment.

When they emerged onto the front steps of the store, Father Prescott waited for them in the dusty street. "Good morning, Will and Finn." He inclined his head but kept his eyes on them. "I want to offer you another chance to repent for the sake of your everlasting souls. Would you come with me to pray?"

Will sighed and moved to push past the preacher with Finn on his heels. "Sorry, Father, but our souls are fine this morning, and we need to get going."

"Going along the path of the Lord or the path of the Dark One?"

"For now, our own path." Neither looked back.

"Then that would be the path of the Dark One, Will and Finn Hennessy."

Now they both stopped to look back. The preacher's smile threatened to swallow his ears, and his eyes glinted. "Yes, I recognized you both when you rowed up in Fortitude. The Lord set me in your path to turn you back to the way of Righteousness. Come with me now and repent while there is still time. Repent, and the Lord and I can still shield you."

"Shield us from what, Father?" The knot in Will's stomach was already grumbling the answer, but he needed to hear it to know for sure.

The preacher pointed back down the main street. In the distance, more than two miles away, a cluster of horsemen rode at a gentle pace toward Sanctuary. "I got to town more than a day before you did and sent a telegram off to San Alonso. I believe that is the posse that has been searching for the last of the Hennessy Gang. Repent your sins now with me before the Lord, and they need never know you arrived. I can offer you the protection of the Lord and His forgiveness."

Before Will could take a step toward the preacher, he felt Finn grab his shoulder. "Time to go." He pulled, and Will followed.

Fortune was with them, and the farrier had completed shoeing their horses. Will tossed the man one of the gold coins. "It's real. Thank you for your help."

It took them several minutes to saddle the horses and stow their gear as best they could. While they were busy with that, the preacher approached once more. "Last chance, boys. They're almost here."

Will looked up. Yes, the posse—he could see they could be nothing else all dressed in Agent's black—was now perhaps half a mile out of town. "No thanks, Father." He undid the reins from the hitching post and pulled himself into the saddle. "Finn."

"Almost there," Finn said as he adjusted the saddle's cinches one last time.

The preacher turned down the street and began to wave

his hands above his head and shout. "They're here! It's them! Hurry before they get away!" Townsfolk emerged from their homes and businesses. They looked up and down the street taking in the spectacle of the screaming preacher, the two otherwise mundane-looking young men, and the passel of black-clad riders approaching their town.

Finn swore and climbed into his saddle. "Okay, let's go."

The cousins turned westward and urged their horses into a gallop.

"Fly you may, but you cannot flee the Judgement of the Lord!" Having alerted the posse, Father Prescott turned his attention back to haranguing the young men. "You'll burn just like your false prophet McPhail, and rot just like that patricidal whore from Mercy who rode with you."

Will pulled up his horse and half turned the beast. One of the rosewood revolvers was already extended in his hand.

Father Prescott was maybe forty yards away spraying bits of saliva to the wind. "You'll burn in—"

Wherever they would burn was drowned out by the roar of Will's gun. A dark red blotch appeared in the center of Father Prescott's forehead. He tottered there for a second with a crazed look in his eyes, as though he had reached some great epiphany, and then fell straight over backward into the dirt like a plank of wood.

"Will, come on," Finn called from down the street. Behind Father Prescott's body, the posse came at full gallop, closing on the other end of Sanctuary.

Will turned his horse again and spurred her after Finn.

They raced from the town together out along the road and into the plains. To their right the end of the Elephants began to rise into the sky; ahead of them, the plains stretched flat to the horizon. Will's horse was a little faster than Finn's, and he soon caught his cousin and began edging them toward the mountains. Behind them, Sanctuary blocked the posse from their sight. Will glanced back once more to see how close their pursuers were and saw it happen.

Finn's horse, at full gallop, mis-stepped or hit a gopher hole or the den of some small animal, and down they both went in a thundering crash of man and beast. Finn's cry of surprise turned to a screech of pain as he fell and the horse rolled over him.

Will reined his horse to a stop and turned her to go back. A plume of dust had enveloped Finn and his horse, but the screams of man and animal told the tale. Beyond that plume, the posse rounded the edge of Sanctuary.

The dust cleared to reveal Finn on his back, his legs trapped beneath his horse who kicked and bucked on the ground in agony. Finn drew one of his pistols, placed it to the base of the horse's head, and fired. The bucking stopped. Now he rolled to look at Will. His face was pale beneath dirt and streams of tears. "Go!" he screamed. "Get out of here! Go, now!"

Will hesitated. The posse had drawn their guns, but both he and Finn lay out of range.

"There's no time!" Finn struggled beneath his horse, but the deadweight pinned his legs tight, and he could not extricate himself. "You have to go now." Finn could see his words made no difference to Will but knew his cousin well. They had grown up together, like brothers, almost like twins. Will would never leave Finn unless he had some higher purpose or goal. Finn had never believed in their quest, but Will did. "You were right. You're the only one left to make sure they pay for what they did to our parents, to Kali, and to Janie. Go, now!"

Finn did not know which of those got through to Will, but he suspected it was the thought of Janie. He was too far away to see the tears in Will's eyes, but he knew they were there, just like they were in his own eyes. Will saluted Finn one last time and turned to gallop off toward the mountains.

Finn lay back flat on the ground and looked up at the wide blue sky above him. The bright ball of the sun was somewhere above his head. He could no longer feel anything in his left leg, but his right screamed and grated enough for both of them. He could smell dust, horse sweat, and urine. He could taste the coppery tang of blood in his mouth. The smooth grips of his father's rosewood revolvers felt cool in his hands. He listened and could hear the approaching hoofbeats and under his back could even feel their thudding in the ground.

When he sat up, the men and horses loomed less than ten yards away. He only had eleven bullets left, but he used them all before they brought him down.

Will found little peace after Sanctuary. He fled north from the posse and his cousin's still warm body and managed to lose them in the Elephants. For a week afterward, he avoided roads and followed game trails. He camped alone in the mountains and shunned people, be they in towns or isolated cabins.

In the end, that solitary and morose existence drove him back toward civilization. A young man befriended him when they met hunting in the mountains. Will returned with him to the town of Honor and spent an afternoon helping move hay into the family barn. That evening, though, the young man sent a telegraph message to San Alonso, and a day later, the posse appeared. They would have caught him had not a soft voice seemed to whisper from around a corner, "Time to go."

For almost a week, the posse dogged him across the western plains of Jefferson, from one city to the next, one night after another. As a lone man, he might lose them in the hills or mountains for a day or two, but inevitably, happenstance allowed them to catch up to him. Before their noose could close, though, that same soft voice, a guardian angel, would whisper in his ear, and he would disappear unscathed like a wisp of smoke.

After slipping from their snare yet again, he skirted Conviviality and headed into the tablelands. Everywhere he turned another city closed itself to him, but he remembered the pueblo atop the mesa and Atsa and Doli. They had once extended them hospitality for a few days. Perhaps they would again, even though he would arrive bearing news of McPhail's death. He thought of Sahkyo, and if she somehow waited for Finn, she deserved to know she waited in vain.

That village was also where Janie had welcomed him into her embrace. She saved the words "I love you" for that final wagon ride out of Triumph, but she had told him she loved him with her actions in the pueblo. Ghosts of the dead floated before his eyes and sang siren songs in his ear as he traveled closer to the village's mesa. Were those songs to draw him on to his death in the village or to pull him away from a village where he might find succor? He could not tell.

One voice rang true and clear through the swirl of voices and songs in his head. As always, Janie's voice spoke to him more and more in his isolation. She was his guardian angel looking down on him. "Wait. Don't go there yet," she whispered in his ear. He could have arrived at the pueblo before dark, but that warning held him back, and he camped several miles away in the lee of another mesa. He suspected the villagers knew he was near, but if so, they did not disturb his rest. Maybe they watched over him as protectors while he slept. He never knew the truth of that.

The next morning when he woke, he mounted up and headed toward the mesa, but before he journeyed far, a group of two dozen or more horsemen rode up to the base of the pueblo. The posse had anticipated his arrival as if they could read his habits and intentions before they even occurred to him.

Will knew he was done for then. He would never escape Governor Hogg and his posse. He had only one choice left. At the end of it all, it had always been the only real choice anyway. He turned his horse toward Mount de Dios, toward Janie.

PART THREE

NOW

When Will's legs pistoned him out of the ground, the scene matched his ear's prediction. One horse and rider were already in the chute with a second rider ready to follow. Two more riders waited to the right and one to the left. Will started with his guns spread wide and brought them together in the middle.

His first two shots were simultaneous. The leftmost rider pitched forward off his mount with a red stain blooming over his spine just below the neck. Down and out.

The rightmost rider must have caught movement from the corner of his eye because he began to turn as Will fired. The bullet caught him on his right shoulder, and he too fell to the ground. Down, but not out yet.

Rider three was the one preparing to enter the narrow pass, and Will's left gun felled him with two shots to the torso. The force of the shots threw the man over the side of his horse, which bolted back down the trail, dragging the cowboy along by his foot still wedged in the stirrup. Even if the shots had not been kill shots, he was out of the fight.

By the time Will's right gun tracked to him, the fourth

rider, second to the right, was reaching for his pistol. The cowboy drew from his far side though, and Will's first bullet took him in the belly. The man stayed in his saddle and attempted to bring his gun to bear, but Will's next shot took him just above the sternum. Down and out.

Rider five, the man already in the pass, could have saved himself. If he would have spurred his horse forward, he could have been out of Will's line of fire. Instead, he tried to turn his horse around in the narrow space and bring up his rifle. Both of Will's pistols tracked to him. Each thundered once. Rider five was down and out.

The horses snorted, bucked, and pranced about from the noise and the smell of blood and cordite. Will stepped out of his hideaway and hurried over to the canyon opening. Rider two still struggled on the ground, writhing in pain and trying to reach his pistol over his deadened arm. Will shot him once in the head.

Nine shots. Five men down. No returned fire. Not McPhail-good maybe, but good enough to start.

Will plastered his body on the outside wall of the canyon and risked a quick peek. The lead horse had fled about halfway down the first leg of the pass. The sound of gunshots echoed in these hills, so surely the rest of the posse was now alerted. With luck, they would still be unsure of the direction of the attack. In the distance, Will could already hear calls, but no one had yet come back to check on the rear guard.

He took the time to empty the used shells and reload both pistols. The cylinders were already warm, but soon they would be hot enough to burn his fingers. He took one more glance to be sure no one had come back to investigate. With the path clear, he ducked around the corner and ran into the defile.

He skittered around the horse, which shied away from him, and approached the first turn. A voice shouting from around the corner pulled Will up short. "Dobkins, you see anything?"

Will backed to the wall of the canyon and kept both pistols high. Two seconds later, a new horseman came around the corner. Will shot him twice, and the man went down.

More yells came from deeper in the pass, as did the sound of boots dropping to the ground. Someone started to pull at the first man's body while another someone took a cautious look around the edge. Will fired, but his shot glanced off the rock face as the man pulled back. "Jesus, it's him," a voice yelled.

Will charged. He fired twice into the opening as he ran, which kept the men back. When he came around the corner, he went low, sliding past the legs of the first rider's horse. The horse reared back, and Will fired into the two men. One was still dragging their fallen companion clear and took Will's bullet dead center in his chest. The second man fired once at Will, but his shot went wide. Will's first shot took him in the thigh, the second in the belly, and the third in the chest.

Will scrambled to his feet. Beyond the horses crowding the way, he could see two more men riding toward him. Seven bullets gone, five to go; three in the left, two in the right. He moved about ten feet forward and crouched behind a boulder.

Bullets pinged off the rock surface as the riders closed. They were too far and riding too fast for their shots to be accurate, but that would change. Will waited and counted the distance in his head.

When his ears measured the distance to be right, Will bobbed a feint to one side of the rock and then rose to the opposite. Bullets stabbed through the air to his right, and a rock fragment ricocheted into his cheek. Will's first shot missed the left rider but must have hit his horse because the animal cried and veered, throwing off the rider's aim. His second shot hit the other rider, as did his third, and the man went down. Will's right gun was now empty.

The final rider tried to hold on to his reins, keep his saddle, and bring his gun back to bear. Will dispatched him with his last two bullets.

With no opponents in sight, Will crouched back down behind the boulder and reloaded. Ten opponents down, a good thirteen to go. Shouts continued to echo along the canyon walls, but no new opponents appeared.

Keep going, Will told himself. *For Ma and Pa. For Kali. For McPhail. For Finn. For Janie.*

He stood and jogged down the path toward the next bend.

The next section of canyon was short but wide and littered with large boulders. At the far end it made a ninety-degree turn to the right and opened into a wide oval before narrowing down again. Will had traveled this route often enough to have memorized the layout.

He was hurrying down the path when the sound of hoof beats echoed back to him. He ducked behind a boulder that stood taller than him. Through the narrow space between it and the canyon wall, he watched the four riders gallop around the corner and come pelting toward him. He cocked both pistols and waited.

As the men rode past, Will tracked the first rider with his left hand and fired with both guns as the second rider cleared the edge of the boulder. Neither saw their end coming and collapsed to the dusty ground. The next two tried to pull up, but Will eliminated them just as rapidly as the first pair.

"Fagan! Hoyle! McDougal!" someone yelled. The face of a bearded man popped around the corner and dodged back when Will fired at him. "It's Deadeye," the man yelled to his companions.

Again Will pictured the landscape ahead: an open space with a narrow entrance. His opponents could arrange themselves behind cover and pick him off as he came through. This could be his blaze of glory end, but he could stop here. All of his pursuers waited ahead of him in the canyon. He could grab a horse and be gone off the mountain before they raised enough courage to come after him. One of the four horses had kept running, but the other three had stopped and stomped nervously about their departed riders. One young man still lay slumped across the back of his horse, dead in his saddle. Will looked at the horses and made up his mind. Janie would understand.

Around the corner, Big Ben Neems tried to still the tattoo of his racing heart. Shots echoed about the pass from everywhere at once. The Deadeye Kid was right on their tail. How in the world he had gotten there was a mystery, but what had happened to the rest of the posse behind them was not. He had two men with him, Gus Cartwright and Midnight Moses Macon. Neither looked any calmer than Big Ben felt, and they were looking to him for leadership, only the Lord knew why.

"Okay boys," Big Ben said though his voice broke into a squeak. "He can only come through that hole. We spread out here and take him when he shows his face. Just like one of them carnival shows." Neither Gus nor Moses looked convinced. In fact, Midnight looked as though his face had not seen a lick of sunlight in years, and Gus looked about ready to toss his lunch along the trail. "Go on, spread out," Ben yelled and waved his arms out to the sides. The other two men took the flanks, and Ben stood his ground in the center.

They heard a "hee-yah!" yell from around the corner and then hoof beats. The three men raised their guns as three of the four horses they had just sent around the corner came charging down the trail. Poor Bobby Rawlings still lay sprawled backward across his horse, his lifeless body bouncing along, caught in the stirrups and reins. Bobby had been a good kid, not much older than the Deadeye Kid they tracked, and still green. Big Ben would hate to have to tell his mama her boy was dead, but at least he had died in his saddle like a man.

"Keep your eyes open, boys. This is just to distract us. He'll be right behind the horses." Ben tried to look around the large veering bodies, searching for a glimpse of movement. Hopefully, one of the others on the wings would get a clear shot first.

The horses were almost upon them when Bobby Rawlings gave up being dead and sat up in his saddle. Only, he had never been Bobby Rawlings. He was the devil Covington himself. Big Ben Neems never had a chance to shift his aim before the darkness took him.

Will was nearing the end of the pass. In just two more turns, the narrow trail would open up into a wider canyon and then the rolling hills leading down off the mountain into the badlands or up to their old hideout all the way to Janie.

He had expected to be dead long before this. The odds were still against him. He had killed seventeen of perhaps two dozen and exhausted an entire bandolier of bullets. He had around seven opponents to go, give or take two or three, and they all knew he was coming, but he felt a sudden clarity that it would make no difference.

He would kill them all.

Then he would take a horse and ride the rest of the way to Janie's grave. He would move the stones and earth so that he could lie down next to her body, hold her one last time, and give her one last kiss. Then he would put one of the big rosewood guns into his mouth, the one Kali had used, that would be fitting, and head off to that big frontier in the sky. They would all be there waiting for him: his real ma and pa; George and Molly Hennessy; Kali, unsullied by Hogg's men; Finn; McPhail; and of course, Janie. Together they would ride the plains under the great big sky of the Lord, just like that preacher had said.

But first, he had a few more men to kill.

He reloaded his right gun and dropped it into his holster and went to work on the left. He slipped the last bullet into the chamber and snapped the weapon closed when three more members of the posse came around the corner. Will dove to his right. Hot lead screamed past his ears and a burning sensation flashed up his left bicep. He fired once as he fell and a second time as he hit the ground. At least one of his shots connected, and one man went down, and the other two withdrew.

Will chased them through the next zig of the pass. He fired once more as the two men disappeared through the final opening and heard a cry as if he had hit one of them.

Blood flowed down Will's left arm, and he gripped it with his right hand to staunch the bleeding, but pain could not fight its way past the adrenaline pumping through his body.

As Will entered the final opening, one of the duo leapt around the corner holding a shotgun, but again Janie's ghost seemed to whisper a warning, and Will ducked down. The man's buckshot whizzed over Will's head while Will's bullets took him in the chest and abdomen.

The final man of the trio remained out of sight near the final exit, but his shadow splayed across the opening. Will dove through low in a roll to bring himself up beyond the cowboy and shot the would-be ambusher once in the head.

Horses snorted behind him, and Will whirled about once more. He had gotten twenty, but that left at least four more, and all four must have him in their sights.

Four horses pawed the dirt in the open space and regarded

him with brown saucer eyes. Three bodies lay sprawled about on the ground. The gun in Will's left hand tracked to the remaining figure still standing, a tall lanky cowboy smoking a cigarette.

"Hello, Will," the man said.

Will held his gun unwavering. "McPhail."

PART FOUR

ONE MONTH AGO

Black smoke billowed up the stairs, and portions of the floor near the front windows had begun to glow and smolder in their own right. An irregular but persistent tempo of bullets whizzed through the broken windows and thudded into the ceiling and walls.

When McPhail had woken to the sounds of stealthy men in the square outside, he had been surprised that Will and Finn had not woken too. He had trained them better than that. When he discovered they were gone, his face darkened. They had betrayed him in the night, stolen out while he slept, alerted the authorities, and disappeared into the bowels of the city.

That was disappointing, but in the end inevitable. Finn's loyalty to the cause had always been questionable, but Will's had been solid, at least until Janie started returning his mooning eyes. Will was smart, and once he recovered from his grief over Janie's death, he would deduce what must have happened in Triumph. He would realize that McPhail had paused for the briefest of moments to let the fatal shot happen, because no one was faster than Ranger David McPhail. At that point, betrayal would be the only option left to Will, but McPhail had thought better of the young man. He would have expected Will to face him like a man, to draw and let the best man win.

By that point in his reverie, the coach had arrived, and McPhail had no more time to dwell on betrayal. Hogg's little speech only reinforced the idea he had been betrayed. The boys had just been clever enough to let Hogg believe all three of them remained inside the fish market. A small part of him still hoped this was some sort of ruse on Will's part. Finn was too slow to come up with a plan like this on his own, but if Will had not betrayed McPhail, then the boys would be hiding in a nearby building. Two extra pairs of guns from a different direction would turn the tables on Hogg's ambush. Perhaps even as Hogg spoke, the boys were creeping up on the governor for the coup de grâce.

Well, Will and Finn were not out there. More than fifteen minutes after Hogg's pompous grandstanding began, no extra sets of guns had come to his aid. Once again, David McPhail, last of the Territory Rangers, stood alone. In the next few minutes, either the smoke would overcome him or the building would give out beneath him and bury him in flames. Hogg was cagey enough to stay ensconced behind his coach, shielded from McPhail's bullets. So it was time to go.

A single window opened over the docks in the back of the building. Given the available space, fewer Agents could guard the docks than the square out front, and so a rear exit afforded the best odds even if he would need to drop through a small window to the ground.

He grabbed a chair from the sitting room as he went. Flames licked up the stairwell, blocking that as an exit in any case.

His eyes watered and the smoke clogged his lungs while the heat wafting up the stairwell singed his skin.

The window broke against the chair legs, and McPhail ducked, expecting a fusillade of bullets. The men outside were professionals and saved their bullets for an actual target.

The Ranger examined the window from a crouch a few feet back. It was narrow and jagged with pieces of glass jutting from the frame at odd angles, but it was wide enough for his frame. He scooted back a few more feet, coughed when he inhaled a thick puff of smoke, and spat tar-colored mucus. When he sprinted at the window, he extended both guns and leapt through the shattered opening and into the night air.

Glass snapped off against his shoulder and a shard grazed his belly. He somersaulted in the air to try and bring his boots around below him. He spread out his arms, at once attempting to balance his looping fall and search for targets. By now, hot lead should have been burning the air around him and slamming into his flesh, but the only gunshots echoed from the front side of the fish market.

He landed short of the wooden docks. His left foot rotated behind before finding purchase in the mud which crashed his full weight onto his right leg. It twisted at the knee and buckled with an audible pop that ignited lighting bolts of pain up into his belly. He collapsed a few feet from the body of an Agent oozing fresh blood from bullet wounds to his chest.

One of McPhail's guns clattered from his fingers in the fall, and the other lay trapped in the hand beneath his torso.

Boots pounded on the ground from the side of the building to his right. McPhail rolled to the left and tried to bring his gun to bear.

Through smoke-blinded eyes, he saw the butt of a rifle swing toward his face. He heard his nose crack with the impact, and darkness overtook him.

McPhail had no concept of time after that, just a confused jumble of images and sensations mixed of memory, delusions, and reality. At any one moment, which was which remained impossible to tell.

He seemed to stumble through a maze of doorways in the dark. Each step through a doorway spun him and churned his stomach as it swept him to a new scene. He stood with the garrison at Fort Vigilant, laughing with Joseph Covington, except Joseph had Samantha's long auburn hair and kissed him on the lips. Those lips smothered and suffocated him. She sucked the air from him. He and Joseph fought in the shadows of the fort, and Joseph shot him in the belly. George Hennessy, wearing Finn's face, drank with him in a saloon on the steps of the Federation capitol. He and Dick Warren and Tommy Hopkins fought off armies of snakes with the heads of men, or maybe they were men with the heads of snakes or birds or weasels or coyotes. Clad in Agent's black, Janie and Will hounded him through a gold mine in North Cali. At every turn, Janie outdrew him and laughed at him with accusing dead eyes and flicked her serpent's tongue across his cheek. A black spire erupted through Fort Vigilant. He and Will and Janie and Finn and George and Joseph and Molly and Samantha stood on the ramparts, repelling armies of men in black and blue and tall thin men wearing bright white. Smoke and flames enveloped them all, and he stood the lone witness as the spire and Fort Vigilant fell. And through all of those images, church bells chimed and hammered on his ears until they bled.

The flames died, and his fever broke.

His nose throbbed, but he could breathe.

The smell of soot faded to a memory.

His shoulder complained a dull ache, but his right knee hollered and monopolized the conversation.

His throat was dry. Someone put a glass to his mouth, and he drank.

His stomach growled. Someone spooned mash into his mouth, and he ate.

His surroundings grew solid. He lay in a narrow, plain room with beige, adobe walls. Two small barred windows near the ceiling let in light during the day, but they were too high up to see out of even if he could stand. His right knee was swollen and stabbed little daggers up his leg when he shifted in bed. He doubted it would support him for long if he tried to stand. In any case, a manacle chained his left leg to the bed, and a handcuff did the same for his right wrist.

Three times a day, a muscular nurse came in to feed him and care for his wounds. Whenever she entered, two Agents stood in the front corners of the room to glare at him, but in his current condition, McPhail doubted he could have over-powered the nurse, let alone his guards. The Agents never spoke. McPhail and the nurse exchanged the meagerest of words.

A week passed.

After the midday meal on a day like any other, when the nurse had finished cleaning him, she exited as usual but re-turned moments later with a chair that she placed facing the foot of his bed. She left again and returned with a small table which she set up next to the chair and placed a thick folder on it. "The governor will see you now."

When she left, Governor Hogg strode into the room wear-ing one of his white linen suits and holding a long white walk-ing cane with a golden alligator head handle. He sat down in the chair and crossed his legs. He gave a dismissive wave, and the two Agents slipped out the door after the nurse. The door clicked shut behind them.

Governor Hogg smiled. "Well, well, well, so we finally meet face to face. Well, actually, I met you a little over a week ago, but you were not in talking shape. That's all well and good though because it gave me time to assemble everything. I didn't have time to bring all my files with me that night. We were all in such a rush to meet you."

He shook his head and chuckled. "You really were very careless, you know. The night of the Winter Gala, I had no fewer than four reports that you and the boys were in town." Hogg held up his fingers to enumerate. "A barmaid from the Loyal Groomsman served you drinks all afternoon and then served you up to me in the night; the daughter of a business associate rode into town in a coach with Master Covington and just about wet herself in her excitement to tell me all about it personally; Mildred Weatherwax, whom you menaced in Humility, spied you outside my front gates; and a pair of my Agents eventually spotted you heading away from my residence and tailed you to your hideout. It was almost as if you wanted to be caught."

Hogg leaned back in his chair and spread his arms wide. "My biggest problem turned out to be how to divide up the reward. Mrs. Weatherwax was out given her husband is my close advisor. The two Agents were just doing their job, though they may get a bonus. In the end, I split it between the barmaid and the young lady."

The governor smiled. "And here we are, together at last." He picked up the file folder and opened it in his lap.

"David Jonathan McPhail of the town of Damnation, former member of the Territory Rangers, friend of the Indians, failed lobbyist, ranch hand, cowpoke, gold prospector, bandit, murderer, desperado, fugitive, instigator, and general troublemaker. You have gotten around quite a bit in the last seventeen or eighteen years. While some people have been trying to build up this world and make it a safer, saner place, you have seen fit to drift about, a piece of detritus, reimagining your supposed glory days, and trying to tear down what your betters have built."

McPhail shifted in bed and glared but refused to speak.

Hogg leaned forward. "Is your head so buried in the sand or deep in your own ass that you have no idea what is happening in the wide world about you? Jefferson, our home, sits on the razor's edge, David. May I call you David?" Hogg waved a hand. "No matter, I will anyway. To our west and south, General Santa Ana and a growing Spanish Mexico hope to reclaim their glory days and territory, much like you I suppose. They plan on driving out the last of us pale skins. Mexican rule is returning unless we all stand tall against it."

Hogg rapped his knuckles on the table. "And don't think the Federation will do much to stop them. No one back east cares about what happens here in Jefferson. They like Tejas well enough for its beef and North Cali for its gold, but we're just a little flag on the map to them connecting it all together. In any case, the Federation is preparing to rip itself apart over whether one man ought to own another just so they can have cheap laborers to abuse. When it falls apart back east, the war will be long and bloody and pointless, and there will be no troops streaming in to turn the Mexican tide. We'll be on our own here in Jefferson to sink or swim as well as we can manage. That's what I've been building here for the last twenty years, a strong, independent state to preserve our way of life."

The two men sat and watched each other in silence for almost a minute.

"Fine. You won't speak. It is your choice. I could use more men like you, David. You inspire people to follow you. You have ideals. You're good with your guns. I also could have used Janie De Casas, Finn Hennessy, and William Covington, but the first two are dead, and the third is in the wind like some rabid dog that may jump out at us at any time."

He saw McPhail's face twitch. He picked up a telegram from the folder. "Just came in a few days ago. Finn Hennessy was shot and killed just outside the town of Sanctuary. William Covington escaped. They've started to call him the Deadeye Kid after a particularly spectacular shot he made there."

He dropped the paper on the stack. "Let me tell you how this is going to go, David. You are no longer a Ranger. You are no noble samurai, no knight of the Round Table, no Swiss Guard, no conquistador, no gunslinger. You will get no last stand, no blaze of glory death. You get no Thermopylae, no Alamo, no stand of the French Foreign Legion, no Jericho Hill. You get to die here, alone, in a hole, uncelebrated and forgotten. You will be no martyr to the cause. You will just be gone."

He locked eyes with McPhail and held up a finger. "Unless. Unless you see reason and help put right the damage you have done. I need William Covington brought in, alive preferably but dead if need be. I think you're the man to bring him in alive if anyone can."

McPhail's voice, unused for so long and with his throat still healing from smoke and heat, came out as a croak. "And why would I help you bring him in?"

"You created him. For once, have the decency to clean up your own mess. How do you think William will feel if he sees this?" Hogg handed over a smudged ledger entry. "That's from Revenue Man DuBois of Tranquility. It seems the day before the raid on the Hennessy farm, a good citizen cowboy going by the name of Daniel McAdams showed up to warn DuBois that George Hennessy was planning on fleeing in the night for parts unknown to avoid paying his taxes. He also claimed Hennessy, a former Territory Ranger, was as dangerous as a grizzly and recommended DuBois bring reinforcements."

McPhail flicked the paper off the bed. His eyes were a snakebite waiting to happen.

Unperturbed by the insolence, Hogg pulled a final item from the folder and tossed it on McPhail's lap. It was a faded daguerreotype. On it, three Rangers smiled back at McPhail. His own young face stared up at him between a young George Hennessy and the dark face of Joseph Covington who never had a chance to grow old.

"Samantha Lambton came from Scotts-Irish extraction. Joseph Covington was born of the union of a runaway slave father and a Cherokee mother." Hogg leaned back in his chair and spoke in low tones. "I am told that Samantha Lambton was a fiery redhead, beautiful, and independent. Her charms caught the attention of two young men, good friends, Joseph and David, who tried to woo her over. In the end, Joseph prevailed, and she became his wife, but perhaps her marriage vows did not dissuade her other suitor. I am told that Samantha, eight months pregnant, moved to the Tranquility Valley to be closer to her sister. Joseph Covington never lived long enough to meet his infant son. I wonder what he would have said on meeting him for the first time? I will be honest, after seeing a better sketch of young William, I cannot find a hint of the Covington line." Hogg paused in thought. "I suppose those Lambton traits must be strong, wouldn't you say, or do you think there is more of his father in him than meets the eye?"

Hogg tidied the papers in his folder but left the daguerreotype in McPhail's lap. He stood and went to the door but rested his hand on the doorknob. Without turning he spoke one last time. "With you, I think William can be brought in alive and rehabilitated. Without you, my men will kill him. Which option do you think Samantha would prefer?"

Governor Hogg left the room, the latch clicked behind him, and the bolt slid home.

A week later, with his knee throbbing but able to bear his weight for short periods and to hold him in the saddle well enough, a McPhail bereft of his rosewood revolvers rode out of town in the company of Dick Warren and Rob Nelson. They crossed the San Alonso bridge and rode south to follow the coach road over Gorseman's Pass and out into the western Jefferson plains. They met up with the rest of the Agent posse in the town of Respect, a town McPhail had avoided on this same route a few months ago.

Agent Julio Palliser had led the search for William "The Deadeye Kid" Covington since the shoot-out near Sanctuary. Palliser was none too pleased with the demotion in command, but since Warren was Head Agent, right-hand man to Governor Hogg, Palliser had accepted the situation with as much grace as he possessed. In Agent Palliser's case, that turned out to be little and ill enough.

"So the Head Man decides to show his face at last," Palliser said when Warren, Nelson, and McPhail walked into the sheriff's office. He looked McPhail up and down. "Looks like all the old men are coming out. Why ain't Hogg put you out to pasture?"

"If you don't shut your mouth, Palliser, I'll knock those teeth so far down your throat you'll be chewing apples with your ass. Now get out of my seat." Warren walked over to the desk and loomed over the younger man.

"Yes, sir, Agent Warren." Palliser pushed himself to his feet and stood eye to eye with his boss. "Guess you must be tired after your long ride. It's tough working out here in the field, not like sitting at a desk in San Alonso." He brushed past Warren and leaned up against the wall.

Warren sat down in the chair and pulled up to the desk to examine the telegraph messages and maps covering the expanse of wood. "What have you got?"

"Sheriff in Honor got a little ahead of himself and thought he could nab Deadeye on his own." Palliser spit a stream of brown tobacco juice in the general direction of the spittoon by the desk, but most of it splashed around Warren's boots. "By the time we got there, he was in the wind but looked to be heading northwest."

Warren stared at the map. "So you brought the posse up to Respect to try and cut him off."

"No, I was headed to Conviviality but was ordered to park here until you and your special friend showed up." He sneered in McPhail's direction. "I would have had him already if they'd let me keep going."

"So after two weeks of chasing him, you know where he's going now?"

Palliser shrugged. "Northwest. He keeps going there he ends up in his old home in Tranquility. Don't have nowhere else to run."

When McPhail snorted, Warren turned to look at the Ranger. "You don't think he'll go home?"

"Tranquility isn't his home. His house is burned to the ground and everyone there is dead. He'll be looking for friends. First stop would be here." McPhail tapped the map over the tablelands.

"Injun country? The big pueblo?"

"Aye, we were there before. He'll expect my friendship with them from my Ranger days to protect him. Probably will, unless I show up to have a chat with them."

Warren's eyes narrowed. "You best be right, McPhail." He looked up at Palliser. "You're in charge of this cowboy. He gets no weapons, and watch him close. He's crafty." The Head Agent stood up. "Nelson, tell the rest of the boys to saddle up. We're heading out in ten."

It took them two days to arrive at the pueblo just after dawn. As McPhail expected, the residents gave a stoic welcome to the Agents, but his presence mollified their underlying animosity.

At the sight of the approaching posse, the villagers abandoned their fields and retreated up the narrow streets of their town. A group of ten braves greeted the posse, including Bidziil, who as the youngest of the group lingered at the rear.

Although the braves declined to invite the Agents into the village, McPhail ascertained that Will had not visited since the quartet's original departure, but something about the way the lead brave spoke made McPhail think they were expecting him. The Ranger was puzzling that out, when Big Ben spotted a lone rider heading northeast away from them. It was Will—the mixed look of distress and defiance on Bidziil's face confirmed that in McPhail's mind.

After that, the chase was on in earnest. It took McPhail two days to be sure, and maybe it took Will that long to realize it himself, but they were headed to Mount de Dios. McPhail had heard it said that home is where the heart is, and although he had never thought much of that saying, it was apparent that Will was going home.

Their quarry outdistanced them by that point, but it was no matter to McPhail. "I know him, Dick," he said to the Head Agent that night when the sun set, and they called a halt for the day. "He's going back to his woman. We don't need to run our horses into the ground. I'll take you right to him."

"You better be right, McPhail. The governor may have said to trust you, and you and I go way back, but you know there ain't no love lost 'tween us. You cross me, and you'll answer for it."

Three days later, with the sun near its zenith, the posse arrived at the narrow pass a third of the way up Mount de Dios.

"Where the hell do you think you're leading us?" His face crimson, Agent Palliser rounded on McPhail. "This is a damn wild goose chase, here. That boy's miles away, and you're laughing at us." Then he turned on Warren. "And you used to be a Ranger. You in on this too?"

"I've had about enough of your insubordination, Palliser." Warren laid a hand on his gun. "Governor Hogg named me Head Agent, and he sent Mr. McPhail with us. If you've got a problem, I can send you back to San Alonso in a wooden box to have a word with him if you want."

"You won't always be Head Agent, Dick."

Warren snorted. "Keep it up, Julio, and you won't be around long enough to see it." He stared down Palliser until the man blinked and averted his eyes. His subordinate in line, Warren turned his anger on McPhail. "What is this?"

McPhail shrugged. "Just what it looks like, a pass heading up the mountain. It's about a mile long and then opens back up. Our hideout is on the other side. Go through or go back down and come up the mountain on the other side. Your choice."

Agent Nelson had joined the little conclave. He eyed the narrow defile and tall walls. "Good place for an ambush."

Warren had made the same calculation. "He's one man. Even from above, he doesn't have a prayer of taking out this posse."

Palliser, who had not withdrawn despite Warren's glower, shot back a sneer. "You wanna bet your life on that?"

Warren narrowed his eyes at the man. "Aye, I'll bet my life on it, and his." He wagged his chin at McPhail. "And yours." He nodded at Palliser. He urged his horse out from the small knot to address the other men. "All right men, dismount and take a breather. Our guide, Palliser, Nelson, Neems, De Angelis, and I are going to scout on ahead." He turned back to McPhail. "Lead the way, old friend." Somehow, the last word lacked the warmth it had in the old days.

McPhail looked back and forth from the pass to Warren. "If there's an ambush, I won't do any good with empty holsters."

"Better not be an ambush for your sake, then."

"Governor Hogg wanted me here to bring Covington in, dead or alive. I'll need a gun for that."

Warren gave him a withering look, but McPhail did not flinch.

"I'm still the fastest man here, Dick. I taught Covington everything he knows, but I'm still faster."

Before Warren could reply, Palliser cut in with a laugh. "You talk pretty big, old man. I've seen Deadeye's handiwork, and I'd like to see how fast you are. Here, take one of mine." He tossed one of his guns to McPhail. "Now let's get going." He rode into the defile first.

After giving the chambers a spin and checking the balance, McPhail dropped the pistol into his holster and followed.

Nobody molested them on the way through.

On the far side, where the pass opened for the final time, they found a small campsite about a day old. They dropped down from their horses and examined the area.

"Made himself a little fire here. Must have thought he lost us entirely." Palliser kicked at the ashes. "Bedded down here and had the horse tied up over there."

De Angelis was examining the old manure. "At least a day old, maybe more."

Warren stared at Palliser's back. "Well, we know we're on the right track. Nelson, Neems, head back and bring the rest of the posse through, twos and threes at a time."

With a grimace of pain and a slight give in his right knee, McPhail dismounted. If he turned too quick, the knee wanted to buckle; but the swelling was gone and if he moved slow, it kept its complaints to a dull ache. His nose had healed and looked much the same as it had since breaking it as a teen when a bull had thrown him at the town rodeo. His strength had returned otherwise, and his faculties remained keen as ever.

Something smelled off. Unless Will had arrived here very late, he never would have bedded down outside the pass. He would have continued on to their old camp. The Ranger squatted, his bad knee protesting the entire time, and examined the fire and the depression in the dirt where someone had lain.

The fire was small, almost not worth making for the time it had burned. The disturbed area of earth where the bedroll had lain was narrow. Will always tossed and turned in his sleep, but the ground suggested the sleeper had lain rather still.

McPhail sat back and rubbed his chin and thought. A campsite that was not much of a campsite along the path the posse would follow. Had someone else passed this way and left these signs? Was Will trying to lead them astray in some way? If they thought he had camped here more than a day ago, they might let down their guard. But if this was to be an ambush, the most likely vantage was from the walls above the pass, and with the posse strung out, the odds were against him. Was he playing another game?

McPhail winced when he stood and stared at the ground in concentration.

Then, the first salvos of gunfire echoed up the pass.

All four men whirled as one to the opening behind them. The shots sounded distant but clear.

"Damn it," Palliser cursed. "It is an ambush."

De Angelis' face was still screwed up in confusion.

Warren turned to McPhail, his eyes narrowed. "You led us right into it." Head Agent Dick Warren reached for his gun as the words left his lips.

Ranger David McPhail was faster than Warren, and he had started to draw as soon as the first echo of bullets touched their ears. His right arm aimed to the left and shot Dick in the chest before the man could draw. He tracked to the right, by-passing De Angelis, because Palliser turned out to be faster than Warren and had already cleared leather, but he was slower than the two bullets McPhail sent his way.

Dick was not through. His left hand clutched at the sucking wound in his chest, but his right hand battled to come up. His first shot went into the ground three feet from McPhail, and he never got a chance at a second as McPhail followed up with two more shots to the gut.

In the middle, De Angelis clawed at his holster, trying to grab hold of his gun. McPhail's final bullet brought him down.

Down the pass, shots echoed, and men yelled and screamed.

McPhail tossed Palliser's empty gun over by his body. He limped to Dick Warren's horse and dug in the saddle bags until he found the rosewood revolvers hidden in the bottom. He checked that they were loaded and dropped them back into his holsters. Their weight comforted him. He had felt naked these past few weeks without them. Now he was whole again. He dug into his pocket for a cigarette and matches and settled in to wait.

PART FIVE

NOW

The adrenaline coursed through Will's blood. His breath came heavy in his throat. His heart hammered in his chest. He gazed down the barrel of his revolver at David McPhail who had mentored him for the past year, who had died in the fire in San Alonso, and who now stood reincarnated before him, not as a friend, but at the head of an avenging posse. The posse's clairvoyant ability to predict his destination had become clear. Will had never stood a chance of escape.

In the distance, the carrion crows cawed over their feast.

McPhail's arms hung loosely at his sides, not touching his guns, but nearby. He watched Will over the tip of the smoldering cigarette. Little tendrils of smoke undulated from the tip before catching in the breeze and vanishing. The emotions seem to dance across Will's face in tempo with the dancing cigarette fumes.

Will's left arm throbbed and warm blood oozed under the hand clutched over his bicep. In the first instant he felt relief that it was McPhail, then surprise at his reanimation, then confusion, and then a hardening of his heart. After that, his mind accelerated, assessing his options. He tried to think. He had reloaded the right gun, holstered it, and finished the left before the last of the posse charged him. How many shots were still in the chambers? He tried to replay that last section of scrambling fight. He tried to focus on the back of the gun while not taking his eyes off McPhail. He measured its weight in his hand.

Then again, did it matter how many bullets he had left? As long as McPhail thought he had one more, they were at a standoff. Will released his left arm and let the right hang down by his side in a partial mirror of McPhail's stance. The blood started to seep faster from the wound and into his shirt. His left hand trembled as fatigue set in, and his adrenaline ebbed.

McPhail kept his face neutral, but inside he recognized the signs. Will was out of bullets or thought he was. Then again, maybe the boy was slyer by far and playing an even longer game, trying to goad McPhail into making a fatal move. He had managed to dupe the posse and Head Agent Warren with the faux campsite. Maybe he was attempting to out-think McPhail.

Either way, opportunities abounded. Will might pull the trigger and shoot him down, but if not, it would come down to who could draw the fastest and shoot the straightest. McPhail could always beat Finn. Janie might have outshot him on her best day, but he was not facing Janie. At full strength, Will might beat him, but Will was neither hale nor healthy.

McPhail's shoulder was stiff from the gash from the window. His right knee throbbed and wobbled at inopportune moments. The cowboy was not at full strength himself.

Perhaps the opportunity was not to gun down Will but to go out on his own terms. He had never wanted to die in bed of old age. Somewhere out there, a bullet wore the name *David McPhail*. Maybe that bullet was in Will's pistol right now. He could die with his boots on like a gunslinger, and Will could take his place as true scion and protégé. This last act of betrayal would become the fulcrum to propel Will on a rampage against Alistair Hogg and his Agents.

Images flashed through Will's mind of a childhood filled with love from his adopted parents, his bond with Finn, Kali's melodious laugh and infectious grin, but most of all, images of the last year with Janie. He saw her smile, the glint of mischief in her dark brown eyes, how her dark hair gobbled up the light, the smell of her breath, the sweet moistness of her lips on his, the soft warmth of her body against him in the night.

"For what it's worth, I wasn't at Sanctuary. I was sorry to hear about Finn."

"Didn't stop you from tracking me down."

McPhail shrugged.

The tremors increased along Will's arm. Time was almost up. "When this is over, take me to Janie."

McPhail nodded. He reached up with his left hand and flicked the cigarette off to the side, away from his gun hand.

Will smiled at the ruse, flattered that the old man thought he needed that against him.

In his left hand, the hammer clicked on an empty chamber even as he drew with his right.

The guns thundered and echoed across the mountain and out into the plains.

The crows screamed.

Pain. Then darkness followed.

Sometime later, the crows scolded the lone rider who headed up Mount de Dios.

ACKNOWLEDGMENTS

Gunslingers, as it exists, would not be possible (or nearly as good) without all the collaboration from my friends and colleagues. Thank you to my early readers who suffered through the initial rough drafts: Elaine, my children, my mother, my brother, Rana, and Tom among others.

A giant thank you to the team at Atmosphere Press, both those whom I worked with directly and those hidden behind the scenes from me. BE pointed out all my confusing passages and tightened and clarified my vision, all with a gentle enough hand that always made me feel positive when they pointed out my errors. Amie and Chris picked through the manuscript with a fine-toothed comb and straightened all my commas, semicolons, and various dashes. I apologize to them that I just have a mental thing for "grey" over "gray". Ronaldo and his design team created the wonderful cover, and in particular, captured the image of Janie that was floating in my mind. Alex ushered me through the process and kept everyone on schedule, even me.

Once more, thank you to Elaine and my family, who allowed me the space to write this story in peace when I needed it, but then accepted this treasure, warts and all, when I was ready to share it. Without your support, I never would have gotten to the finish line. I love you.

Coming Soon

Janie
by Kendall Roberts

In the town of Triumph, a sniper's bullet struck and killed Janie De Casas, and her death pushed Will Covington onto a self-destructive path of revenge.

But in the town of Victory, that bullet struck Will instead...

Bereft of her only friends and betrayed by her mentor, Janie is set adrift in the state of Jefferson, but she has knowledge few other people in the state have. Janie's father was a member of Governor Alistair Hogg's vaunted Agents, and so Janie knows the secret that lies beneath the governor's mansion in San Alonso. It is a secret she plans to use to her advantage.

On her journey, Janie will face obstacles and dangers, loneliness and despair, but she will also find support from unexpected sources and learn that we are never as alone as we think we are. With newfound friends, maybe Janie really can find the happy ending she is hoping for, but to do that, she may have to sacrifice the very people who profess to love her.

ABOUT ATMOSPHERE PRESS

Atmosphere Press is an independent, full-service publisher for excellent books in all genres and for all audiences. Learn more about what we do at atmospherepress.com.

We encourage you to check out some of Atmosphere's latest releases, which are available at Amazon.com and via order from your local bookstore:

Icarus Never Flew 'Round Here, by Matt Edwards

COMFREY, WYOMING: Maiden Voyage, by Daphne Birkmeyer

The Chimera Wolf, by P.A. Power

Umbilical, by Jane Kay

The Two-Blood Lion, by Nick Westfield

Shogun of the Heavens: The Fall of Immortals, by I.D.G. Curry

Hot Air Rising, by Matthew Taylor

30 Summers, by A.S. Randall

Delilah Recovered, by Amelia Estelle Dellos

A Prophecy in Ash, by Julie Zantopoulos

The Killer Half, by JB Blake

Ocean Lessons, by Karen Lethlean

Unrealized Fantasies, by Marilyn Whitehorse

The Mayari Chronicles: Initium, by Karen McClain

Squeeze Plays, by Jeffrey Marshall

JADA: Just Another Dead Animal, by James Morris

Hart Street and Main: Metamorphosis, by Tabitha Sprunger

Karma One, by Colleen Hollis

Ndalla's World, by Beth Franz

Adonai, by Arman Isayan

The Journey, by Khozem Poonawala

ABOUT THE AUTHOR

Kendall Roberts lives in California. In his spare time, he enjoys writing, biking, and board games. This is his first novel.